THE SENATOR

MAYA GOLDEN BETHANY

RISING ACTION

Text copyright © 2024 by Maya Golden Bethany

Cover Illustration © Nat Mack
Distributed by Simon & Schuster

ISBN: 978-1-998076-19-2
Ebook: 978-1-998076-20-8

FIC031060 - Thrillers/Political
FIC031000 - Thrillers/General
FIC049000 - African American & Black/General

#TheSentator

Follow Rising Action on our socials!
Twitter: @RAPubCollective
Instagram: @risingactionpublishingco
Tiktok: @risingactionpublishingco

For MomE and Granddad

THE SENATOR

PROLOGUE

The three-year-old's snaggletooth reveals itself within a bored grimace behind the nebulizer face mask. White plumes of mist float out from either side of the face covering which was molded in purple, pink, and clear plastic to appear as a Triceratops. With each of her strained exhales, little cloud-like puffs frame Felicity's cherub face. The snaggletooth could have easily been the horn of the Triceratops.

A strip of purple elastic stretches from one pale cheek to the other, tight around the back of her head and her sandy brown curls. Plump legs stretch out towards the edge of the sofa cushion. Pudgy toes wiggle and flex as she sways her feet from side to side to a version of Skidamarink that only she can hear in her head.

"Three more minutes." Her mother's voice is intentionally loud so that Felicity can hear her over the industrial buzzing of the blue and green Brontosaurus nebulizer on the floor next to the sofa. A clear white tube connects from the dinosaur's butt to the chamber filled with a clear liquid at the bottom of the face mask.

Her mother's footsteps pounded over the wood laminate flooring, rocking the sofa and the entire mobile home as she strode from one side of the kitchen to the other. She sat Felicity's favorite red bowl, filled with a few clunky scoops of macaroni and cheese, and a box of chocolate milk down on her Elmo placemat at the kitchen table.

The bright red stamp on the opened mail stacked up on the table caught her mother's eye. She snatched the tri-folded paper up and shoved it back into the hastily ripped open envelope.

Felicity could not yet read, though she knew her numbers to 10 and could sing her ABCs thanks to *Sesame Street*. She didn't know what the letters E-V-I-C-T-I-O-N spelled out for her future.

Her mother scooped up the mail and shifted it from the table to the kitchen counter.

Felicity reached her tiny hand in the air and gave her mother an exaggerated down gesture as she wagged her head from side to side.

"I want down, now!" the toddler whined.

"Three minutes," Aubrey said.

Felicity's brows knitted into her mean face. It would have been comical if Aubrey didn't feel so damn tired.

"I'm not arguing with you today. You know you have to have your medicine." Aubrey shook her head, exasperated.

Felicity curiously examined her mother's worn face and began to hum the tune Mama is all too familiar with. Aubrey Fischer sang it to her daughter every night as she playfully poked at her sides and her belly, emphasizing with each tickle, "I looooove you!"

On good days, the tickling and laughter didn't result in minutes-long fits of coughing. On good days, Aubrey was able to sing every verse without becoming winded.

Part I

The Lede

Chapter 1

April 16

H is own name howls in his ears like a siren's song. Carried by the early spring gale blowing across the Mall, Oliver discerns the three syllables against the funnel swirling around his lobes.

"Oliver!" The voice came to him like lyrics from a song of his youth. He hadn't heard the tune in years, but he knew the melody immediately. Few people address him as anything but Senator, Senator Michaels, or even Mr. Michaels, these days.

Oliver flinches and tightens his grip on the leash in his hand. Montana, his golden Labrador, stops as well, though he tugs on the crimson nylon strap before conceding and sitting on his hind legs.

"Alex?" A flood of energy comes over him, a rush of adrenaline he hasn't felt since running out of the tunnel during pregame.

The smell of petrichor hangs onto the wind like a briar. The darkening gray sky silhouettes bloated charcoal clouds that threaten to release a deluge.

Alex tucks a copy of *The Washington Post* under her arm and shoves her hands into her wool coat pockets, appearing to brace herself from the sting of April wind in the capital. A fat raindrop splatters on the cement between them, and she gives a furtive glance at the sky.

"What ...?" Oliver's thoughts become fuzzy.

Oliver watches as Alex's gaze drifts down to the dog. His tail becomes a blur of golden fur as it wags with expectation. Alex pets the top of his head as she steps in front of Oliver.

"Hey!" The beauty mark at the left corner of her mouth lifts with her lips as she smiles. Alex Broussard could easily be a catalog model, or at the very least, selling cars in local television commercials.

"It's him. The famous Montana. I follow you on Instagram," she says, scratching behind the dog's ears. He gives her hand an appreciative sniff.

"He has more followers than I do." Oliver forces a false smile. Like kissing babies, shaking hands, and posing for selfies, it's a mask for his dissociation.

"Pretty brilliant idea—getting kids interested in politics by watching him go around the Capitol Building with you and sit in on meetings," Alex says.

"I have to do *something*. I don't know if you are aware of this, but politics have become taboo and politicians less than popular. Montana could probably get more votes than I can in the next election."

"Montana's turds could get more votes than many of your colleagues," Alex quips.

"Ouch. True." Oliver chuckles. The banter is nice; two old friends chit-chatting about nothing of major consequence. Her presence, however, does not make sense to him. "I have a strong feeling this isn't some coincidence that we are seeing each other."

She licks her lips, her gaze darting around, but her smile remains in place. To the casual observer, it is likely a chance reunion of two old buddies passing each other by. "I didn't want to call, and I didn't want to show up at the main office. I didn't want it on your visitor's log."

"So, you were just hanging out here waiting for me to come out?" His eyebrows jet towards his hairline.

"Pretty much."

"It's freezing! It could have been hours!"

"Posts on Montana's feed show that you usually are walking in this area about this time of day. I took a chance. If that didn't work, well, I was prepared to wait as long as I needed."

The Blue Norther pushes across the nation's capital as spring quells the dying gasps of winter. The tail of Oliver's trench coat flaps up behind him as the gusty air catches it like a flag on a pole. Montana stands and becomes restless, pacing under the restraint of the leash.

Oliver leans towards Alex. At thirty-two, he is the youngest sitting US senator. He rubs his lower lids which are swollen with lack of sleep. "What's going on?"

She surveys their surroundings again before lifting her eyes to his.

"I need your help," Alex says. She winces as the cold falls over them like a drum fill. She glances around the Mall, again, and Oliver wonders what she's looking for. Or who. "We can't talk here. Is there somewhere we can meet later? Somewhere we can go, privately?"

"Yes. 575 Danube Avenue ... apartment 323," he says. "Tonight. Ten o'clock? We should be wrapped up from session by then."

"Are you sure it's private?"

Oliver gaze lowers to his old friend. "No one but my assistant knows I'm staying there," he admits.

Alex tilts her head, her eyes silently questioning him. "575 Danube Avenue, Apartment 323," the reporter repeats.

Oliver nods.

"I'll be there," she says.

US Senator Oliver Michaels has had enough with his colleagues on both sides of the aisle.

"What are we doing?" He stands on the floor of the US Senate Chamber, his hands open as if gripping a small invisible box as he implores the nation's elected officials to take action.

"The American people voted for us and put their faith in us that we would serve them. How have we repaid that trust? With petty bickering, finger pointing, and serving not our constituents but big business." Oliver tightens one hand into a fist and uses his other thumb for emphasis as he continues his list. "We're serving lobbyists with ambiguous moral codes and leaders with questionable ethics. *Not* the interest of the people who put us in this very room."

With a pause, he slides his hands into the pockets of his navy-blue suit and paces slowly away from the podium. His forehead creases into an equal sign before he turns back to the microphone mounted on the podium. He grips the edges of the dark wood and exhales so audibly it echoes on the speakers mounted around the chamber.

"So, I ask you again, *what are we doing here?*" As the passion in his voice rises, so does the native Maine accent that he has learned to quash during most speeches and interviews. "Doing" is dragged out slowly like a pebble floating down to a creek bottom. The department store suit, flag red tie, and crisp white shirt are the only polish about Oliver now. The niceties of bureaucracy are forgotten along with the emphasis to complete his R's.

"The Adequate Income for Americans Bill is before us and we have a chance to improve the lives of every American, not just the wealthy. Sadly, in my home state of Maine, the average cost of living is $45,000 a year. The average income is $31,000 annually."

Oliver reaches up and rubs his fingertips against the creases in his brow. "You don't have to be Albert Einstein to see the math is off. To live with basic human needs, it's almost eleven grand more a year than what the average person brings home. That's not living. That, ladies and gentlemen of the senate, is surviving!" He clutches a fist and slows the speed of its descent before his knuckles rap against the podium. "Tell me how it's fair that in what is *supposed* to be the greatest country in the world, our citizens move through life day to day in survival mode." He grips the sides of the podium again as he leans towards the microphone.

"My colleague from Texas argued earlier that with proper education, every American has a chance to succeed and increase their income. I challenge Senator Giles to take another look."

Oliver opens his worn, leather-bound portfolio, pressing the palm of his hand against the sheets of index paper with an almost illegible cursive scribbled on every free space. Upon his election as a state representative almost ten years ago, his mother gifted him the now tattered brown leather folder.

Oliver turns a paper and surveys his notes. "We know not every American has access to equal education. We know that college graduates have been entering the workforce with an average of twenty to $25,000 in debt. In Senator Giles' home state, the minimum wage is $7.25 an hour and education ranks 28th of the states. Oh, and the cost of living in the great state of Texas?" Oliver lifts a hand and slices it through the air. "It's $39,000. Now factor in student loan payments, childcare for a single mom of two, or a cancer patient with insurmountable medical bills for life-saving chemotherapy, and you tell me how anyone can do more than survive?"

From his seat behind the bench, Senator Giles flares his nostrils.

Oliver continues his spiel. "The American people deserve better. A few weeks ago, I gathered several of my constituents during a town hall meeting in Maine. I met with Naomi Bowman, a sixty-three-year-old widow and daycare worker who was hoping to live off Social Security. Naomi began working her first job at fourteen and hasn't stopped, and you know what? She's not going to be able to retire in two years or any time soon. On her single income, with her treatments and prescriptions for diabetes, monthly rent for her apartment and the rising costs of groceries, Social Security won't even cover a third of utility and medical bills. I refuse to leave this chamber floor in good faith that I didn't do everything I could to help people like Naomi and millions of others. If we aren't helping the people we serve," he continues, shaking his head as he taps his thumbs repeatedly on the podium, "then what are we even doing here? We don't deserve these seats. Not when poverty and homelessness are on the rise. I am begging you to put aside the interests of big business and Wall Street and vote in favor of the Adequate Income for Americans Bill because of basic human decency and empathy. If you believe in the Founding Fathers as many of you so claim, then remember these words from the Declaration of Independence, 'All men are created equal that they are endowed by their Creator with inalienable Rights that among these are Life, Liberty and the pursuit of Happiness.' They never intended for Americans to have Death, Subjugation and Strife. We have a chance to help our people live life without fear of eviction, bankruptcy or lack of healthcare. We have a chance to do the right thing. Vote yes."

Oliver closes the old portfolio and tucks it under his arm as he returns to his seat. There are no further appeals to be made. The bill had passed in the House of Representatives and now awaits approval at the next level of Congress.

Senate Chair Bill Ackerman opens the voting.

There is a spattering of "yea" as the senators' votes are called for alphabetically by the clerk. The first no comes from Senator Travis Chickman of Kentucky. Thus begins the chorus of "nay." Senator Giles of Texas cuts his eyes across the room to where Oliver is trying to sit tall, and it's no surprise to the Maine senator when Giles gruffly says, "Nay."

Oliver's voice is loud and strong as he says "yea" when his name is called. He ticks away at something in front of him with his pen.

When they reach the final vote, Senator Zilsky of Nebraska, Oliver examines the tally he's been keeping on his notepad. He doesn't need to hear the chairman say it. His shoulders drop before he recovers. With a vote of 76 nays to 34 yeas, the bill doesn't pass.

———————— ◦•◦ — ◦•◦ ————————

A rap sounds at the door. Oliver moves around the coffee table, with Montana hopping up to inspect the visitor waiting on the other side of the door. Oliver removes the chain and then unlocks the double bolt before pulling the door open quickly. He finds Alex looking down the hall. She steps inside, a battered messenger bag draped across her body. Oliver shuts the door behind her, locking it before turning to face her.

They stand inches apart, peering back at each other, curiosity in their gazes. The old friends had kept in periodic contact over the years. Alex was the first of the college friends to call and congratulate Oliver on each night of his campaign victories: as a state representative, a state senator, and most recently the US senate race. She has clearly followed his political career as he has followed hers, reading her stories in *The Times*, blown-away by the intricate, in-depth pieces she has put together over the years. He remembers when she began writing for *The Daily Campus*, the University of Connecticut paper. She's come a very long way since writing a hype piece about him when he was captain of the football team.

"It's good to see you, Oliver." The words come out unsure, lacking her usual confidence.

"You too." He nods. He lifts his arms, apprehensive at first, but wraps them around her, pulling her against him. She returns the hug, resting her cheek against his arm as he holds her. His arms pull her tighter, resting against her warmth. He rests his cheek against her curls as they grip each other. Oliver pulls back when he feels the hug has lingered a heartbeat longer than it should. Alex lifts her gaze up into his eyes before dropping her arms and walking away from him to pet the top of Montana's head. "You're staying here?" she asks, her back to Oliver.

He puts the chain in place on the door and bolts it. "Yes, I moved in about three months ago."

"You and Lydia ...?" She glances at him over her shoulder.

He puts a hand into the pockets of his cutoff sweats and tugs at a loose string on his old UConn T-shirt.

"It's not working," he confesses softly. "We separated. Trying this for a while but we both know it's over." He shakes his head.

"I'm so sorry, Oliver." Alex's words seem sincere.

His stare lingers on a dust bunny on the floor before leaning against the wall. "So, what's going on, Alex?"

She takes a deep breath and opens her messenger bag. She pulls out a piece of paper rubber banded around several photos.

"I got this at my office the other day." She puts the packet down on the coffee table and sets her messenger bag down beside it.

Oliver steps forward, reaches down and picks up the photos. Frown lines deepen on his forehead as he looks over each one. There are multiple pictures of a creek littered with dead fish. Another shows a large factory with a barrel tipped over oozing thick chemical sludge onto the soil. He flips and there is a photo of the Administrator of the Environmental Protection Agency, Rupert Ingelman, along with US Senators Travis Chickman and Martin Eisenhower, and a fourth and fifth man Oliver does not recognize. Chickman is shaking hands with one of the unidentified men. The photo appears to have been taken with a long-range lens from an elevated position, perhaps from a balcony or maybe even from a tree.

"That's Lonnie Cobert." Alex points with her index finger, answering Oliver's silent question. "I did a scan and a Google Lens search. Image recognition came back from a LinkedIn profile. Not a trace of him on the company website but he's CEO of Takestrom Chemicals," she explains. "That factory is just outside of Marktown, Indiana. A letter I received claims that the factory has been putting toxic chemicals in the soil and water sources for the town. It's killing the wildlife. The emissions and working conditions are also being linked to respiratory illnesses and some cancers. Despite complaints from residents and a few attempts by workers at lawsuits, it's all being swept under the rug."

"Who is this?" Oliver studies the image of a short man with black hair.

"I don't know yet; I'm working on it," Alex replies. "But I'm guessing not simply an upstanding and interested citizen."

Oliver holds the photos and takes a seat on his sofa. Alex sits down beside him, placing her messenger bag on the coffee table.

"I pulled this up. It's a report from the EPA from about five years ago," Alex says as she takes a paper from her bag and hands it over. "A list of violations you could wrap around the equator. That's just a summary. Somehow, Takestrom has never faced a penalty, or a single civil administrative or judicial action."

Oliver skims the paper, then returns to the pictures.

Something jogs Oliver's mind when he sees Ingelman's face in the photo. A grouping of numbers comes to mind but it's foggy. He elects not to mention the vague recollection to Alex. He moves his attention to the other pictured faces.

"What are Chickman and Eisenhower doing with Ingelman and these guys?"

"Insurance. At least, I think," Alex replies.

Oliver stares curiously.

"You remember voting on a resolution under the Congressional Review Act last year? It would have required companies to report any labor violations, even alleged violations, that they had had in the last three years before they could bid on a federal contract?"

Oliver's head moves in the affirmative. "I voted for it. I believe it would have been a requirement if the contract was going to pay them anything over $500,000."

"Exactly. No small chump change, but big contracts. You remember what happened to it?"

He licks his lips. "It didn't pass. We didn't have the votes," Oliver sighs. "I've come to learn that there are never enough votes for that type of thing."

"You and four others were the only senators who were in favor of the requirement. Every other senator, every single one except for you five, voted against it. Now, for two of them at least, I know why."

Oliver puts the photos on the coffee table and listens to Alex intently.

"Takestrom Chemicals was awarded a $10 million federal contract to help dispose of toxic waste and slush last year. They should have never been awarded the contract in the first place. They already had a shitload of EPA violations, until suddenly, they got this massive contract. Not a single violation has been reported against them or is on record since. But from these photos, if we can get to Marktown, the evidence of what they are doing is right there."

Oliver stares down at the picture of the factory on the coffee table.

"Oliver. This is where you come in," Alex begins. "I think Chickman, Eisenhower, and Ingelman are getting kickbacks from Takestrom to keep all of this hush-hush. Whoever sent me this information knows it, too. I don't have a connection yet regarding the involvement of the fifth man, but I will find it."

"Maybe that's who had the photos taken?"

"Maybe."

Oliver shrugs. "I don't know what you want me to do, Alex. I mean … what could I do about it?"

"You're a senator, for Christ's sake. These are your colleagues. You have access that no reporter could ever have." Alex gestures wildly with her hands, pushing her head forward and lifting her brows.

Oliver blinks. "Even if I can get you some information, what good would it do?"

"Oliver! You have to know someone that can help get us some kind of proof of the under the table dealings between these guys."

"Alex," he says, shaking his head. "Yeah, probably, but ... this is Washington. This type of thing goes on all the time."

Alex's eyelids flutter and then she frowns deeply. "What, we just turn a blind eye to it?"

"No, that's not what I'm saying—"

"What are you saying?"

"You pick your battles." Oliver's voice rises. "Do you know how many lobbyists and corporations pull the strings on campaign donations and pressure people to vote this way or that? It's not going to change. The system is rigged. It always will be." He lets out a defeated huff.

For a full minute, silence ensues like that of outer space, a silence of distance and vastness.

Montana sneezes next to the coffee table, the first noise to break the quiet. He shakes his body and yawns.

"I should have known better." Alex yanks the photos and sheet of paper from Oliver's hand and stuffs them back into her bag.

"You should have known what?" Oliver inventories her profile, searching.

"That you would be of no help. The American government doesn't give a shit about its people." Oliver opens his mouth to speak but Alex continues her tirade. "We've got the proof right here!" She jams a finger at the photos in her hand. "The EPA doesn't care. The senate doesn't seem to care. FEMA sure as hell didn't care." She speaks with such ire her face contorts into someone Oliver doesn't recognize.

With the mention of one acronym, Oliver comprehends this situation is about much more to her than just Takestrom. "Alex."

"What happened to you?"

"Alex—"

"No!" She lifts a hand and eyes him up and down with a look that makes him feel small. "What happened to the campaign promises of Oliver Michaels? You sold us all on a message of hope and optimism. What happened to the man out there fighting for the little guys and trying to do the right thing?"

He sighs and rests his elbows on his knees, looking down at the floor. "I got to Washington and saw that nothing was going to change. It's always going to be business as usual here. I had such big hopes with the Live and Learn Initiative and the Adequate Income for Americans Bill. Those got shut down so quickly my head is still spinning. It's about the buck here, not the people. Democracy died in this country a long time ago. We were just too caught up in football games and Big Macs to notice."

Alex puts her hands on her hips. "Okay, so, you had two initiatives that didn't pass. You go back and try it again from another angle. Oliver, look at these pictures. Look at what's happening in that town. Your colleagues are responsible for this. You help me blow the lid off this whole thing, and we'll shut it down. Do we disinfect all of DC? No. But do we make changes one step at a time where we can? Hell yes."

Warily, he lifts his head, about to speak, but she continues.

"The Oliver I knew would be furious about this. He would rally people together to put a stop to this kind of thing. He would be outraged that politicians were behind this. He would blow the whistle on it. Jesus! Has Lydia sucked that much life out of you, really?" It leaves her mouth with such force and contempt Alex's countenance registers her own surprise.

Oliver sits up straight, his jaw clenched. He gulps and closes his eyes.

Alex pauses and puts her hand to her forehead. "Oliver ... I'm sorry, I—"

He waves his hand. "No, no. You're right," His eyes are fixed to the floor.

She takes a seat beside him. "I didn't mean to bring that up. I just ..."

He lifts his eyes to her.

"This isn't you. I know you. I know you stand up for people. I know your heart," she pleads.

It's clear she is worried about the man her friend has become. Oliver's mind flips like an automated card shuffler from one idea to the next as he tries to speak anything but the truth nagging him.

He exhales, the blustery release of air deflating his body. "I'm sorry. I can't help you."

Chapter 2

Aubrey Fischer's maroon minivan clanks as she drives, the sound followed by a series of rapid sputters, then a sizzling like bacon frying in a skillet. The smell of sulfur blows through the vents and she punches a button to turn the heater off. With a prayer and a few swears, Aubrey wills the old minivan to keep powering out of the parking lot of Tony's Meat and Fruit Market in East Chicago to her home in Marktown, Indiana.

She flicks her gaze to the rearview mirror where Felicity is strapped into her car seat, eyes trained to the window and the passing town. Felicity's legs bounce and her feet wag to whatever melody is in her head. Aubrey and Felicity were both having good mornings when she made the decision to venture to the store. Aubrey's gaze returns to the road.

She had a few extra dollars from her husband, Jessie, for the trip to Tony's and the luxury of purchasing the breakfast meat and stretching it to make BLTs for dinner. The cubed cuts of chuck for stew had taken all the bills in her wallet. She pushed coins around on her palm and ignored the line of customers behind her while she counted out enough to buy Felicity a lollipop. Today, every dollar and cent went into buying something other than ramen noodles and mac and cheese. Tomorrow, they would worry about paying tomorrow's bills.

Aubrey, Jessie, and Felicity Fischer's mobile home slumps at the edge of Marktown in the forested shadow of a chemical plant. Marktown had once been considered a tourist attraction, a wonder of the world. The streets were walkways, and the sidewalks served as parking spots.

It is the only truly remarkable oddity about the Indiana community. Now, its singular claim to fame is that it neighbors the Mascot Hall of Fame in Whiting. Otherwise, it was just another manufacturing town that failed to keep up the type of economic growth to label it anything different.

Aubrey drives past townhomes that are carbon copies of each other, though the original factory in town had produced steel. The wall of one neighboring townhome ends where another starts, each painted in varying but now fading colors to give the addresses some distinguishable characteristics. Most of the residences had been built in the mid-1910s and few renovations transformed them.

The edge of the town where the Fischers live ends abruptly. The dilapidated homes bookend where World War I stopped development. Marktown had been a planned industrial residence for millionaire Clayton Mark's steel factory, but when the boys were needed in Europe and the influx of immigrant workers slowed, Mark sold his factory. The plans for building dropped with the bloodied bodies on foreign soil.

Most of the duplexes and almost all the storefronts are boarded up with two-by-fours, plywood, and in some cases nothing more than cardboard. Commerce had left Marktown for more fruitful sales in nearby Gary.

There isn't even motivation by local riffraff to graffiti the soft, rotting boards. Even deviants lack the heart to deface the grim properties.

Mobile homes, like the Fischer's, are positioned diagonally and horizontally from each other at the town's borders, as if someone had left Legos scattered across the sinking marshlands.

Aubrey rolls the minivan onto the sand and gravel outside their gray and white house. She cuts the motor and the minivan shudders hard before it stills. It shakes so hard, Aubrey is reluctant to try and start it again, fearing another disappointment. She exits the van and slams the door, the wind whipping around her thin body and knocking her off balance. Marktown is far enough inland that there is only a faint waft of fish from Lake Michigan. The wind blowing over the freshwater carries enough moisture to create fat snowflakes that fall to the earth and make the streets treacherously slick in the winter.

The energy Aubrey started the day with is waning. She slides open the van door and smiles at Felicity. As Aubrey leans in to unfasten the belts of Felicity's car seat, the little girl takes her mother's face between her clammy hands and places a kiss on her cheek. Despite her world weariness and winded breaths, Aubrey smiles as she scoops up Felicity. She places the little girl on her hip as she opens the screen door and unlocks the front door.

The walking, wind and weight of Felicity bring on a tightness in her chest as if there isn't enough oxygen in the atmosphere. She places Felicity down on the couch.

"Mama will be right back. Stay put."

"'Kay!"

Aubrey swallows hard before she trods back out of the house and leans against the minivan's passenger side door, her forearm resting against the cold metal in her thin jacket, her head resting weakly against her arm. She gazes down at the ground, wanting to hurry to get back inside to her daughter and not leave her unattended. Eyes to the ground, she inspects the dust and gravel outside their home. She'd tried to grow a garden no less than three times so her family could have fresh fruits and vegetables for nutrition. But the produce never seemed to flourish in the soil outside their home.

Despite the many businesses that had moved away and the lack of farms, one corporation has remained for the last twenty-seven years. MacAllen Industries bought out the bankrupt Paradigm Steel and, with it, revived and resurrected it into Takestrom Chemicals. Takestrom produces many solvents found in products under the kitchen sink, including the Fischer's, in the containers where food was stored, and even in the walls that held homes together. Benzene was the top output from the company, unless one counted the limitless byproducts: leukemia, lymphoma, and myeloma specifically.

Most of Takestrom's workers didn't live to see the retirement benefits and pensions for their years of service and exposure. Most of the Marktown residents didn't leave this world peacefully in their beds but were, instead, hooked to ventilators and oxygen masks, gasping until life left them.

It takes Aubrey a minute to regain her breath. She thinks of Felicity and with a mother's resolve, she picks up the bag of groceries from the middle seat and with a grunt, pulls the sliding door shut.

Alex's messenger bag thuds against the floor as she sits a brown paper bag down on top of her keyboard. Reaching inside, she retrieves the hot sandwich, wrapped in yellow paper already greasy with drippings from the melted cheese and roasted beef. She pushes aside a stack of papers and old newspapers cluttering her desk to make room for lunch or dinner—at this point in the day, she isn't sure which. Tossing her head back, she guzzles a can of soda like she did beer more than a dozen years ago in college. After plopping down in her chair, Alex shifts the brown bag over to the newly freed spot on her desk.First, powering on her computer, she then grips the sandwich in both hands, cheese dangling in a string from her lips as she chomps into the meat and groans, reveling in the satisfaction of a hot meal after so many hours on the job. Her toes ache, cramping like a printer paper jam and folding even in her loafers. The bottoms of her feet are sweaty in her shoes—even in the fifty-degree weather. Alex hadn't just been pounding the pavement, she had resurfaced the streets of New York City.

As she chews, her eyes lift up to the double-height skylight above the newsroom. The light is less sharp with the setting sun. The desk clock confirms the time. It's neighbored by a photo of her at age nine, seated on a piano bench with her fingers on a baby grand. Another is a framed photo of her and her father, a tall, bald man with a round belly sticking out from beneath his too-small polo shirt.

It's 7:08 p.m. and this is her first chance at any semblance of a break all day, since arriving at the office before nine this morning.

Even though official office hours ended a little over an hour ago, the newsroom still bustles with reporters, copy editors, and digital content creators trying to beat out the clock before deadline.

After working in medium markets including Hartford and Austin, Alex's keen eye and commitment to upholding the ethics of journalism caught the attention of staffers at *The Times*. She'd written a piece for *The Austin American-Statesman* that exposed a Texas representative for getting his not-quite-20-something intern plastered and having drunken sex with her. Alex's interview with the former intern had picked up national attention once the state representative was forced to resign. For the last three years, she has been a member of the esteemed Times' investigative unit. Alex has built her career on exposés and in-depth profiles on the world's most influential people.

Her computer screen comes to life. Holding the sandwich in one hand, she pecks out the keys for her password with the other. Her wallpaper appears: a navy blue, white and gray theme with the UConn Huskies logo in the center. She glances at the photo of her at thirteen years old wearing braces and standing next to her father. They'd been the exception rather than the norm, cheering for the Huskies all those years from their home near the banks of the Mississippi River in New Orleans ninth ward, instead of the local favorite LSU Tigers. During the month of March, for most of her childhood, they had ordered pizza and wings and not left the sofa for the entire weekend watching the tournament and UConn basketball. She was nine when they celebrated one championship and fourteen when they danced and hugged for another national crown. She pauses for a moment as she scrutinizes her father's big smile in the picture. It was taken just one year before the levees burst amid the hurricane's fury.

She thinks of home. She lays the sandwich in its wrap on her desk and reaches into the messenger bag on the floor. She retrieves the envelope that had come to her three days ago in the stack of mail that was dropped off on her desk sometime during the day. It had blended in so easily with the other piles of paper, Post-its, and half-used reporter notepads, she had almost overlooked it. There was no return address. She'd grabbed the large envelope, feeling its weight and thickness. Alex tore open the top, reached in, and pulled out a printed letter with no name and no address on a plain sheet of paper. It was typed—but with the almost archaic strikes and misalignment of a typewriter. The kind of anonymous, cryptic letter that had been featured in every suspense and horror film over the last sixty years of cinema. "How very cliché," Alex whispered to herself. There were several photos included with the letter. The lines in them indicated that they had been printed on a regular home inkjet printer. The pictures, though riddled with broken lines, were clear in what they showcased. She knew Senator Chickman from his weekly media blitz on a cable network that she felt drummed up conspiracy theories and fear. Senator Eisenhower was tenured and though he didn't make as big a spectacle of himself, he was easily recognizable in American media. His appearance reminded Alex each time she saw him of the snowman in the motion-captured adaptation of *Rudolph the Red-Nosed Reindeer* she'd watched every Christmas as a child.

The face of one of the other men had been familiar to her since she was a teenager: Rupert Ingelman. She'd seen his face in the press for months when he'd been with the public affairs office for the Federal Emergency Management Agency, FEMA. He'd moved on to become the Administrator to the EPA.

It had taken more digging that night to find the name and likeness of Lonnie Colbert. Once Alex had most of the players, she'd headed to Washington and Oliver's front door.

Now, she flips through the pictures as she runs her tongue over her lips. Someone wanted her to have this, but why her? Why now? What were the stakes for someone coming forward?

The questions cycled like a View-Master in her mind before the mental interrogation was interrupted.

Her co-worker Coleman Chester stops beside her desk. "Alex, you just getting back? Almost quittin' time!"

Alex turns the photos over and lays them on the desk. Her eyes lift to meet Coleman's. He is wearing a no-nonsense black suit with a black and blue tie. His blond hair is gelled and slicked back, and when he smirks at her, his dimples are as deep as canyons. His warm brown eyes are appealing, draped with lashes that rival false extensions. His nickname around the office is The Human Ken Doll. His smirk is the type that seems to compel women out of their clothes and into his bed. Alex has, at least up until this point, been able to avoid any such a rendezvous with her co-worker.

"You know, Coleman, some of us real journalists are just getting started," Alex retorts, grabbing her sandwich and chomping for emphasis.

"And some of us have appointments this evening." He grins. He drapes his coat over his arm, shifting the briefcase he is carrying from one hand to the other.

"Is tonight's appointment brunette or blonde?" Alex's mouth is full as she puts a finger to her chin as she pretends to ponder her own question.

"Neither." He winks. "Redhead. Bottle job, but still red."

Alex chuckles. "Good luck with that."

"Oh, I won't need it," he says over his shoulder as he begins to walk away. "See you tomorrow."

"Bye Coleman." Alex shakes her head incredulously. He gives her one more wink and a glance before turning and walking towards the elevators.

She takes another sip from her drink, glancing at the stack of over-turned photos and then her desk phone. The blinking light indicates she has voicemail. She grabs a pen and notepad from the chaos of her desk and lifts the phone receiver to her ear. She has a few messages in response to the zoo story. There is only one complaint message, which she deletes, and a few others praising the story and requesting follow-ups with details on how citizens can help.

There is also a message from her mother. "Alex, you aren't answering your cell when I call so I thought I'd try you at your office." An exaggerated sigh is part of the recording. "Please call me when you have the chance. Okay?"

Alex sucks at her teeth in response and presses 2 to delete the message. The last few weeks, she has been working on an investigative piece about the impact of school choice in urban communities and its effect on public school standards. Today, she made the rounds, visiting several schools in Harlem and the Bronx, talking with teachers, parents, and a few high school students about the conditions in stark contrast to some of the private schools with years-long waiting lists. She's excited about the piece but still faces several more weeks of digging and interviews. Not surprising at all, the communications office with the New York City Department of Education has been dragging its feet on forking over all the data she submitted in her Freedom of Information request. She hasn't submitted a formal complaint about the filing, yet.

Her eyes dance back to the stack of photos, and she flips them over, studying the men photographed during the covert meeting. Alex stares until every line and grain of the printed photo feels memorized.

She types a search on her computer now that it's booted. Scrolling down the page, the cursor hovers over a link and date. She glances at the desk calendar.

A thought strikes like a five-ton vehicle. She thrusts her chair back as she stands and bolts towards Patrick's office, hoping he hasn't left for the evening. She needs a ticket.

Oliver's front door key still works, a surprising revelation. He wasn't sure if his wife, Lydia, had changed the locks by now. It's been a month since he took so much as a step in the direction of their DC townhouse.

She'd left a message on his cell, reminding him of the photo shoot and interview they had early in the morning. He had already forgotten about it. His assistant, Yvette, reminded him of it again before she left him alone at the office earlier that evening. He looked at the calendar, sighing heavily as he realized he was to take center stage the next day in his role of keeping this farce alive.

He opens the door, and the house is dark except for the blue glow of a television in the living room. He hangs up his gray wool coat on the rack next to the door, sitting his briefcase underneath it.

Two mastiffs lounge in wool-lined dog beds in the foyer. One lifts its head quizzically at Oliver, studying him before resting his long lips back down on the bed. The other is snoring and unmoved at the return of one of its owners.

"Good to see you guys, too," Oliver huffs.

A singing competition, one of Lydia's favorite shows, blares from the television. A teenage voice hits a note, not quite off-key but not on it either. There is no movement in the house. Diffusers pumping the joyful scent of citrus throughout the house almost mask the stringent smell of disinfectants and cleaning products. She'd likely hired a cleaning service to come in earlier that day and prepare their home for the cameras tomorrow. Optics were everything, and he highly doubted she had done the scrubbing herself.

He strides across the hardwood flooring into the living room, peeking around for any sign of life. He is about to call out to her when he sees her blonde hair in a luminous blonde beehive, swirled about her head, highlighted by the TV light like a messy halo.

She is laying on her stomach, her face buried in the cushions of the sofa. Her high heels are on the floor just next to the coffee table. An arm hangs limply off the side of the sofa, her fingertips almost reaching the oak boards.

Finding her in such a state would have caused him alarm if he had not seen her like this so many times before. An empty bottle of red wine sits on top of the coffee table, beside a half-full stemmed glass. A highball sits next to it. He picks it up, taking a sniff of the residual brown liquor. The sharp inhalation stings his nostrils, making his head jerk. He sighs, running a hand over his face, and loosens the constricting tie for a third time that evening.

"Lydia." She does not move.

"Lydia!" he repeats. The arm hanging off the sofa jerks and the blonde hair tumbles to the side as she turns her head. She groans and rolls over onto her side, wincing from the glare of the television. The rims of her eyelids are pink, her face red on one side where the blood had pooled, imprints of the sofa stitching wrinkling her skin.

Oliver reaches for the television remote on the coffee table, turning the sound down before dropping the remote on the coffee table. The loud whack forces her to squint in response.

"Wasn't sure you got my message," Lydia breathes out, rolling onto her back. She rubs at her eyes, squinting before sluggishly shifting to a sitting position. She is wearing a satin slip, and a thin strap dangles off her pale shoulder, dangerously close to exposing one of her surgically enhanced breasts. The dress she had been wearing was thrown into the seat of a nearby chair.

"Yeah," he grunts. He takes off his suit jacket, folding it and laying it across the arm of the sofa. "I'm here. I figured we better not risk it in case there is traffic or something in the morning and I have trouble getting here on time. Best for me to stay tonight since they're coming so early. I'll sleep in the guest room," he spells out for her flatly.

She nods and runs a hand through her disheveled hair, pulling at the knots to free the tangles then places both hands on the edge of the couch and blinks.

A sleepy smile stretches her lips. "You came home."

He sighs. "Let's get you upstairs and in bed. You need to sleep this off before the morning." He bends down, loops an arm around her waist, and helps her to stand. As he does, she stumbles and leans into him. He lifts one of her arms, guiding it over his shoulder, as he helps her. Liquor and wine permeate her skin like toxic perfume.

They move to the staircase, Lydia's toes all but dragging over the floor as Oliver carries most of her alarmingly thin frame. She's lost at least five more pounds since he last saw her. He knows she won't make it up the stairs this way, and he bends down, scooping her up into his arms as he heads up the steps. She rests her head on his shoulder, her face inches from his. She lifts her other arm, looping it around his neck. Oliver feels her eyes, heavy with the effects of her many drinks, locked onto his profile.

He makes his way to what used to be their bedroom, clutching her against him as he quickly lifts a hand to flip on the light before returning it to cradle her. He moves to the bed and slowly lowers her down on top of it, but Lydia keeps her arms draped around his neck and shoulders."Oliver ..." Her voice is hoarse. He can smell the cocktail of wine, liquor, and maybe even pills on her lips as he lowers her down, her breath tickling his cheek. She bites her lip as she looks up at him from underneath her lashes. He recognizes this look. When they were in college, he saw it daily, her insatiable appetite for his body needing to be placated every night and sometimes again in the morning just before football practice.He stares at her as she lies back on the bed, her head resting on the pillow as she peers up at him. She slides her hands from around his neck to cup his face.

"Lyd—" he begins, but he is cut off when she pulls his head down to hers, her mouth seizing his. Oliver is paralyzed in her grip. He wants to resist. The virulent nature of their coexistence has turned the heart that once complied with her every demand and desire to driftwood.

She runs her fingers into his dark brown hair, her tongue pressing against the seam of his lips and pushing its way inside. He tastes the alcohol first. He doesn't remember the last time he kissed her and didn't taste it. Lydia slides one hand down from Oliver's neck, over his chest, fluttering down his stomach until her hand rests comfortably against the juncture in his pants.

Oliver's eyes shut as he tries to feel pleasure in her touch. He wills himself to feel. Her mouth smacks against his and with the hand behind his neck, she pulls down, indicating for him to join her on the bed. His body eases on top of hers, but he lets her lead the way. The last time they even attempted to make love was twelve weeks ago in an effort to save their marriage.

She pulls away, breaking the kiss, and, breathing hard, as she inspects his face. His eyes are open. She grips his shoulders, rolls her body, flipping him onto his back. Lydia straddles his waist, smiling in her intoxicated state down at him as she rolls her hips against him. She pulls her slip over her head.

Oliver stares up at the ceiling. Something becomes painfully clear after several breaths. Lydia stops her movements, glaring at him in frustration. She sits up, her head lolling forward with her slurred speech.

"You can't get it up, can you?" She scoffs. "Wow."

"Lydia, I'm just not in the mood, all right?"

She covers her bare breasts with her arms. "This is so pathetic," she says, throwing her legs off his body and the mattress. She stands beside the bed, swaying.

"And you're drunk," Oliver sits up on his elbows. "You're always drunk. Maybe for once I'd like to try this and have you remember it in the morning."

She scowls at him. "Maybe just once I'd like to feel like my husband gives a shit about me."

Oliver throws his hands up and climbs off the bed. "We've both known this was over for a long time now, Lydia. This isn't something that happened overnight. We don't even live under the same roof anymore!"

"Get out," Lydia turns away from him as she runs her fingers through her hair.

Oliver studies the back of her head before turning with a deep sigh and heading back downstairs. He opens the door to the guest room, taking off his tie as he sits on the edge of the bed. He rests his elbows on his knees as he puts his face in his hands.

CHAPTER 3

Light bulbs and metallic backgrounds on stands surround Lydia and Oliver, illuminating them as a photographer snaps pictures and a videographer rolls during the interview.

Before dawn, Lydia had held a frozen spoon under her eyelids to take down the swelling. Each breath reminds her of the skull-splitting headache she'd chewed ibuprofen to ease. She guzzled Pedialyte as soon as the alarm clock blared like a foghorn in her ears. Lydia's dark blue dress complements Oliver's attire, her hair is neatly swept into an elegant updo, and a string of pearls is around her neck.

Tamara Jones leans forward in her chair. The veteran reporter for *People Magazine* has interviewed dignitaries and movie stars over the years and is in full control of this conversation. She is as much of a celebrity as the people she interviews, making appearances on Good Morning America, Entertainment Tonight, and CNN. Her ebony skin is accented in a dark orange, sleeveless dress, with perfectly placed gold jewelry and her short hair slicked and waved in the style of Josephine Baker.

Tamara sits across from the young couple, holding hands on the sofa. A light kit is set up in the living room. Her husband is dressed in a pale blue sweater with a white-collared shirt underneath and gray slacks.

"Our lives have really been an open book." The smile Lydia flashes has been practiced and cultivated for years; it neighbors sincerity. "Quite literally, we are an open book." She laughs as she gestures to a scrapbook one of the campaign assistants had made for Lydia to help her appeal to the Pinterest voters during Oliver's at-home senate run that sits open on the coffee table.

"May I?" Lydia asks, pointing to the album with an unwavering, enthusiastic smile.

"Absolutely." Tamara folds her hands over her knees and watches as Lydia carefully stands, ducking underneath the shotgun mic and out of frame for just a moment to grab the blue and white picnic blanket bound book with ruffles. "What can you show us?" Tamara grins with intrigue.

"This one," Lydia spins the book around as Tamara leans forward. Lydia indicates with a red-tipped nail a picture of four people sitting at a table: a younger looking Oliver in a department store suit with his hair neatly gelled; his mother, Andrea, a blonde with short cropped hair and wrinkles at the corners of her pink lips and tired eyes; his kid sister, Leah, looking unimpressed by the hoopla and uncomfortable in her dress complete with petticoats and Mary Jane shoes; and lastly, his brother, Andrew, who is a miniature version of his big brother in his suit and clip-on tie.

"This was the night of the draft," Lydia explains as Tamara leans in. "Twenty-eight overall picks in the first round," Lydia recalls. "I don't think Oliver breathed once until the commissioner announced his name as Tampa Bay's pick."

"I sat in that chair a very, very long time." Oliver's brow lifts as he nods. "Don't let that smile fool you, I was a nervous wreck thinking I was going to be left sitting there and get passed over that night."

"But they did call his name," Lydia interjects, "and Oliver loved his time with the Buccaneers."

He had loved the Tampa Bay fans as long as they loved him. Oliver's pro quarterback days lasted two seasons before a UCL injury and Tommy John surgery weakened his right throwing arm. As the interception and incomplete pass stats rose, the fans started calling for his replacement.

Rather than dwell on the disappointment of a short-lived pro-career, Oliver seized the opportunity to put his political science degree from UConn to work. The NFL dollars and the face that had garnered several product endorsements deals left Oliver and Lydia with a comfortable financial status to support her and pursue her husband's political aspirations.

He first ran for Maine state representative in District 6, which included his hometown of South Berwick. It was the kind of town where the local bank posted the athletic scores on the electronic marquee out front—win or lose, and they'd rarely lost. Oliver had helped lead Marshwood High School to a state championship, earning him an athletic scholarship offer from the Huskies.

Oliver's movie star good looks, coupled with Lydia as his charming and beautiful wife, his status as a former college and pro football standout, combined with his youth and optimism for the future of American politics, drew the attention of the nation to his household.

Lydia lifts her chin high. Tamara flashes another smile. "People are comparing you two to a modern-day Jackie O and JFK; what do you think of those comparisons?"

Oliver's pause gives Lydia the chance to respond. It's in these moments that she shines.

"It's obviously very flattering," Lydia says after a moment of contemplation. "They were very influential as a couple on the social and political landscape here in Washington. I think Oliver and I don't quite compare." Lydia gives an amused gasp. "He's not from a wealthy family with powerful roots in this country. Everything Oliver has achieved, he worked for and accomplished on his own," Lydia places her other hand on top of the one he holds. "He's truly a story of what can be achieved when you believe in yourself, work hard, and have the blue-collar mindset to make your dreams a reality. I'm just a girl from California who was lucky enough to fall in love with him," she says, looking into his eyes. Oliver blinks slowly and squeezes her hand as they stare back at one another.

After the US Senate election, Oliver's lack of free time got worse. With his NFL money, he'd purchased the $3.5 million townhome for Lydia, giving her the means to decorate it as she saw fit. He had hoped the task would occupy her mind and her time. But she had found it harder to adjust to life in DC than in Maine. She was the wife of the youngest senator and low in the pecking order with the other wives. Many had shunned her because of her age and their lack of children, but also because Oliver was a celebrity who now occupied a seat in Congress.

"Beautiful," Tamara says. "What's next for the senator and his wife?"

Lydia flashes a theatrical smile as her voice lifts. "Continuing to follow our mission of supporting American families and the future of this nation. Ollie and I will be attending an environmental justice gala over the weekend. The health of our legislature is equally as important as the health of our planet."

Oliver shifts in his seat. The vague memory that lurks under the surface waters of his memory releases a pebble of information when Lydia mentions the gala. The thoughts launch at him with a bullet's speed: The EPA. Ingleman. The grouping of numbers he couldn't clearly remember during his conversation with Alex was a date.

Alex flashes in his mind, standing side by side with his feelings of hypocrisy. He recovers by smiling and squeezing Lydia's hand.

"Sweetness," Oliver says, turning to Lydia. "I'm sorry to rush but I've got to go to the office."

"Always ready to do good." Lydia laughs and reveals bleached teeth to Tamara before turning to Oliver. "Have a good day." She rises up onto her toes in her navy-blue pumps and plants a kiss on his lips. He gives her a warm smile then kisses her forehead. He bids them farewell before grabbing his coat and attaché case and heading out the door.

Oliver darts across the small front yard, the sprigs of wet, soft brown grass mixed with budding green crushing under the hard soles of his dress shoes, and heads over to the stand-alone, two-car garage. The black pickup truck beeps as he taps the key fob. Swinging the door open, he climbs inside, eyes on the rearview mirror as he backs away from the townhome.

"Coleman, don't give me any of your bullshit, I need you to look into something for me," Alex says, leaning against the side of her co-worker's cubicle, not caring that she's interrupting his phone call.

Coleman glances at her and purses his lips before holding a single finger up. Whatever the caller on the other ends says garners a boisterous laugh from Coleman.

"All right, Dexter, man. I'll holler at you later. Be safe, brother."

He hangs the phone up, gawking at Alex with a serpentine grin.

"Yes." He spins around in his chair to face her fully. The back of his chair reclines as he man-spreads his legs and leans into the cushion. His blond hair is again immaculate, and his freshly shaven face reveals his deeply set dimples as he speaks. He grabs a pen and begins to chew the top as he peers back at her, his rows of pearly white teeth like a seductive vice grip. "You want me to take a look at your online dating profile? Help you fine-tune it? Make it more ..." He looks her up and down "... appealing?"

"Ugh," she groans and rolls her eyes. "Didn't you write all about the #MeToo and #TimesUp movements? Have you learned nothing?"

"I learned plenty. Extremely eye-opening about what women deal with in the workplace and the harassment they face," he admits. "But this is me and you we are talking about here." He winks. "You flirt, I flirt; that's the hamster wheel we've been in for two years now, Alex."

She gives a wary huff. Her curls bounce as she shakes her head at him. "I need you to be serious about this. It's something really important. I wouldn't trust this with anyone else here but you." Her statement is followed by a fixed stare.

He takes the pen out of his mouth and sits up straight in the chair. "What's up?"

"I'm working on a piece ..." She peruses the faces in the raucous newsroom. Reporters speak into phones and type ferociously away at their computers. There are many with DC contacts and sources, some who have exchanged story information for a few positive pieces about congressmen. She couldn't rule out anyone tipping off one of their contacts if they were aware of what she was developing. Even their editor had been given a very vague summary of the story when she requested funds for a rental car and hotel in DC. "You know what, let's go into the conference room." She tosses her head in the direction of one of the closed, soundproof rooms.

Coleman chucks the pen onto his desk, stands up, and follows her. She opens the door for him, letting him enter before shutting it behind him.

He leans against a wall, folding his arms over his chest. "What's up?"

"Two dirty senators, a corrupt head of the EPA, and an entire community and workers literally being poisoned to death," Alex explains. She leans forward and places the palms of her hands on the conference table.

Coleman lets out a whistle. "Shit."

"Exactly."

He reaches up and his fingers indent his gelled coif as he scratches his scalp and thinks. "What do you need from me?"

"If you've got something else you are working on and you can't—"

"It can wait." He shakes his head. "What do you need from me, Alex?" He repeats.

"Marktown, Indiana. I need you to do what you do best. Go there first. Takestrom Chemicals has a factory close by where the chemicals are leaking from and the workers are getting sick. I need you to go and talk to the locals, find out about the quality of life, talk to doctors about any unusual illnesses. Maybe shake down a few Takestrom employees, find out what's really being done with the chemicals and what is in that crap they are putting out."

"On it," Coleman says.

"Do you need to write any of this down?"

He waves her off and taps his temple.

"Good. Take a few pictures but be careful. I know you'll be as discreet as possible, but when you start asking questions, someone who probably doesn't want us getting answers is going to find out."

Coleman rubs his chin. "What are the other elements of the story?"

"On the surface, from my best guess at this point, it appears Senators Chickman and Eisenhower and EPA Administrator Ingelman are getting some cash under the table to ignore violations by Takestrom. They're probably receiving kickbacks for getting them a massive government contract. There's another player, but I am not sure how he fits in."

"You got concrete proof?

"No ..." Alex rubs at her brow in a moment of dismay. "I tried to get a contact, a Washington insider on board. I thought they could really help me get what I need to piece everything together."

"No dice?" Coleman questions.

"No. I think they are ... afraid." As the words left Alex's mouth, she couldn't believe she had ever used those words to describe Oliver Michaels. "I'm asking for your help, Coleman, because you are good at blending in and charming people into talking," Alex admits. "They see me coming; they will know I'm an outsider. They will take one look at you and trust you."

Coleman shrugs. "Some old work boots, a faded pair of jeans, flannel shirt, let the beard and hair grow in a bit. I'll make it work."

Alex smiles. "Thank you, Coleman. I swear, we get this done and there will be a lot more than just a dual byline with both our names on it. The implications of this story have the chance to really change things in DC."

"I'd help you even if it wasn't." Coleman licks his lips and uncharacteristically glances away from her face.

Alex tilts her head and gives a tiny smile. "Thanks."

"Who tipped you off to all this?" He presses his tongue into his cheek and folds his arms over his chest.

She shakes her head and shrugs, standing up straight. "I don't know. I got a letter with no return address and some photos. Whoever the source is obviously knew the underhanded crap that was going on with these senators and the EPA but didn't want to step forward."

"Maybe some senator had a change of heart along the way."

"Doubtful, but you never know."

"I can leave for Indiana tomorrow. Let me get with Rubyth in accounting and make the travel arrangements."

"Thanks again," Alex replies. "I'm heading back to DC soon. I need to shake a few trees and see what falls."

"All right," Coleman says, pushing away from the wall. He walks towards Alex and her brows lift in surprise. "Do me a favor will you? Be careful in Washington."

"I plan to keep a low profile with a very good cover."

"Even the best covers can get blown and you may piss off a lot of people by digging."

Alex nods. "Same for you in Indiana."

"I can handle things. It's you I'm worried about," Coleman counters.

She sighs and reaches out to embrace him. He hugs her, giving her a gentle squeeze and rubbing her back before letting go. There are no comments laced with innuendo, no inappropriate lingering gropes, only genuine concern.

Alex tilts her face all the way up at her tall colleague. "Take care of yourself."

CHAPTER 4

Oliver enters his office and is greeted with a bark and a wagging tail. He bends down and ruffles the fur of his four-legged friend. The gentle, golden Labrador retriever laps at his hands to greet him.

"Hey Montana, how's it going today, boy?" Oliver smiles at the dog he named after his football hero.

"Happy to see you," Yvette, his assistant, says. She stands up and moves around her desk.

"Thanks for looking after him last night." Oliver straightens. "Appreciate it. I just didn't want to leave him at the apartment by himself, and I didn't want to take him back to the townhouse with Lydia. Her dogs don't get along with him, and he's not too fond of them either."

"Oh, no problem. He was great company," Yvette smiles. "I don't see how anyone couldn't love him."

Yvette is small in stature but big in competence. A graduate of Howard University, she applied for the office assistant's position with Senator Michaels the day it was posted. Oliver had several people who had worked on his campaign that he could have hired for the role, but during the interview process, Yvette Graham was the strongest candidate. She not only had a tenacity for completing the tasks in front of her, but she also believed in the vision the new senator had for Washington politics. Of biracial upbringing, her parents had taught Yvette to appreciate the culture and struggle of her Black and Hispanic ancestors. Oliver's vision for the Live and Learn Initiative at the federal level was one of the first things that garnered her support and her vote.

During the first election of his career, the former quarterback easily won against the incumbent, sixty-four-year-old Benjamin Ryder, whose constituents had deemed the twenty-three-year term as out of touch. Oliver ran a financially transparent campaign with a platform promoting education and healthcare reform. He served in the Maine state house for one two-year term before he decided to advance his career from the house to the senate. After a successful first term, and a commitment to helping local organizations, Oliver won the senate race handily for District 35 at the age of twenty-eight.

He decided that although making an impact in his home state was crucial, he had a true chance to garner real change at the federal level. As soon as he was eligible at the age of thirty, he announced his candidacy for US senator.

"How'd the interview go?" Yvette asks as Oliver opens his office door. Montana trots in ahead of them both and curls up under Oliver's desk.

"Without a hitch." Oliver sighs. The ease with which he can deceive the media and his constituents these days is unsettling for him.

"Details on Senator Baskins legislative proposal on cell phone data access," she says, laying down a folder in front of him.

Oliver nods. "Anything on the schedule?"

"You've got that two o'clock with the representative from Lone Star Oil." Oliver stares fixedly at her when he hears the disdain in her voice. She's arched an eyebrow steeply at him.

"These damn lobbyists." He rubs his temples and squints up at her. "Any way I can cancel?"

She smirks. "I'll see what I can do."

"Thank you." His exhale flows long and slow.

He opens the folder with the Baskins proposal and skims it before losing interest. He flips the proposal closed and blows a raspberry with his lips. He can't seem to focus today. Maybe it was starting the morning out with that sham of an interview, but something feels off. He barely slept in the guest bed, thinking of the woman he once loved that was sleeping in the bedroom above. How had they gotten so far off course? He had made her a promise to stick this out publicly, while privately, they were living separate lives.

He had told her if she determined to file the papers, he would sign without any legal headaches or hesitations. Lydia was not ready to concede. Of all the reasons she was sticking with him, Oliver didn't believe love was one of them. He was beginning to question her motives more each year the calendar rolled over to their next anniversary. He tosses the file folder onto his desk and peers down at Montana. "Walk?"

The dog's head lifts, and his tail slaps the floor rapidly in response to the word.

Oliver slides on a jacket, stands up, and heads to Yvette's desk. "You have Montana's leash? I think I'm going to take him around the block once before I get to it." She turns and grabs the leash off a cabinet beside her, handing it to Oliver. He snaps it onto the 49ers collar around

Montana's neck as they exit the office and take the elevator down to the first floor.

Oliver walks through the lobby of the building, Montana keeping up with his strides as they push through the main door and step out onto the sidewalk.

As the cold slaps against his neck, he flips the collar of his coat up as a shield. Shoulders hunched, he retraces the steps on the Mall where Alex had found him two days before.

What happened to you? she'd shouted at him in his apartment.

As Oliver walked up the sidewalk with the Capitol Building coming into view over the tops of partially denuded trees, he wonders the same thing.

•◆◇ — ◈◆•

Oliver strides over the marble floor of the Capitol Building underneath the frescoed ceiling of the rotunda. School children on a tour walk in single file behind a guide pointing out 150-year-old paintings of George Washington, Pocahontas, and the Discovery of the Mississippi by De Soto. Below the murals and statues of the Founding Fathers and great battles in American history, the young and once idealistic politician heads to the Senate Chamber.

Oliver smiles at the students as he passes by, lifting his hand to wave at their teacher, whose chin hits the floor.

Ten minutes ago, he left his public office at the Hart Senate Office Building for the Capitol, where session was about to resume for the day. A quick call to Yvette at his private office on the edge of town and she was beginning the carefully detailed tasks he had laid out for her.

As Oliver enters the hallowed territory of the Senate Chamber, he is pleased to find Kentucky Senator Travis Chickman and South Carolina Senator Martin Eisenhower already huddled together and engaged in conversation.

Oliver finds his desk, between the 10-year veteran senator from Massachusetts and the relative rookie senator from Maryland, and sits his briefcase down, taking his coat off and sliding it over the arm of his chair. He greets them both with morning salutations and handshakes but keeps his eyes on Chickman and Eisenhower.

After giving his arrival enough time as to not raise suspicion in his haste to talk with the pair, he begins to move towards them, greeting other senators, smiling, and nodding as they update him on their children's sports activities or curse and grumble about issues in their districts back at home.

"Gentlemen." Oliver smiles politely at the senators when he reaches them.

"How's it going, Rook?" Chickman grins and sticks out his hand. Oliver forces a chuckle at the teasing nickname he has been given for his rookie status in Congress. He shakes Chickman's hand before looking at Eisenhower. He wants to recoil from their grasps but reminds himself of the task at hand.

"Oliver, I think a thank you is in order," Eisenhower says. The older man adjusts his glasses over his tiny brown eyes made smaller by his large nose. His belly is big, bulging over his saggy black suit pants and belt. His knees turn inwards towards each other under his thick thighs, and his fingers are each as big and round as the cigars he smokes. A metal American flag is pinned to the lapel of his jacket. His face is dimpled with pockmarks and dotted with age spots as big as bullseyes.

"For what exactly?" Oliver shoves his hands in his pockets.

"My daughter's newfound interest in politics." Eisenhower guffaws. "I've been in politics since before the day she was born, and she never expressed any interest in it until you came on the scene. Now, she is suddenly asking me about internships and if so, can she be assigned to a specific senator," he explains with an arching brow.

Chickman laughs. Oliver keeps the smile on his face.

"So, I ask her, 'Well honey, what senator would you like to intern with?'" Eisenhower folds his arms over his chest, his elbows resting on his bloated belly. "She doesn't skip a beat. Looks me dead in the eyes and says 'Oliver Michaels, Daddy,'" he continues and Chickman bends over as he begins to laugh.

"What did you tell her?" Oliver inquires with a faint smile.

"Oh, I told her absolutely not. No way am I letting my lovesick nine-teen-year-old within fifty feet of you unattended. That's for your safety, not hers," Eisenhower adds and begins to laugh. Chickman lets out a howl and laughs harder.

"All I know is, I'm calling it now. I want you on my team for the flag football game. I'm willing to cross party lines and join up with you if it finally gets me a victory," Chickman jokes.

Oliver chuckles again. "I'm a little rusty. I don't know if the arm is as good as it once was after all those surgeries."

"Nonsense," Chickman interjects. "You are still in better shape with one injured arm than most of us are here with two good ones."

"I don't know; you look like you could pick up a few rushing yards," Oliver replies. Travis Chickman is in his early 50s. His hair is a mix of mostly silver and a few remnants of dishwater blonde. He is a few inches shy of being nose to nose with Oliver's six-foot-three frame. His face is smooth but there is a slight double chin from age that only shows when he famously jerks his head back at what he thinks are asinine comments made by his colleagues. His vacant brown eyes, highlighted by dark crescent moons underneath, seem to either dart in perpetual motion or hold you in a glare of contempt.

The ringing of bells and a series of light flashes above the chamber signal the start of the day. Chickman slaps Oliver on the back.

"Better get to our desks," he says to Eisenhower. "Some of us actually rely on the salary we make as senators to pay the bills, you know." He cuts his eyes to Oliver.

The young senator's eyes narrow. "What does that mean?"

"Means some of us don't have NFL dollars to fall back on if times get tough," Chickman continues. "What we make for doing this and the cost of living here in DC just ain't right."

Oliver's back straightens at Chickman's words. He regards Eisenhower, who gives an amused half-smile.

"The two of you have your own successful businesses, though, right?" Oliver swings his gaze back and forth between them. "Chickman, what is it, real estate? Eisenhower, you've got your tech business, right?"

The two senators exchange glances before looking back at Oliver.

"When times are tough in the economy, it affects all of us, not just the taxpayers out there. But yeah. I'm doing all right these days." Eisenhower puffs his barrel chest. "Despite paying two private university tuitions for my oldest kids."

Senators move around and head to their desks.

"I'll catch up with you later," Oliver says as he moves away from Chickman and Eisenhower.

"Sure thing. Don't forget what I said about flag football!" Chickman calls over his shoulder as he walks away.

Oliver heads to his desk, rubbing his forehead as he takes a seat with a heavy sigh. *They have a motive*, he thinks. *It's not much, but it could very well be something.*

Part II

The Source

CHAPTER 5

The Washington Post had published the intended guest list for the annual fundraising gala for DEEDS (Delivering Environmental and Economic Demand and Support) United, a DC-based nonprofit. The list included EPA Administrator Rupert Ingelman, South Carolina Senator Eisenhower, and the freshman Senator Michaels.

Alex came across the event page during her online search of Ingleman three days prior. The gala provided her an opportunity to get closer to him.

She'd paused when she saw Oliver's name. Never did the thought of not attending the gala enter her mind as an option. They had not spoken since that night in his apartment. She was uncertain of the future of their friendship after he'd declined to assist her investigation. But she knew this night she held the advantage of being prepared to see him. She'd made the choice to pursue this story and not even old romantic inclinations could deter Alex.

Swedish college student and face of global climate change Clara Goransson would be the gala's keynote speaker. The twenty-year-old had made a name internationally as a teenage environmental activist. DEEDS mobilizes urban and rural communities to build healthy neighborhoods with locally grown and sourced organic produce at reduced cost for low-income communities.

Clara's trip across the Atlantic Ocean was an opportunity for Alex. Thanks to Pat, *The Times* reporter had been submitted for a small pool of press credentials issued to American news agencies covering Clara's visit. Each news outlet was provided with a brief ten minutes for a one-on-one before the event.

"It was a pleasure," Alex states when it's signaled that her time is up.

She shakes Clara's hand as she stands and moves from the press room to the ballroom of the JW Marriott Hotel. Alex's high heels create a pristine cadence as she crosses the buffed marble flooring of the hall and enters the carpeted ballroom. She wears a sleeveless, contrasting black and white jumpsuit with a skirt overlay. Her thick hair is smoothed into a low bun.

Overhead, halogen lights are dimmed, bathing the room in bronze. The front of the ballroom is staged with two conversation chairs, a podium, and a black backdrop with a screen framed by green light.

A server disappears behind the stage to refill a pitcher of iced tea. The jazz band positioned in the front corner of the room plays acoustic instruments as the ballroom fills with attendees.

At the center of each white and black linen covered table rests a cylinder vase with floating tea lights made of beeswax. With a meatless menu for the American-grown, environmentally friendly event, a preset salad of spinach, strawberries, and pecans is set at each place sitting. The earthy scent of the spinach and the sweet, buttery scent of the strawberries and pecans invade Alex's nostrils and cause her empty stomach to growl.

The tension in Oliver's body conjures a headache. There was more inaction in the Senate this week and he has not found a peaceful night of sleep since Alex stepped into his new living space.

"How long are we going to keep this up?" Lydia asks during their commute. The week since the photo shoot feels like it has been months long instead of days.

"You tell me." Oliver responds, his tone glib.

"I'm not walking away, Oliver. There's too much invested here," Lydia spits the words.

"You make this marriage sound like a business deal."

"Yes, I am expecting a return on my investment," Lydia returns with a snark of her own.

His gaze shifts for a breath from the traffic ahead to Lydia's left hand clutching her right in a fruitless attempt to try to stop the shaking.

"When was your last drink?"

"Yesterday morning sometime. Why?"

"They're serving alcohol at this thing tonight. Are you going to be okay?"

Lydia gave a sardonic snort. "I can handle it."

"Are you sure?" Oliver squints.

"I said I can handle it, Oliver!" Lydia snaps. She huffs as she flips down the visor and pushes back the slide on the mirror. A small light shines on her pale face. Her blonde hair is curled in a half updo. Concealer is caked under her eyes. Red veins reach out from her pupils like bloody brooks.

"I'm doing this for you ..." Lydia turns her head and watches Washington DC with the attentiveness of a toddler.

Oliver rubs at his gritty eyes and his shoulders curl towards the steering wheel. He doesn't offer her a response which draws her ire.

"You just couldn't get a limo for tonight, could you?" she mumbles.

"No. We *aren't* the Kennedys. I don't have endless income and neither do you. I'm not going to have the taxpayers footing the bill for a driver either."

Lydia removes eye drops from her clutch, her hands twitching as she attempts to place the replenishing liquid on her pupils. She had not always been the wife she was now. For thirteen years, he'd been Ollie to her.

After letting go of her life as an NFL spouse, she quickly settled into the social scene of Maine high society. She proudly helped organize fundraising galas and sat on several boards for various charitable organizations. She appeared happy to watch her husband dedicate his life to helping his home state, and she enjoyed her role as the loving wife who gave her time and energy to the causes they were both passionate about like the Children's Advocacy Center and local chapters in Maine of the American Cancer Society.

It was not until Oliver's run for the US Senate and the blinding spotlight on their lives, that he'd noticed her adjusting with about as much ease as an ant trying to climb the inside of a highball. She had always enjoyed a party here and there, and time with the other socialites. What became a meeting during Happy Hour to unwind and avoid politics, became mimosas for breakfast, Bellini's at lunch, and scotch at dinner, chased by a bottle of wine. With Oliver's busy schedule, they saw each other less and less.

Oliver and Lydia arrive at the valet kiosk near the hotel entrance as the orange sun descends for the evening, creating a fiery halo behind the obelisk known as The Washington Monument. The structure's pyramidion peaks over the rooftops of businesses and townhomes in its needle shadow as the valet opens the door for Oliver and his wife.

The senator buttons his suit jacket as he steps to the passenger side door and waits for an attendant to open it for his wife. She places an opera gloved hand into Oliver's and gives him a smile as they head into the hotel.

The sounds of light jazz greet them as they step into the ballroom and breeze past security. A photographer glides into the space in front of them, their shutter clicking rapidly with a flash that stays on for the couple.

Lydia the Chameleon appears. Her back straightens with a demure smile. *Never too much teeth, almost like you have a secret,* she'd once advised. *Keep them wondering.* Oliver had ceased being astounded at her ability to shape and mood shift with the speed of an Olympian sprinter. This was simply what Lydia did.

She ventures off and away from Oliver's side as quickly as her performance begins. Kissing both cheeks, she greets the wives and girlfriends of other Washington bureaucrats and firmly shakes the hands of their partners.

The pounding in Oliver's temple grows stronger. He turns away from the crowd to conceal his grimace. His eyes dilate when the phantom of his past moves along the ballroom wall.

He spies Lydia, busy with the mindless small talk of energy vampires. Giving diplomatic head nods and smiles, he strides across the floor towards the apparition in black and white. His heart beats faster with each step.

"Alex."

He watches as the bones in her spine seem to stack robotically one on top of the other, an alignment that makes her head lift like a queen, before she stops and turns to face him.

"Oliver." The corners of her lips lift in a cordial smile, but her gaze moves about the room.

Oliver's incredulous stare accompanies the tipping of his head from side to side. "What—"

"Working. Same as you," Alex replies, words rushing to meet the speed of her lips.

Oliver smooths the front of his tie, making sure it's still tucked into his jacket, and lowers his head briefly. He gulps before his eyes meet hers again. "You look great."

"You're here with Lydia?"

"Yes."

"I should go say hello." Alex takes a step but Oliver's large hand encircles the entirety of her bicep, fingers overlapping.

"No." He halts her steps. Alex looks down at the hand on her arm and he releases her with an apologetic glance. "She's not good tonight."

Above the jazz music, Alex and Oliver watch the blonde throw her head back in a delighted cackle as she stands in the center of a small crowd increasing in numbers.

"She seems fine."

"Yes, of course. She always does," Oliver retorts. "Seeing you will only set her off."

Alex concedes with a curt tilt of her head. Oliver twists his neck, moving it around trying to ease the migraine thumping at the base of his head. Enough attention had already been on him when he entered the ballroom, his conversation would be sure to draw attention, particularly

Lydia's—something he hoped to avoid along with any more of her wrath that evening.

"Do you have anything you wanted to say to me?" Alex's gaze is that of inspection, and somehow it makes him feel smaller than a mountain tick.

He shakes his head.

"If you'll excuse me then; I need to do my job." Alex's eyes meet his in a meaningful stare-down. Oliver pinches at the bridge of his nose before he retreats, moving back towards Lydia, the journey interrupted every few feet by a greeting or handshake.

After twenty minutes of banal banter, Oliver disappears from the ballroom into the men's bathroom, seeking refuge, a moment away from the flashing cameras and selfie requests. Awkwardly posed photographs have been uploaded to social media of attendees with him seconds after they were taken.

He steps to the urinal and unzips the front of his slacks. When the bathroom door swings open, he glances up in usual fashion, ready to avoid eye contact. He does a double take. Martin Eisenhower gives an out of breath gasp as his bulky body crosses the threshold. He pulls a handkerchief from his pocket and dabs at the tracks of sweat rolling from what's left of the hair on his almost bald head.

"Well, Rook! I saw that lovely wife of yours a minute ago." Eisenhower bellows, his voice echoing off the bathroom tiles. He swells as he inhales and then clears his throat. "You know, you better be good to that one or she's going to end up in the bed of someone with more status than you! She's got a fire in her, that one does."

Oliver fumbles with his zipper, no longer feeling the need to urinate.

"Good evening, Martin."

"What kind of event doesn't have any goddamn meat? I'll be going to get a burger after this."

"This doesn't exactly seem like your scene," Oliver remarks. "Vegan menu, tree huggers, climate truthers."

Eisenhower walks towards the stalls pushing against the partially opened doors before bending at his hips to peek for any legs or feet. Once he seems assured of the stall's vacancy, he responds.

"Agriculture is the number one economic sector in South Carolina, brings in almost $50 billion." He walks to the urinal next to Oliver and fumbles with the belt buckle below his belly. "Almost a quarter of a million in jobs. As much as I hate to see it and say it, appeasing these Impossible Sausage-eaters is good for business if you know what I mean."

"Good for the pocketbook?"

Eisenhower grunts. "We do the dog and pony show, but really, who cares?"

Oliver turns to the sink to wash his hands. "I do."

Eisenhower chuckles. "You and your righteous indignation. I've been watching you and your big flashy speeches and your 'we can do it' rhetoric. You remind me of a baby fawn trying to stand up for the first time. Clumsy. Eventually, you'll learn."

Oliver didn't appreciate being likened to an infant anything. He'd faced his fair share of career politicians like Eisenhower past their prime. Oliver had challenged Dan Lions, a silver-haired, sly fox who had represented the state of Maine in Congress for the past twenty-six years. Oliver campaigned with an idea that had been effective for him in college during his student government presidency at UConn. He advocated for a student loan forgiveness program that would apply to anyone not earning a livable wage based on the state's medium cost of living five years after graduating with a college degree. He called it the Live and Learn Initiative. Oliver also touted better healthcare support for women and children, influenced by having grown up in a home with an absentee father since the age of five.

He defeated Lions, unseating the veteran senator in a lopsided victory.

"Now son, we've all been patient with you. But Jesus himself had his moment of table flipping when he felt disrespected."

"I'm not your son, Martin. Thank God for that." Oliver dries his hands with paper towel, a smirk on his lips. Eisenhower resembles a bull facing an unfazed matador.

Eisenhower's scowl melts into a sneer as he labors towards Oliver. "Fawn. Yeah, I like that a lot better than Rook. Hey, Fawn? Remember what happened to Bambi and his mother? He almost got put down too when he got in the way. Stay in your lane, son." Eisenhower slaps him hard on the back, stinging his shoulder. "Now, I think I'm going to go and have a dance with that pretty wife of yours." He exits the bathroom without so much as turning a faucet to wash his hands.

Oliver grips the granite of the sink, searching his reflection in the mirror.

Alex stalks around the ballroom as more guests arrive. She watches for the faces that are her focus for the night, their visages now part of her brain like emotional wounds.

Rupert Ingelman does not have a plus one. He arrives solo as he often does. He takes a seat near the front center of the ballroom, pretending to read over an event program. Senator Eisenhower's yowl is one of the few things louder than the jazz band as he presses a hand to the small of his wife's back.

Alex finds the table reserved for the press and takes a seat next to Miranda Kipling from *The Washington Post*, a woman she's sat beside at numerous press conferences. They exchange the customary complaints about the job's long hours, a rite of passage for journalists who would not prefer it any other way. As Miranda speaks, Alex flicks her gaze repeatedly to the neighboring table where Ingelman is seated alone. Her head on a swivel, she notes Eisenhower, chatting it up with leadership from the evening's nonprofit host.

Five minutes pass and Oliver takes a seat with Lydia as the chair of the board for DEEDS steps to the podium. Oliver leans back, as he drapes his arm across Lydia's seat back. They smile at one another before Lydia's attention returns to the stage.

The chair of the board gives an update on the projected donations and sponsorships raised from tonight's event before he turns the program back over to the MC. As the woman steps to the podium, from her peripheral, Alex sees Ingelman push his seat back and duck his head as he moves hastily out of the ballroom. His smile is nervous and apologetic as he tries not to disrupt the program.

Alex's first thought is that the EPA administrator is venturing out for a bathroom break. As the MC begins to read Clara's biography, Martin Eisenhower kisses his wife's temple and bumbles alongside the ballroom wall to the darkness of the back. Alex's gaze tracks him out the ballroom door.

Her train of thought is interrupted by the outbreak of applause as the crowd welcomes Clara to the conversation chair. Alex stands and claps, taking advantage of the moment to slip away from the table and towards the door at the back of the ballroom. When she gives a fleeting glance across the room, Oliver's gaze meets hers. Lydia is smiling as she claps for Clara and watches the twenty-year-old take the stage.

Alex steps outside the ballroom door and gives a polite smile to one of the security guards. She counts to twenty-five in her head and then moves about the foyer.

She takes a seat at the bar across the hall and watches the foyer and ballroom door, waving off the bartender who asks her if she'd like a drink.

Her eyebrows shoot towards her hairline when she sees Oliver enter the hallway.

Oliver walks about the space in front of the ballroom and then notices a security guard standing near a door to one of the meeting rooms.

Oliver adjusts his tie, his movements quick and nimble, as he steps to the door and pushes the silver bar, thrusting the door open. He catches sight of the two men inside as Eisenhower tucks a small envelope into the interior pocket of his suit jacket. At the sound of Oliver's entry, Ingelman takes a step back from Eisenhower.

"I'm sorry, sir." The guard puts a hand out as his large body blocks Oliver. "This area is restricted."

"Oh!" Oliver smiles and feigns surprise. "I was looking for Senator Eisenhower."

"Can't let you in, sir," the guard emphasizes.

"I'll catch him some other time then." Oliver scratches the side of his nose and turns away. He paces the foyer for a moment before he sees he's not the only tail Ingelman and Eisenhower have that night. He smiles at a few hotel guests who recognize him and gives them a wave. Clara's voice is not muted by the hotel walls and even in the foyer, Oliver can hear her speech vibrating from the speakers.

Oliver passes the corner of the bar, his stare above Alex's head as he passes her swiftly. "I'll help you."

CHAPTER 6

The train car blows past Oliver as he stands on the platform of the Capitol subway system. He paces fifty yards behind Travis Chickman.

The next car will run in ninety seconds. Chickman stops near the base of an escalator, the metallic steps sliding upwards behind him without any passengers. Chickman checks his wristwatch. A briefcase is in his hand, and a wool coat draped over his forearm. Oliver stops, pulls out his phone from his attaché case, and pretends to scroll.

The fluorescent light bulbs glow with an unnatural blue, like an aquarium, drowning out the whiteness of the tile and gray cement space of the underground rail system. Oliver hadn't been prone to claustrophobia until he regularly began the descent 350 feet below the Senate chamber to take the subway between buildings. When possible, he preferred the long walks with Montana as an alternative.

Peering over the top of his phone, Oliver watches Chickman, now 40 feet in front of him, roll his shoulders down, lifting his chin high as he stands close to the edge of the platform, beyond the yellow caution line. Oliver glances down at the electrified rails, taking another step back.

In the distance, a sound like a mosquito buzzes before it whirs like a weed eater. It's a half hour after the evening rush, when public officials and government employees clear out and head home.

Oliver and Chickman watch as the four-car red, white, and blue train approaches. The brakes screech as the wheels grind and come to a stop in front of Chickman, who steps inside as soon as the doors slide open. He throws his coat and briefcase onto one of the blue seats. As he turns to remove his suit jacket, Oliver jogs up the platform and slips inside a car. Chickman in the front car, Oliver takes a seat in the second, holding his attaché in his lap, watching the Kentucky senator through the glass enclosure. A series of polyphonic chimes announces the train's departure. The brakes release as the train jerks forward, jostling from side to side as it picks up speed.

Behind Oliver are a few congressional staffers who were already boarded in the tail car, turned sideways in their seats as they cackle and chit chat, making plans to get drunk at the bar near the hill to trade war stories and bitch about their bosses.

Oliver had left his office at the Hart Senate Building and caught a glimpse of Chickman roaming the halls. It wouldn't have seemed out of the ordinary if it weren't for the fact that Chickman's office was in the Russell building. A month ago, Oliver would have scarcely blinked, nevertheless thought it out of the ordinary.

As they roll along, Chickman holds his rigid posture—military neck—without any bend or curvature. Oliver's eyes stray to the passing walls, the banners of allied nations overhead as the subway rolls past a pair of bullet holes in the tile. John W. Bicker had survived the attempt on his life from a disgruntled capital police officer in 1947, but the holes remained. They were once a talking point for tourists before terrorist attacks had ended visitors journey into the subway. They now served as pseudo historical markers of the volatile lives of congressmen and women.

Chickman remains as stiff and unyielding as PVC pipe despite the swaying of the train. The car's wheels thump like a heartbeat as the rail flows through the veiny turns and reaches the end of the line near the Capitol exit.

"He's a tight ass and a liar." Yvette had scowled as she pushed down hard on a three-hole puncher in the office earlier that afternoon. The contraption pushed down and sprang back in her hands like a defibrillator as it stabbed through stacks of copies she was filing.

Chickman had appeared on Eagle News as part of the morning chat with a mannequin blonde and former political advisor. Among the topics Chickman addressed were the president's lack of response to a humanitarian crisis overseas and the failure of the Adequate Income for Americans Bill that Oliver had authored.

Oliver had to hide his amusement at Yvette's response. "You're angrier about it than I am."

"You should get angry, Oliver!" Yvette whirled around. "He's got no right to go on that so-called news network and say hateful things about you. All it does is get the crazies worked up into a frenzy and make you a target."

Chickman made the barbed comment that, "Maybe Oliver got his bell rung a few too many times during his football days and his brain is scrambled like an omelet. That's the only reasonable way to justify him thinking we'd ever pass such a communistic piece of trash like that bill.

He's another example of this new wave of progressives who are being elected. They are dangerous for the future of our nation."

"He's the one that's dangerous!" Yvette shouted at the TV screen in the office before Oliver reached for the remote and turned it off.

He kept his response to Chickman's interview subdued in front of Yvette, deescalating her anger before he thought steam might blow from her ears. But Oliver *was* angry. His bill had failed and he didn't want to admit to himself he was still licking his wounds from its defeat. Chickman was gaslighting millions of Americans into believing he had their best interest at heart while his hands were covered in the residue of dirty money. Meanwhile Oliver was steeping in the shame of not making any significant accomplishments and wondering if he'd see a second term.

The Kentuckian grabs his coat, suit jacket, and briefcase and strides out of the car at the final stop. Oliver continues behind him, the cadence of their hard sole shoes falling in rhythm with each other. Chickman whistles a popular country tune as he strolls with a hand in his pocket. Oliver remains several feet behind. Reaching the steps of the east side of the Capitol, Chickman swings around. Oliver halts his stalking, switching his attaché case from one hand to the other.

Chickman surveys the younger man, plastering a smile on his face. "Rook. Not used to seeing you in this area this time of night."

Oliver did not offer up an answer. His mind fumbled with a response. *What had led him to follow Chickman exactly?* He marches down a few of the steps towards Chickman, keeping an arm's length between them as he stands on an upper step.

The May evening air feels warmer than earlier in the week. The last hues of purple from sunset are turning black. Above Oliver and Chickman, lights beam up at the raised US flag, still waving in the approach of darkness.

Oliver shrugs before turning away and looking off into the distance. When his gaze returns to Chickman, his stare is glassy. "Saw you pass by earlier. Thought I might have a word with you, Travis."

"It's been a very long day—"

"Yes. You were up early this morning for another big TV appearance. All that hot air you were blowing must be exhausting."

Chickman barrels his chest. "Is this really what you want to do right now, Michaels? You trail me like a puppy dog at the end of the day to bring me your holier-than-thou soap box?"

"You insulted me on national television."

"Insulted? Well, ain't you just pretty *and* sensitive. It's politics. You do realize that's part of my job, right?"

"It doesn't have to be. We can do this respectfully. At least I'm giving you the courtesy to talk to me face-to-face. What kind of a man would I be if I didn't respond?"

"I've often wondered what kind of man you are. Because from where I'm standing, you're just a boy."

Oliver stood up to his full height, his voice raised. "Now, wait a damn minute—"

"No, you wait! The grownup is talking." Chickman jabs a finger in the air towards Oliver's chest but doesn't make contact. "You think you're smarter than me. That I'm some redneck hick thinking from the Old Testament. That's the problem with younger generations. They don't realize the experience that comes from walking up and down these steps every single day. It's not for my fitness goal. This is my life."

"I may not have as many years in office as you, but this job matters to me, too. I could have gone into the booth and done broadcasting. I could be coaching. I chose to do this because it's important to me and what we do in there matters."

Chickman moves up one step closer to Oliver. "How's that going for you?"

Oliver sets his jaw as he feels heat rising inside him. His smartwatch chirps that his heartrate has increased.

"You are playing this all wrong, kid. You need allies, friends, partners. You haven't shown loyalty to your own party. What makes you think any one of us would trust you? Publicly support you? Make deals to benefit you? Help you pass bills?"

"They should pass on their merit! Not because of whose ass I'm willing to kiss!"

Chickman's veneers gleam. "Then your days are numbered. You better start learning to pucker up."

"Then maybe I'm not fit to be here."

"Finally. Something we agree on."

Oliver blows out a breath. "You have a daughter, don't you?"

Chickman's impossibly straight neck tightens. He moves up two steps, now perched above Oliver. "What about her?"

"When you are on air spewing all that bile ... talking about taking rights from women or making a brighter future for Americans ... I wonder what you think about *her* future?"

"She's a kid."

"Yes, but there are twelve million kids in the country living under the poverty line that don't have a tenth of the privileges your daughter will have. While you are looking out for yours, I'm looking out for everybody else."

"You leave my family out of this."

"You leave my name out of your mouth when you're trying to campaign. Say what you have to say to my face, don't wait for a television camera."

"You are one to talk about using the media. Oliver Michaels. Handsome former NFL quarterback who once had shaving cream and shampoo endorsements. Hell, didn't you endorse hemorrhoid cream at one point? You want to point fingers but when is a camera not on you? You've got that damned mutt of yours on social media. Don't act like you don't know how to play that game."

"I'm not peddling lies and fear."

"No, but you're trying to sell hope which is just as much bullshit."

"Since when did it become a crime to get into office and do what we said we were going to do?"

Chickman snickers. "You play it too safe, Rook. You are afraid of getting your hands dirty. You don't have the balls to put your foot on the gas and push ahead. That's what it takes to do this job. You are parked in dreams and hopes of revolution. This isn't fucking *Hamilton*. This is Capitol Hill. There isn't a black and white, a right or a wrong. Reality here is gray."

Oliver squints. "Do you hear yourself right now? Does it sound intelligent in your head or is it like a dog whistle and a long tone?"

"You worry about pissing people off. You want to be the poster boy, the All-American hero. You've never seen a battlefield or had to defend this country. You are as much a charlatan as anyone else in that building."

"You're right. But neither have you."

"You're a crossing guard, Michaels! You are telling people to look both ways. Ow, Washington is corrupt! But you are walking the same path. You are leading them in the same direction while telling them to watch out for the same group you are a part of." Chickman sucks in a breath. White foams of saliva form at the corners of his mouth. "Save your persona for the Met Gala. We don't pass a bill, you blame us. Are you working with the people who can get you what you want? Are you willing to step into the trenches to get results, to get in the game? Or are you going to sit in the bleachers watching while the men play?"

Oliver opens his mouth to speak but closes it.

"Night, Rook." Chickman trots down the stairs to the parking lot.

CHAPTER 7

Yvette Graham had learned to take up space in places not reserved for her and to walk into rooms with the confidence that she belonged there. She needed that skill this afternoon as she parks near the Federal Triangle.

She makes her way through what once had been called Murderer's Bay. The district had spent millions on security a decade before to clear out the drugs and prostitution in the area. Yvette believes the authorities should have done a clean sweep inside most of the buildings in the area as well. At least the criminals out on the street had the gumption to do their worst without secrecy.

Dressed like a college co-ed, she keeps a tall back as she moves against the crowd walking in opposition to her. She eyes the curved limestone and granite facade of the William Jefferson Clinton Federal Building. Making her way past the neoclassical columns, porticos, and arcades, Yvette walks into the building and presents her identification before stepping through the metal detector. She's met other former Howard University students here for young alum gatherings of all those who work civilian jobs or in the congressional offices. Otherwise, her arrival on the log may raise suspicions later.

She moves to the library, her white sneakers squeaking over the parquet. Entering the robust multi-floor facility, she finds herself still in awe of the starburst chandeliers overhead that catch the light and cast it around the mahogany paneled walls, so they appear to be inlaid with diamonds.

Her contact from the EPA, Ray, sits at a table near the back of the stacks, His hair cut in a high fade of textured obsidian waves that look like cooled magma on the top of his espresso skin. When he sees Yvette, he quickly hops up from the table. The chair legs screech, making some of the other library patrons glare when their peace is disrupted.

Yvette inhales his bergamot and cedarwood cologne when they embrace. He pulls back and a shy grin spreads on his lips as he gives her a probing visual caress.

"What do you have for me?" she asks in a hush.

Ray sweeps his hand over the stacks of paper on the table.

⸻ ❖ — ❖ ⸻

"Here," Yvette says excitedly as she opens the door to Oliver's office. He is seated behind his desk, brow furrowed, as he stares at his computer screen.

She drops a massive stack of papers on the desk in front of him, proudly putting her hands on her hips as she grins.

"What's all this?" Oliver asks.

"Travel logs, visitor logs, and some decent phone records for Ingelman," Yvette says.

Oliver's eyes widen. "How'd you get all that?" he asks. He rolls his chair over and lifts a few of the pages, eyeing them as he thumbs through them quickly.

"Guy at the EPA was in a brother fraternity to my soro at Howard," she says. "He also hates his job. I worked that connection a bit." She hunches her shoulders meekly.

Oliver steeply arches a brow.

"We may be having dinner this weekend, but that's not the point. The point," she says, tapping the massive stack of papers, "is this."

"Do you trust him to keep his mouth shut about this?"

"Absolutely. I didn't really tell him what it all was for specifically. He couldn't care less. Any excuse he had to talk, he was down for." She chuckles. "Your name never even came up."

"He knows you work for me?" Oliver asks.

"Yes, Oliver." She nods. "He knows. I mentioned something about a congressional review, and he grew bored pretty quick. Like I said, your name never came up and even if there is any fallout, he wouldn't say anything to anyone about you. I trust him. I mean, I'm having dinner with him."

Oliver's pulse quickens, and his chest tightens slightly; he's not exactly comforted by her words but trying to find some level of peace in her own ease with the situation.

"Thank you, Yvette." Oliver lifts his eyes to her, amazed. "I owe you."

"No, you don't. This is why I wanted to work for you," she says, her voice suddenly strong with youthful passion and determination. "This is what I signed up for."

Oliver stares up at her and she paces towards the door, turning back to him.

"There are a lot of people in Washington that I could have worked for," she says flatly. "I had some direct job offers before I even graduated. But when you got to the senate last year, when you publicly started championing the Live and Learn Initiative and more opportunities for women and children and even mass-incarcerated populations, it did something to my soul. I had always been interested in politics, but for the first time, I actually believed in a politician. I wanted to help."

Oliver sighs and places the papers in his hands down on the desk. His head drops. "I had all these bright ideas when I campaigned, and when I first got here. I'm sorry, Yvette. I know I've let you and a lot of other people down."

She shakes her head. "You haven't let me down at all. You are still out there casting votes for what you believe in and speaking up for the things you feel are wrong. When you called the other day and asked me if I could maybe find a paper trail on this EPA stuff, for the first time in months I legitimately felt excited. Your tone was different."

Oliver grins.

"If this gets back to me, that I was part of this bust up, it could be the end of my days here. I've got a lot to lose. I'm a rookie senator with no track record of any real legislative change," he says glumly.

"Maybe this *is* your record," Yvette replies.

Oliver frowns, not grasping her meaning.

"You said you had a desire to change things in DC, to shake up the status quo. You may not always be able to do that with votes and being outnumbered on a lot of things, but you could have a record of keeping your colleagues honest. It might not make you popular in the House or the Senate, but you'd be a rock star with the voters. That's what people need, Oliver. To see someone out there trying to clean this place up and make sure the people representing us really represent us."

He stares at her and blinks. After a few moments of reflection on her words, a sudden lightness releases with the tightness in Oliver's shoulders.

Papers are strewn about the coffee table in Oliver's single bedroom apartment. The scent of roasted coffee swirls with the rush of air from the heater that has not cut off all evening. Another unseasonably late cold front blasts through, sending the already chilly DC temperatures plunging. A rumble of thunder reverberates in the distance as the frontal boundary approaches.

Montana is curled up on the floor between his owner and his guest who's seated on the sofa. Alex's feet are tucked underneath her as she skims through Ingelman's travel log. She's circled a few locations that are not coincidentally close to Indiana.

Alex takes a sip of her coffee, then sits the mug back down on a coaster as she examines the document in her hand. She grabs a highlighter and marks an area on the copy.

Oliver is reclined on the sofa, his body molded into the plush, over-stuffed pillows as he flips through Ingelman's abbreviated phone record. He scratches his head and grabs a pen, circling something on the page. Montana softly snores, drawing a quick glance from his owner.

Oliver grabs his phone off the table and types in a search.

"I think I've noticed something here," he says.

Alex sets down the paper in her hand.

"This 812-area code is on Ingelman's phone record a few times," Oliver explains. "The calls always seem to be in clusters, but I just looked it up and that's an Indiana area code. There is no business link to it on the search, but it's definitely Indiana. You'd think they would be smarter and more careful when making calls."

"We can run that number down. Our tech people at *The Times* can trace it back," Alex says. "That's awesome, Oliver, thanks for catching that. Let's start a stack over here of important items," she says, pointing, and Oliver lays the paper down.

"There's something else," he says. "When I was at the office today, I went into the system to review the federal contracts that were out there. I checked on the Takestrom contract. Ten-million-dollar, massive deal, right?"

Alex nods.

"Frequent reports are required with any federal contract and there's a ton of burden put on the contract recipient to update the status throughout the course of the year. I checked, and the Takestrom contract was awarded in February of last year. It's been almost a year and a half and there has been only one report from them."

"One?" Alex gapes.

"Yes. Companies or people that don't meet the reporting requirements can face criminal or even civil action. But when I tried to check on why there was just one report from Takestrom and there had been no reported violation of their contract, the system information ended there. There was no flag or anything placed on their contract. So, someone out there marked it okay for them to get a massive deal and never update the government on what they were doing with the money."

"Holy shit! Oliver, thank you! That could be the foot in the door that we need to get this going!"

Oliver's cheeks rise.

"I need to check-in with Coleman." Alex grabs her phone and taps in a quick text message. A minute later, her phone rings, causing Montana to stretch his paws before collapsing back down and returning to his sleep.

"Coleman?" Alex accepts the call.

"Hey," he replies. She taps "Speaker" on the phone and sets it back down on the coffee table.

"Coleman, I'm here with my DC contact." Alex glances at Oliver. He stares at the phone but says nothing.

"Okay, well I'll make it quick," Coleman replies. "A few people figured out I'm a reporter poking and digging around here for a story but, surprisingly, one or two have been receptive. I talked to a doctor whose office is about twenty minutes outside the town. He was clear that everything he shared was off the record. Said he's seen and treated people for a ridiculously high number of respiratory illnesses, sometimes the same person multiple times in a year, and increasingly in the last few years. But the biggest thing is the early and swift onset of cancer in people around here. Of course, he couldn't give me specifics, but when I asked if any of them worked at the factory, he nodded."

"That's terrible." Alex sighs. "Did he say what he thought was causing it?"

"He advised that I look into the chemicals Takestrom produces, so I did. I hit up the municipal office in East Chicago for some copies of permits. That's when folks got suspicious. From what I read, any number of the chemicals could be causing it, but evidence would show it's benzene. Nothing in-depth yet, but hell, you can just Google it.

There's an undeniable link between benzene and a number of cancers. The time between diagnosis and death is quick."

"Did the doctor blame benzene for all his sick patients?"

"I stopped back by his office. Off the record? Yes. He was adamant that the factory is polluting the town and killing its workers. He didn't mince words about that. On the record? He never talked to me. I couldn't get him to give me a statement or link his name. He lives in a town an hour away just to be out of distance of that factory. It was a helpful start, but I'm going to have to do the rest of my digging without him. We all know he can't tell me any names of his patients, HIPAA laws and all that. I can probably knock on any door and find someone he's treated. Doc said people have two attitudes about it all. They seemed to be resigned to this being what it is and that this is home and always will be, but then there are the people who are angry. They want things cleaned up. I'm telling you, Alex, when you drive in, there's something that just latches hold of you. Feels like death creeping in."

Alex glances sideways at Oliver. His eyes are narrowed in anger. The thought of people suffering in this way and that Ingelman, Chickman, and Eisenhower not only know about it but are profiting from it, disgusts him. He closes his eyes and runs his hand over his head with a heavy sigh. He feels nauseous when he thinks about the greasy handshake Chickman gave him with that rotten smile of his.

"You've barely been there twenty-four hours and you've already uncovered so much, Coleman. This is why I recruited your help. You're amazing." Alex beams.

"Coming from you, that means everything. This is just the tip of the iceberg. After I find some patients, I'm going to try to get close to the factory, see what I see. I figured when I get back to New York, we can make a formal request together to speak to their management."

"Sounds good," Alex agrees. "I'll see what research I can pull up on benzene, too. Gives us some more teeth on the medical side. My contact found some reporting violations with Takestrom, but it's going to be hard to get many details from them or about the government contact. The *Freedom of Information Act* doesn't apply to private companies or anyone who receives federal contracts."

"Damn. You're right," Coleman huffs.

"But we've got a story."

"We absolutely do."

"Thank you again, Coleman."

"How are things in the nation's capital?"

"Thanks to my source," she says, anchoring her attention on Oliver, "I've also gotten some phone records and travel logs to go through. Starting to see some stuff that doesn't add up."

"Alex, just be careful out there. I know you aren't afraid of anything, but these career-politicians will do just about anything to avoid going down."

"You be careful around that factory. Don't need you arrested for trespassing."

"Alex, I've had years of practice sneaking out of girls' windows or out the front door before my date's husband gets home. I won't get caught."

She laughs, tossing her head back slightly. Oliver sucks in a cheek.

"Take care," Coleman says. "I'll call you tomorrow with another up-date. I really appreciate you bringing me in on this. I'm really happy to work with you."

Oliver sits up now and Alex meets his stare. She bashfully stares down at her phone as though trying not to meet his gaze.

"Me too, Coleman. Talk to you tomorrow. Goodnight."

"G'night," he says, and her phone beeps as he ends the call.

Oliver rests his elbows on his knees. "Sounds like he's making a lot of headway on this."

"Yeah, Coleman's a great reporter." Alex clears her throat.

"So, what's up with you and him? You guys dating?"

"No! Why do you ask?" Alex runs her fingers over her hair and shifts on the sofa.

"Because he sounded like he was worried about you in a way that goes a lot further than just being a co-worker." Oliver frowns slightly.

"Is that wrong?" Alex glares back at him. "That someone is concerned about me?"

"No. I could tell from the way he talked to you that he's into you. Do you like him? You wanted to work with him on this."

"I wanted to work with him because he's incredibly talented and good at investigative reports. Even if Coleman and I were dating, what would it matter?" Alex asks pointedly.

Oliver shrugs and licks his lips. "I guess I'm used to you being single. If you were dating someone, I ..."

"You what?"

He licks his lips again. "I don't know how I'd feel about it," he says, softly then casts his gaze down to the floor.

Alex stares back at him, stunned. "Oliver, I've been in a couple of relationships since college. It's not like I've never dated someone else."

"I know, it's just ... now ... with you here ... showing up again." He rubs at his neck. "I don't know what I'm saying."

The heater hums as they look at the papers.

A brilliant flash of white light fills the apartment for a split second. A crack of thunder follows, and the building vibrates. Montana suddenly sits up, whimpering a bit.

"Easy boy." Oliver rubs Montana's head to calm him. Oliver stands up and goes to the balcony door, then pushes aside the vertical blinds and peers outside. A few large and heavy raindrops slap down against the balcony. The trees outside of the building sway wildly in the high winds. There is another flash of lightning and then, suddenly, the bottom seems to drop out from the sky. Rain falls in sheets over his apartment building.

"You parked in the garage a few blocks down, didn't you?" Oliver asks, turning and looking at Alex, wincing slightly. He knew she had tried to avoid any areas with surveillance cameras that would put her in proximity to Oliver's apartment.

"Yeah." She sighs. She grabs her phone and opens a weather app, looking at the radar. The screen is a mix of green, yellow, and red. "Shit."

"It's not looking like that's going to let up for a while either," Oliver says as she holds the phone up, displaying the radar.

"No, it doesn't." She huffs. "Well, let's just work, and I can deal with it when I have to." She reaches out, grabbing another stack of papers, frowning deeply.

"Alex." Oliver lets go of the blinds. They slosh and scrape against each other as they swing back into place behind him. Montana shifts from his spot in front of the sofa to under the coffee table.

"There's no way I'm letting you walk out of here into that," he says, motioning towards the window. "Plus, you don't know your way around DC that well. It would be easy to get turned around or even in an accident with the weather like it is." He takes a deep breath. "Look, why don't you just stay here tonight? You can sleep in my bed. I'll sleep on the sofa," Oliver offers.

She shakes her head. "Oliver, I don't want to put you out."

"I would be more put out if I knew you were out there trying to drive around in a monsoon," he replies. "It's fine. Besides, I've had many a night of Netflixing and chilling on my own and passing out on that sofa. It sleeps just fine." He grins briefly before gulping.

"Well ..." Alex chews her lips. She blows out a slow breath. "Okay, thank you."

Silently Oliver grabs a paper and pretends to look over it, but his mind is on a college dorm rooftop, fourteen years ago.

Oliver sat with Alex on the roof of their dorm building, beneath string lights that their suitemates had mounted above a few outdoor cushions. It was just the two of them perched under the lights, and the starless sky stretched over them, their shimmer dimmed by the city lights below. It had been well after midnight, and if the RAs or administration knew the students had created a rooftop oasis, they'd have all been in trouble, so the lights were rarely turned on. The sting of cool air filled their lungs. The Louisiana girl, sitting next to Oliver of Maine, hugged her coat around herself but didn't mind the chill. They could see most of the University of Connecticut campus from that rooftop: the white steeple of Storrs Congregational Church pointed up towards the starless sky; the winding cement pathways that led to the square and seating spaces outside the Student Union; and the dome of Gampel Pavilion.

"Dad would have loved to have seen the pavilion," she said, her solemn words full of grief. "We loved the Huskies. I wish he were here to go to a game with me." Her gaze shifted beyond the dome to somewhere where the memories resided. Five years ago, when Alex was 14, the warnings had come, but no one could have expected the category five hurricane that was going to be unleashed on their city of New Orleans. In anticipation of the storm, Alex's father, Craig, had sent her and her mother ahead of him, so that he could stay behind and board up their home, securing it as much as possible from any potential looters. It had taken Alex and Camille almost five hours to reach Baton Rouge from the I-10, which was normally just about an hour and a half away. They'd phoned Craig, who was outside putting up another layer of plywood on the windows and some homemade sandbags on the front porch when the first rain drops began to bomb their meager home. He told them to cut west, and he would meet them in Nacogdoches, Texas. They'd be further inland and safe. The wind had started to kick up, and Craig decided it was time to leave the city.

But the roads were so congested, cars scattered like a child's Hot Wheels across the lanes trying to merge, that Craig never got past downtown. He'd left his Chevy truck parked in an attempt to escape on foot. Alex learned that much once it was identified. The two-ton vehicle had been lifted like a raft and swept away when the flooding began. They found it wedged against a tree trunk, suspended in the heavy branches like hands holding a toy. They didn't know where Craig was when the levees broke. They'd called but received no answer. The phone lines were down, and the cell phone towers were toppled by the storm's winds that beat like the flapping wings of Lucifer, assaulting New Orleans. Alex and Camille had returned to a splintered structure of matchsticks. They'd found Craig's decomposed body two months after the storm, under a pile of debris four blocks from where their home once stood.

Alex recounted the horror and then how they had waited for help and aid that took almost a year to manifest. When FEMA payments finally came, she and Camille permanently relocated to east Texas.

That night, she had done something she almost never did. She cried. She wept in Oliver's arms as he tried to soothe her but did not have the words.

Fourteen years later, he still felt he failed at his words around Alex. She intrigued him as much as she intimidated him. He sees her determination, knowing this investigation is Alex's reckoning.

Alex scans the travel log and stops highlighting. Giving an exhausted groan she relents. "I think I'm going to turn in now."

Oliver scratches the back of his head. "No problem," he says and returns to his spot on the sofa. Montana opens one eye before shutting it again.

"Okay. Um, do you need towels or anything?"

"No, I'm just going to go straight to bed." She stands up.

"All right, let me just get my pillow and a blanket." He leads her towards his room. Alex follows with an uncharacteristic timidness and Oliver turns on a lamp. It glows to life on the nightstand.

He swipes one of his pillows and pulls the extra blanket off the foot of the bed.

"If you get cold or need anything, don't hesitate to get me, okay?" He faces her as she lingers near the door.

"Okay." She nods. Holding his pillow and his blanket against his chest, Oliver eases past her.

"Goodnight."

"Night."

CHAPTER 8

Coleman taps on the screen door of the mobile home and waits. He'd pulled the silver rental car into the driveway behind a battered maroon minivan. He was knocking on doors today. He'd had no luck so far in obtaining more information, but then he'd spotted a single mobile home just off Highway 912. It was about a quarter of a mile away from the Takestrom Chemicals factory.

So far, most of the doors he'd knocked on remained closed. From his conversations with Dr. Peterson the day before, it was clear the people in Marktown knew each other, attended kindergarten through twelfth grade together, or were some form of relation. Despite Coleman's ability to camouflage as a local, strangers knocking at the door weren't taken to too kindly. He braces as much as a person can for the real potential of being greeted by the barrel of a gun.

Standing outside the door, he registers the increased volume of a television commercial from inside. *Someone's home.*

He tries to keep his hands free and revealed to look relaxed, but the wind beating at his back feels like he's in a one-sided snowball fight with mother nature.

There's movement at the window next to the door. A sheer curtain is pulled back and a thirty-something woman with sunken eyes studies him with unveiled suspicion. Coleman offers a cheery smile and lifts his hand, wiggling his fingers in a wave.

He's come to learn that hard working folks can spot a pair of unscarred work boots and BS easily. He hadn't gelled his hair, so his blond strands lift in the air. The stubble on his face has grown in patchy splotches of wheat gold.

He'd folded the collar of his red, plaid flannel shirt over a fleece-lined jacket. When packing for the trip, he'd shoved his oldest pair of jeans and a pair of boots he'd distressed years ago in an old gym bag.

The woman lets go of the curtain. The flimsy red door that could have been made from two layers of plywood opens behind a tin and glass storm door, and she uses it as an extra shield between them.

"Yeah?" She shoots him an irritated glance.

"Hello ma'am, my name is Coleman, Coleman Chester. I'm in town for a bit." Coleman usually reserves this part of the speech for later in the introductions, but he gathers from her scowling face that she is two seconds away from slamming the door in his face if he doesn't get to the point. "I'm here working on a story about the Takestrom place." He tosses his head in the factory's direction.

The woman pauses and then hugs her arms in front of her concave belly as she releases the door. She's in a pair of jeans that are worn to the seam and hang loosely on angular hips, and a gray V-neck T-shirt he assumes she borrowed from a man based on the size of it. Her hair, the color of coyote fur, is pulled back into a bun.

"Go on."

"I'm wanting to talk to residents about living around here. Not trying to pry or be in your business. I talked to a doctor yesterday. Doctor Peterson."

Her head lifts with recognition. Her face softens and her eyes are more attentive.

"Some people suspect that pollutants are coming from the factory and exposing the folks working and living around here to them. They think it's making them real sick." Coleman tucks his lips. "They" is a conjuring at the moment but from the widening of her eyes, he hopes she may make the fictional collective real.

He's dropped the pretty boy polish and the charm. He's not talking down to her. "Have you dealt with anything like that? Would you be willing to answer a few questions for me?"

The woman looks down at something that touches the back of her leg. She bends and Coleman's eyes follow her as she lifts a curly haired toddler to her hip. The woman lets out a hacking cough after the effort.

"Who you with?" She rubs the child's back. The sandy-haired little girl stares at Coleman and smiles, showing plump cheeks and a snaggletooth. Coleman grins back.

He turns his attention back to the woman. "*The New York Times.*"

There's a slight angling of her head. "Well, ain't that something. You got some ID, some kind of proof?"

Coleman reaches into his pocket. He pulls out his wallet that has his driver's license. He then reaches into the pocket of his jacket and pulls out the ID card with the metal clip holder. Both show his name, but the ID Card is marked with the *Times* logo and in bold letters, **MEDIA**.

The woman licks her teeth.

"I assure you. I'm a reporter. I'm here to do my job, not cause any harm to you or your ... daughter?" Coleman cocks an eyebrow and the woman gives a reticent nod, clutching the child against her breasts. "I want to ask you a few questions and then I'll be on my way."

The woman silently mulls things over and then unlatches the storm door. She holds it open for Coleman as he crosses the threshold. He steps into a home the temperature of a sauna. A jet of hot air rushes over his skin from a vent in the floor.

"Hi," the little girl greets him.

"Hello. What's your name?"

"Felicity."

"Felicity. That is a pretty name."

She smiles at his reply.

"Ma'am. I'm sorry, I didn't get your name?"

"Aubrey. Aubrey Fischer. My husband Jessie works down at Halifet Dock 22, the steel company. He won't be back till this evening, but I'm sure he'd want to talk to you, too. We all got something to say about how things are around here. He worked for Takestrom for years but quit and got a little salary increase and some benefits when he took on at Halifet. Good thing, too. We needed every bit of his medical insurance."

In his award-winning journalism career, Coleman had learned that most of the time people were looking for an opportunity to talk and be heard. The best thing he could do was give them the chance and listen. Aubrey Fischer was willing to talk.

Coleman scans her pale skin. She can be no more than thirty, but she appears much older and wearier. She lowers Felicity to the ground in front of the television, grunting as she does. A children's program plays on PBS. Felicity grabs a toy alligator and holds it up to Coleman from the floor as she plops down onto her knees. On the entertainment stand next to the TV is a family photo of Aubrey, Felicity, and a man with skin the color of coffee that he assumes is Jessie.

"What's your alligator's name?"

"Mr. Alligator," Felicity replies.

"She sleeps with that thing, too," Aubrey explains. "Go on, have a seat. You want something to drink?"

Coleman lowers himself onto a dark brown sofa. The mobile home is small but neat. A pot of water is boiling on the stove in the kitchen, and Aubrey heads in and turns it off.

Felicity's toys are strewn about the living room floor. In the corner, Coleman notes an oxygen tank. He reaches into his jacket pocket and takes out a small notepad and pen and a digital audio recorder.

Aubrey returns to the living room and sits in a wooden rocking chair across from him. A small coffee table that looks like it was bought at a rummage sale and is a carryover from the 60s stands between them.

"Mrs. Fischer, do you mind if I take a few notes and if I record this?"

"Not at all." Aubrey eases the rocker back and forth. Her feet are in a pair of thick socks and fuzzy, blue house slippers.

He turns the recorder on and places it on the coffee table. "You seemed to be familiar with Dr. Peterson when I mentioned his name."

"Yup. He's been my doctor for the last five years. He's Felicity's doctor, too. Can I get you something to drink?" she repeats.

"Oh, no, thank you. I'm not thirsty." The last thing he wants is a drop of what Takestrom is offering. "You said he's Felicity's doctor, too? What does he see you both for?"

"Felicity has asthma, born with it. Since she was three months old, she's had constant respiratory infections and chronic bronchitis attacks. The asthma is the worst part though. She uses a nebulizer three times a day, at breakfast, lunch, and dinner."

Coleman jots this down, balancing his notepad on his thigh as the pen swirls before he peeks at the toddler as she pushes the toy alligator across the floor, the TV displaying puppets that are now singing.

"And uh, the oxygen tank?"

"For me," she admits. "I was diagnosed with AML—Acute myeloid leukemia. Dr. Peterson was my primary care doctor and first suspected it. He had me undergo some tests. It had gotten to where I was wheezing and got tired real easy from short breath. I'd get weak going out to check the mailbox, and Jessie said, 'Hun, you best see a doctor.' Thought it was anemia at first but things got worse. That's what led me to get checked out and them finding the leukemia. Then it got really bad."

Coleman's eyes narrow as he writes. "In what way?"

"Started coughing up blood. Had a clot in my lungs and an embolism. They were able to catch it in time. Otherwise, Felicity would only have one parent now."

Coleman lifts his head from the attention on the notepad and the maternal reverence beaming on Aubrey's face. "I'm very sorry to hear that. How are you doing now?"

"In remission," she replies, giving a crooked smile. "I did chemo. I still get winded. The oxygen is for some of the rougher days. Especially in the winter and early spring when it's cold like it is right now and that air makes you bark. I've got to watch my activity level."

"You lost income?"

"I'm on disability. Jessie's insurance helps with some of the medical bills, but we are still paying for my hospitalizations from the embolism and my chemo. I was let go from Takestrom when I got sick," Aubrey adds.

Coleman's head pops up.

"You worked at the factory?"

"Yeah. Right out of high school like most everybody else. I got hired and they put me to work. I was a process operator."

"What did you do?"

"I operated the pumps, compressors, and monitored the heaters, reactions, and distillation columns."

"Petrochemicals?"

"Yessir. Stuff used to make some rubbers, dyes, and detergents. Doctors tell me it's bad news."

"Your doctors are right. Benzene?"

"Yeah!" Aubrey's affirmation is swift. "Benzene is Takestrom's biggest output. Unless you count leukemia, lymphoma, and myeloma."

"You know people who were diagnosed with any of those? Family, friends, former coworkers, maybe?"

"A few. Some are gone now, but there are others hanging on like me."

"Any with children?"

"All of us around here got mouths to feed. I got pregnant with Felicity when I was first in remission. We didn't plan the pregnancy. When she was born sick too, we started really wondering if it was safe around here.

Working at the factory was one thing. Jessie and me have lived here our whole lives. Things from that factory have deteriorated over the years."

"What type of things?"

"The air. Funny tasting water. Water flows from Lake Michigan down through the Indiana Harbor Canal. There are factories all through these parts, but when it rains or floods, that runoff empties here. Matter of fact, there's a creek that flows right behind Takestrom and guess where it empties? Right next to the dam where we get our water. Folks have raised this with the town aldermen and filed complaints. You want to know what it did?"

"What?"

Aubrey leans forward so Felicity can't hear. "Not a damn thing," she whispers and leans back in the rocker. "That's what."

"So, you believe exposure to chemicals directly at Takestrom's caused your leukemia and the pollutants caused your daughter to be born with respiratory issues? You're willing to go on record and say that?"

Aubrey points a thin, shriveled finger at Coleman's notepad. "You put down that I said it, and I want it printed."

"You ever thought about moving?" Coleman observes Felicity. She scoots on her knees around the floor until she begins to cough. It's hacking at first, then wheezing. Aubrey rises from the rocker and scoops her up, holding Felicity to her chest. She reaches for something on the kitchen counter—an inhaler she holds up to Felicity's mouth. The child seems accustomed to the routine and wraps her small mouth around it as Aubrey gives her a puff of the Albuterol inside.

When the coughing subsides, Aubrey levels a glowering look at Coleman. "Every day, my morning begins with pain. Mister, we can barely afford the food on the table with what we pay in medical bills. You think we got money to move?" She glances at Felicity and lowers her voice. "We might have to move involuntarily."

Her pointed look helps Coleman to understand. "How much time do you have?"

"Got a notice the other day. Trying to work things out with the landlord since he knows about my health and the little one's. We got ten days."

"Ten?"

"Indiana law. We're fortunate he's giving us more time."

"Ever considered legal action? For your health and with your landlord?"

At this, Aubrey blinks rapidly.

PART III

THE PITCH

CHAPTER 9

The next day, after leaving Oliver in Washington, Alex knocks on the glass office door of the managing editor of *The New York Times*.

"Come in," he booms in his baritone voice. He doesn't lift his eyes from the piece of paper in his hands. Pat Bowman, a journalist for almost forty years, is reaching retirement age but has told his young reporter he has no plans of stopping or slowing down. The art of storytelling and the duty of a free press are attached to his DNA.

"Hey, Pat." An expanding file folder is tucked under her arm as she steps in front of his desk.

Pat continues to skim the paper he is reading, his head moving from left to right as he goes over every line, and a pair of bifocals rest against the edge of his nostrils. His gray hair is slicked back, and his even grayer beard is neatly combed. She can smell the burnt stench of cigarette smoke clinging to his customary black blazer. He takes a cigarette break once every forty-five minutes during the course of the workday.

He is currently smacking on gum until he can take his next break.

He finally sits the paper down and adjusts his bifocals and grins. "What's up, Ace?" He's called her his ace investigative reporter since she began working for *The Times*.

"This." She hands the file folder to him.

He plucks it from her hands and picks out a section to begin thumbing through.

"Hmm, some travel records and phone records?"

"Plus visitor logs. For Rupert Ingelman."

"The administrator of the EPA?"

"Yes. I got a tip about Ingelman being involved with Senators Travis Chickman and Martin Eisenhower in what may be some type of cover-up with a chemical company called Takestrom. At first glance, it looks like they are getting money under the table to keep quiet on some things and to get kickbacks from the massive government contract Takestrom was given."

Pat's gum chewing quickens. "Huh." He blows out a breath. "Who tipped you?"

"Anonymous." She shrugs.

"Where'd you get these documents?"

"A source in DC," Alex says flatly.

"That's a hell of a source to come through for you like this."

"They are a great source. I brought Coleman in on this a few days ago," she explains.

"That's why he dropped my requested piece about the Port Authority to head to Indiana of all places?"

"Yes, sir. He's already talking to residents and getting some things together about how Takestrom is polluting a town near its biggest factory, endangering its workers, and causing illnesses and maybe even a few deaths with the poison they are putting out."

"Alex," Pat says, his voice rising in astonishment, "do you realize the implications of this story?"

"I do, yes. I have reached out to the CEO of Takestrom a few times to try and arrange a chat."

"No dice?"

"He's a very busy man, Pat. He may not be able to contribute to any piece that we do." Alex folds her arms. "At least that's what his assistant keeps telling me."

Pat chews his gum and inadvertently the inside of his cheek as he scratches at the bald patch forming on the back of his head. "We need to get our attorneys rallied and ready. What else do you need?"

"I need research and tech in the investigative unit to go through that stack of papers, trace some of those numbers that have been highlighted and circled, the same with the travel and the visitors' logs—any names of note or destinations of interest to see if there are direct connections to Takestrom employees. We are getting closer but nowhere near done. I need definitive proof that the senators are getting money under the table."

Alex's face drops, morphing from enthusiasm to gravity. "I attended a gala where Ingelman and Eisenhower were there. My DC contact and I saw some type of exchange between them, but it's not a magic bullet."

Pat slides the papers back into the folder and hands it across his desk. "Go downstairs to research and talk to Ezrah, get his team to work on this immediately. I'm going to send him a top line right now saying that you are headed his way and this is our biggest priority."

"Thank you. I appreciate the support."

"Alex, anytime you have a lead, it is always a pleasure."

———————— •♦> — <♦• ————————

The tip of her index finger swirls over the trackpad on her keyboard, eyes skimming over pages of internet content. She leans closer to the monitor, unaware of her proximity to the screen as she digests page after page of information about benzene.

As Pat had instructed, she'd dropped off the phone records and travel logs to Ezrah and the team down in the investigative tech department, returning to her desk promptly.

Hours have passed since she's eaten a bite of food or had a sip of anything. Not even the vending machines can provide her with sustenance today.

Coleman texts, advising her to look into AML, one of many forms of cancer caused by benzene exposure.

Alex reviews images of symptoms from AML first. Patients with mouth ulcers, missing teeth and bloody gums are captured for the recording of the disease's degeneration of the body. Small bumps and blisters of fiery red, unnatural purple and bubonic-like black dots pepper bodies with low platelets.

She snorts when she reads the Centers for Disease Control and Prevention's page dedicated to benzene. The fact that a government agency had so much detail on how deadly benzene is, but other agencies were partnering with the chemical's makers for production and disposal was an irony not lost on Alex. *It can kill people, but we also need to make money off it.*

Her fingers leave the keyboard, and she clicks a pen into place before jotting down notes from her search. Benzene ranks in the top twenty of most produced chemicals in the United States. How many thousands, maybe even millions, of workers are suffering from the same illnesses as Takestrom employees and the people of Marktown?

By now, it's midday and most reporters are on assignment or so busy pecking away at their own keyboards that they aren't engaged in banter with their colleagues. A few content producers and interns have ventured out for lunch or to pick up lunch for someone else.

Pen in hand, the nail of her index finger runs over her thumb's cuticle over and over. Her mouth is dry, but she does not want to leave her desk to get a drink. She glances around once more, feeling like someone might be watching her before she shakes the sensation away.

She continues to click links, reading research articles about benzene and its impact on the body and the environment.

The EPA had already had some issues in East Chicago, Indiana where Marktown was a community within the larger municipality. In the last decade, the Agency for Toxic Substances and Disease Registry advised the EPA that breathing the air, drinking water from the tap, or playing in the soil in East Chicago neighborhoods was harmful to people's health due to lead contamination.

A government housing community—with mostly Black and brown residents—had been built on top of a former lead smelter. The town was ultimately evacuated.

Seven years after the first reports, a study found that children had developed heart disease, cancers, elevated blood lead levels, or had been born with brain damage—all linked to lead exposure.

Alex's pen begins to glide over the ruled paper again when she reads that benzene evaporates into air quickly; however, the vapor makes it possible for it to sink into low-lying areas. It also doesn't completely dissolve in water, but floats on the surface with a yellow-like sheen.

Alex spins her chair around and pulls her key chain from her messenger bag. She unlocks the top cabinet drawer and retrieves the color photos sent to her anonymously. She looks at the fog-like cloud hugging the bottom of a few overturned barrels, like a toxic dewy mist in the early morning sunlight. The yellow grease that surrounds the bodies of the dead fish had done far worse for the creatures than batter dipping and frying them would have. Even the flies that had landed on them had not been able to fly away and were piled up like little winged corpses on bloated, rotting boats.

Another photo was of a doe that appears to have died while drinking from the pernicious waters. Likely not its first drink from the creek. Yet this particular lap had been a solvent-laced liquor that made the doe's knees buckle and her pink tongue hang from her mouth; it skimmed along the surface as life left her.

Alex puts the pictures down on her keyboard and leans her elbows on the edge of her desk as she presses the pads of her hands against her closed eyes.

She'd been dreaming more in the last few days. Haunting nightmares of rain that falls so fast that the flood waters are already rising to the sky to meet them before they settle. She is often trapped in those flood waters, grasping at passing tree limbs or even the hand of a lifeless body. She fights to keep her head out of the waves, as her arms and hands move through the quicksand of hopelessness. Waking with her hands balled in fists and the sheets clutched in her death grip.

Alex slides the photos back into their envelope and locks the cabinet. Her key ring jingles.

Her eyes flick over to the framed photo on her desk and the man pictured beside her.

"We're gonna get them, Dad."

CHAPTER 10

A lex gazes at her laptop screen, her reflection marred by fingerprint smudges on the glass, as the black background flashes with the opening of a new window. Lonnie Colbert's airbrushed photo greets her before he does when the Vroom application opens. The dots in the corner indicate Lonnie is trying to connect his audio, as Alex examines his stiffly posed corporate studio portrait in front of a marble background. There are fewer wrinkles and puffy eyes in this photo compared to the snapshots that arrived on her desk.

She clicks her pen, resting her hand on her notepad inside the second story NYT's conference room. Early morning coffee chats, the tapping of keys and ringing of phones are muffled by the double glass doors, as if someone has turned down the volume in the office. Sixty feet below, the sounds of New York City are louder than her colleagues: the hiss and screeches of city bus breaks, a police officer's whistle, and the blowing of cab horns.

"Ms. Broussard? Can you hear me?" Lonnie Colbert's nasally voice is raised, as if speaking louder will improve the connection.

Alex bolts from her slumped posture to attention. "I can hear you."

"One moment please. We seem to be having some trouble with my video."

When Lonnie Colbert, CEO of Takestrom Chemicals and Senior Vice President of MacAllen Industries, switches on his camera, Alex addresses the man she has been trying to arrange an interview with for the past month.

"There we are!" Colbert's grin is feline. He straightens his gold tie and smooths the front of his double-breasted suit jacket. He adjusts the camera over his screen, retracting small hands. His smaller eyes and ears are aligned under a pompadour of black hair.

"Thank you for making the time to talk," Alex acknowledges.

"Yes, of course. Typically MacAllen Industries doesn't permit employees or management to speak on camera, but we felt this was an opportunity to clear the air so to speak."

"You've made an exception?"

"For *The Times*, yes."

"Well ... thank you." Alex smiles. "How is it today in Chicago?"

Behind Colbert's onscreen visage is his skyscraper office view. The backdrop framing his head is the rippled caps of Lake Michigan and a smog-free sky. Where the blue of the water and that of the sky ended and began was hard to tell from the horizon.

"Beautiful day. Yes, stunning. I may take a walk around Millennium Park later," Colbert says. Alex didn't really care if the events of the Book of Revelations were unfolding in Chicago. She had a job to do.

"As you are aware, we are doing a story on companies that are correcting EPA violations."

Colbert folds his elbows and leans over the desk. "Yes, let me first say—"

"Do you mind if I record this?"

Colbert's head snaps up as he looks at something above his computer screen, his eyes darting from whatever is offscreen back to Alex's face. He grips the edge of his desk before tapping it like a drum. "Not at all. Whatever helps you accurately report the story."

Alex leans towards the screen finding the section to begin recording. A red dot appears in the upper left corner of the screen on her computer.

"As I stated, we are doing a story on corporations that have had major EPA violations and are working to correct them. I have a list of some of MacAllen Industries violations but specifically those of Takestrom Chemicals near Marktown, Indiana." Alex holds up print outs as thick as a one-inch binder to the screen. Colbert's face goes as pale as the printer paper in her hands.

"Could we do better?" Colbert says. "Absolutely. Are we working to make improvements? Absolutely."

Alex skims the bullet points of notes she made. "In the last ten years, Takestrom Chemicals has faced criminal and civil charges from the state of Indiana and from the EPA for violations of the Clean Air Act, the Clean Water Act, Safe Drinking Water Act, and Toxic Substances Control Act."

She watches the screen, but he offers no comment.

"It seems to be an issue of the company's disposal of chemicals and solid waste. What's been the problem?"

"First, let me say that we are in fact turning things around. These violations were a wake-up call to our company to do better for the sake of our workers and for the community."

"Yes," Alex presses. "But why were there so many violations to begin with?"

"We chalk it up to employees trying to cut corners and save time."

"You're blaming your employees?"

"Now, Alex," Colbert begins, leaning back in his chair and folds his arms. "That's not what I'm saying at all. Our employees are the heartbeat of our company. What I am saying is that when the clock is ticking and it's time to punch that timecard, well, sometimes things get rushed or hurried. We have implemented additional waste disposal training as part of our new employee orientation. Everyone knows the rules."

Alex takes her time writing down a note. When her gaze returns to the screen, Colbert's jaw is set in a hard line.

"Takestrom is your largest factory under MacAllen Industries?"

"Yes. We employ approximately 300 at that location."

"How many of those are new employees and have received this orientation and training that you mentioned?" Alex lifts her eyes from the notepad back to the screen, maintains a neutral expression.

"I don't have those numbers in front of me right this minute, but it's a large percentage of our workforce."

"When did you begin the waste disposal training?"

"Three or four years ago," Colbert replies.

"Would it be possible to confirm what percentage of your employees have received this training? Is it something that is required universally?"

"No." Colbert pauses and his eyes flick above the computer again. "I mean, yes, it would be possible to confirm the number of employees who have received this training but no, it is not universally required. Our veteran employees know company policy regarding disposal of chemicals and substances."

"Would you say there is however, a separation between policies and enforcement? Employees can know the policy but is it not up to management and company officials to make sure those policies are being followed and enforced?"

Colbert tugs at his earlobe. "Yes, and department heads and managers have improved enforcement and correction."

"How?"

"Excuse me?"

"How?"

He flexes and curls his fingers before resting his chin on his fist. His eyes move above the computer screen again and he lowers his hand and sits tall. "Walking the floors ... proper demonstration ... checklists for task completion."

"These are new implementations?" Alex's insistent questioning continues.

"We've stepped up our efforts in the last few years."

She writes something with a flourish and underlines it.

"Your company was forced to comply with reductions of air pollutants, stormwater pollutants, and solid wastes."

Colbert seems hesitant to speak. "Yes."

"Where does your compliance and update stand today?" Alex interrogates.

"We have had no further violations charges from the EPA."

"None?" Alex's neck bends forward then stiffens back up.

"We can proudly report we've had no violations in the last two years."

"That's a rather unusual achievement for a company in your industry and of your size, wouldn't you say?" Alex lifts a single brow and cocks her head.

"It's a fantastic achievement. We put a challenge out to our employees to do better and they responded." Colbert's smile lacks warmth.

"Takestrom received a ten-million-dollar federal contract to help dispose of toxic waste last year, did I read that correctly?" Alex peers back at the screen quizzically.

Colbert's desk chair twists underneath him and rolls back before he stops it. "Yes, that's also correct."

"Would a contract of that nature grant your corporation a level of immunity from facing prosecution or additional violations?"

A vein throbs in Colbert's forehead. "Ms. Broussard, I am not sure exactly what it is that you are getting at, but I would advise that such implications border on defamation or slander. We are doing you a courtesy by even speaking today. We would hate for you to regret this use of your time." He shakes his head at her, a warning.

Alex takes a moment to write another note. She presses her lips into a soft smile. "Forgive me. It merely begs for closer examination when a company has pages of violations for years, then none." She rests her elbows on the conference table.

"We have worked to rectify those issues and leave them in the past. We want to show the public that we are better than our shortcomings."

"Lonnie ... there is a belief by some in Marktown and neighboring cities that Takestrom's outputs are causing health issues—"

He talks over her. "That's preposterous! I'd challenge anyone who makes such a claim to provide medical evidence to support it."

"We're working on that," Alex confirms. "If there is any link, we will find out."

Colbert stills before he grabs a paperweight from the corner of his desk, clutching it.

"According to the EPA, in areas neighboring Takestrom, air and stormwater pollutants were found to be abnormally high, and the company was being forced to reduce the release of mercury, zinc, aluminum, copper, and also aerosols."

"That was part of the original violations case and, as I've already stated, we have policies in place now to correct those mistakes of the past."

"How much does it cost to properly dispose of chemicals and waste?"

Colbert opens his mouth to speak but closes it. He looks up. "Ms. Broussard, that's not a figure I have readily in front of me, I'll have to get back to you on that."

"What would you say to citizens who claim that safety and proper waste disposal are being sacrificed for profit. That Takestrom Chemicals, MacAllen Industries, values profits over lives?"

Colbert is silent. His eyes leave the screen and the background noise is quieted. Alex notices that he is muted for a few breaths as his stare shifts above the screen.

When he unmutes, he scratches his eyebrow. "Ms. Broussard. The nature of your story is the correction of EPA violations by companies such as Takestrom, correct?"

"Yes, I—"

"Then let's focus on the facts that we do have rather than speculation and sensationalism. I would suggest you not pursue this type of questioning."

Alex stares at the screen, her gaze locked virtually with Colbert. "The facts are concerning, Mr. Colbert. Not just the EPA violations but also OSHA. In looking at both, the community outside *and* inside of Takestrom, there are the pollutants in the water sources and air, as well as worker safety at risk. The facts show that 3,500 workers were hurt on the job in the past eight years across MacAllen Industries factories."

"Worker safety is our top priority, as well as ensuring the quality of life for residents. I'm sure you'll find in your continued research that MacAllen is invested in the growth of every city that we do business in. We make contributions to support education and human services initiatives because we want to support the families of our workers."

Alex's eyebrows pull close and then down. "Takestrom's primary product output is benzene according to my information."

"I can confirm that, yes."

"Benzene as a chemical is one of the deadliest to handle and be exposed to, is that true?"

"All handling of chemicals comes with some risks."

Alex pauses and writes on her notepad again. Colbert licks his bottom teeth as he waits.

"Lonnie, we appreciate that you've made an exception for our paper to interview you. Would you permit our photographer inside Takestrom to snap a few photos? Maybe capture your employees using the training on proper chemical and waste disposal that you mentioned."

"That is out of the question."

"It is?"

Colbert glances up. "It's against our policy to allow cameras inside of our facilities."

"Would we be permitted to speak to employees who have trained—

"Ms. Broussard, I have another meeting to get to. We must call this meeting short."

"Oh." Alex's eyes widen at Colbert's abrupt departure. "Thank you for your time. When can I expect those numbers you mentioned?"

"I'll have my assistant follow-up with you. We'll make every effort to get it to you before the piece runs."

Alex views the NYT logo on her screen as Lonnie Colbert leaves the call.

CHAPTER 11

"Lydia?" Oliver calls from the doorway. He presses the buttons on the security keypad and surveys the house. Samson and Delilah are nowhere in sight, and neither is his wife.

It is the middle of the afternoon, the only light in the home comes from the sunlight beaming in through the windows.

"Lydia!"

From the kitchen comes the sound of a wooden chair squealing over tile. Oliver pauses. He steps back into the hallway and a second later, Lydia appears and walks towards him, her high-heeled shoes pounding over the hardwood floor. She is not only dressed but also in full makeup. The two dogs stand near the kitchen door, licking their lips before retreating, uninterested in their latest visitor.

"Oliver?" Lydia stops mid-stride in her heels, almost stumbling into the hall's wall. Oliver is accustomed to seeing Lydia stagger. Today, however, he is struck by the clearness of her eyes. They are vibrant, not red and lazy. Her skin is rosy not ghostly; his name on her lips is enunciated not slurred. She smells of Chanel No. 5 not brandy. Her stutter step is from the surprise of his visit, not another drunken haze.

"Hey," he says, taking off his trench coat. He hangs it on the rack and loosens the Windsor knot on his tie. It feels tighter around his neck than when he put it on earlier that morning.

He'd thought he could live with a transactional marriage. He'd really believed he could continue the masquerade with Lydia as DC's bright and loving, young, political couple. The despair he felt for his career had vacuumed his desire for a Camelot marriage. Oliver's tenacity had been rusted over and wedged like the sword in the nation's bedrock.

Alex's return had dislodged him from the spell, but he wasn't entirely free. He'd been thinking. The type of thoughts a man thinks about a woman when he can't focus on his work and the nights are lonely. The kind of thoughts that pictured a future with her out in the open, not hidden from the world. When she'd slumbered in his apartment bed nights before, he lay on the sofa listening to Montana's snores. With Alex close, he wanted to be selfish, to no longer sacrifice his own happiness for the sake of others.

He and Lydia had conversations about their fate together not long after the move to Washington. They'd never reached any type of reasonable compromise. This time, however, is different.

Lydia stops a few feet in front of him as he pulls at his collar. "I was going to call you." Her eyes implore him. He frowns slightly, but quickly picks up that he needs to play along with whatever she is about to say. "Look who came into town this morning."

Lydia's father, Jamison Ainsworth, emerges from the dimly lit kitchen. He is wearing a black suit, starched white shirt, and a black and gold tie. Jamison is a tall man, six foot one, almost as tall as his son-in-law.

"Mr. Ainsworth," Oliver extends his hand. He clears his throat and corrects himself. "I'm sorry, Jamison, how are you?"

Jamison swats Oliver's hand away. "Son, how's it going?" He laughs and pulls him into a bear hug. Jamison's show of boisterous affection compresses Oliver's chest as he gives a jolly laugh. Oliver's arms are pinned to his side as he looks to Lydia, eyes pleading for interference. She covers her mouth from the laughter.

When Jamison lets Oliver go, the function of his lungs returns.

"It's going well, sir." Oliver gives his father-in-law a sincere smile.

"Ah, you don't have to shine shit with me." Jamison pats Oliver's shoulder. "I follow the news. I've seen how the pack has been all over your tail."

"It's Washington." Oliver slides his hands into his pockets and rocks back onto his heels. "What brings you to town?"

"Well, I had some business matters to tend to unexpectedly, and after I was done taking care of things, I decided to stop by and see how my oldest daughter was doing." Jamison wraps his arms around Lydia's shoulders and gives her bicep a squeeze.

"Must be pretty important business if it brought you all the way from California?"

"Yes, it is. During my last visit here, I'd picked up some information around town, I'm not sure where exactly, about a bankruptcy attorney that could help get me back on my feet. I put a phone call in to him, we talked, and determined a meeting in person would be best."

"Daddy was just explaining how things were turning around when you came home."

"Good to hear, Jamison. I'm glad things are looking up."

"The market was volatile these last two years. Unpredictable trends ... natural disasters globally impacting trade and stocks. Hopefully, we've weathered the storms now and everything is going to be fine."

Oliver gives a smile of encouragement to his father-in-law, once a wealthy stockbroker with lavish California homes and multiple cars. He and Lydia's mother divorced during Lydia's junior year of high school. Jamison was living in a single bedroom apartment these days.

"Lydia, sweetheart, I hate to have to run, but I was only in town for the day, and I've got a 6:15 flight."

Oliver reads the clock hanging on the foyer wall. It's four minutes after three.

"Do you need me to take you to the airport? I can," Lydia offers.

"No, no, I'll grab a cab. It was good to visit with you, Lyd."

"You too, Daddy. Oh, I wish you could stay longer."

"I'll call, and we can set up something soon or you can come out to California for a while. I think being on the west coast again might do you some good. Get some sunshine on your skin!"

"Maybe so." Lydia reaches out and hugs her father, who kisses her on the forehead.

"I'm going to head up the street to wait for a cab."

"Daddy, you can wait for one here," Lydia chides.

"No, I want to give you both some time together. It's so rare that I speak to Lydia these days and you are actually around. Take care of her." Jamison places his hand on the doorknob. Lydia moves around them both and types the security code into the keypad.

"You sure you got enough money for a cab?" Oliver asks in an upbeat tone. "A ride to the airport could be costly."

"Daddy's got it covered. Things are better, Ollie."

"I'll call you when I make it home, Lydia. I love you."

"I love you, too." Lydia bolts the door behind him and resets the security alarm. "I had no idea he was planning to be in town today until he called late last night," she rattles out. "I was going to call you to let you know. I wasn't expecting you to come by."

"I know," Oliver bites his bottom lip. "Look, Lydia there's something—"

"Oh! Look what else came today! FedEx delivered it early!" She throws up her hand and scurries to the kitchen, heels sounding like tap shoes. When she steps back into the hallway, she is carrying the glossy stapled pages of a magazine in her hands. She grips the sides of it as she holds it up.

It's People Magazine, and on the cover, Lydia and Oliver are side by side, Oliver's arms wrapped lovingly around Lydia as her unveiled adoration peers into his emerald eyes, both smiling. "Mr. Michaels Goes to Washington: His DC Life" is the headline in the corner of the picture.

"Tamara included a thank you card to both of us. She said the magazine will be on stands tomorrow." Lydia opens the magazine to the center story featuring her and Oliver. There are snaps of them on the sofa together and one playful shot of them with Samson and Delilah in the small backyard behind their townhome.

"The article is so great. Do you want to read it?" Lydia thrusts the pages towards him.

Oliver swallows and takes a deep breath. "No, it's cool. I..." the words are suddenly a struggle. "I needed to talk with you."

"It's really good." She stares at him.

Oliver replies with a tremulous voice. "None of that is real Lydia. We both know it."

Her face is crestfallen as she snaps the magazine closed.

"Yeah." She runs her fingers through her hair. "I know." She hesitates but takes a deep breath. "Oliver, there's something you need to know."

"What is it?"

"The last three nights, I've gone to a support group. Twelve-step for people with alcohol problems." She closes her eyes and steadies her shoulders, freeing herself with the truth. "For alcoholics. I'm an alcoholic. I realize that."

She opens her eyes one by one and exhales, balling her hands into fists.

Oliver blinks slowly. "Lydia, wow, I—"

"I said when I first went that I was doing it for us. That after the interview and the gala, I couldn't go on this way with you. But then, I realized I had to do this for myself. If there is any hope of us rebuilding our marriage, I have to be comfortable with myself. I have to accept that who I am and what I am is enough, especially for you." Lydia's face is etched with the pain from self-realization and self-acceptance.

"Lydia." Oliver scratches at a frown line. Shame courses through his veins, flowing to every part of his being. "I never intended to make you feel like you weren't enough for me."

"I guess I've felt that way since college, like, someday I was going to lose you. I realized when we did this interview; I do still feel like the luckiest woman on the planet to be with you. I don't want to pretend that we are this couple," she says, pointing to the photo, "I want us to *be* this couple again, Oliver. There is still love here. I know there is?" Even in the darkened hallway, he can see her face wet with tears.

Oliver takes a deep breath to stare directly into her eyes. He opens his mouth. He sees it before he says anything. He sees her brace herself, as if she has already accepted that he won't give them another chance. He glances down at the magazine cover in her hand, their two faces tilted adoringly towards one another.

Lydia is oblivious to the fact that her one-time romantic rival has returned to Oliver's life. Inhabiting a separate living space and sleeping in a separate bed has not made Oliver's safeguarding of this life change an easy task. Along with the behind-the-scenes investigation into his colleagues, he feels like a sentry at Fort Knox.

Seeing the fear in her eyes, he knows Lydia's sobriety is as fragile as a newborn. He does not want to drop this precious new life he feels responsible for.

"Hand me that." He motions at the magazine. She places it in his hands.

Oliver opens the magazine, reviewing the article. His own eyes meet his gaze from the page.

He gives her a faint smile. "This is good."

CHAPTER 12

The Red Maple Office Park in Fort Wayne, Indiana, looks like a nursing home from its exterior. White awnings extend like small front porches on white dulcimers outside of three sets of black French doors. It's a long, red brick building with individual suites, one of them leased by Grayson Dwyer of the Dwyer Law Firm, LLC.

The rental car is parked in the lot in front of Suite 402-B, and Coleman makes his way to the door. A sign instructs him to press the red button on the black box next to the door. As he presses, there's a chime inside the building. With a metallic click and pop, the door cracks open enough for a woman's face to appear.

She stares him down and then asks, "Coleman Chester?"

"Yes." He fumbles in his coat pockets and holds up his press badge. She nods and opens the door fully and steps back.

"I'm Bonnie." She secures the door behind him. "We spoke on the phone."

"Yes." Coleman gives the redhead a deep, dimpled smile as he assesses her. She'd interrogated him for several minutes about the nature of the story he was working on and vetted him and his credentials before calling back with a time for him to meet with environmental and toxic exposure attorney Grayson Dwyer.

Coleman wonders why there is so much red tape at a law office before remembering the people Grayson has gone up against.

Bonnie wears fitted dark blue jeans and a pair of all-white Keds. Her attire surprises Coleman given her professional intensity on the phone. Her right hand is in an over-the-counter brace people use for carpal tunnel syndrome.

She walks past Coleman and leads him through a short waiting area with leather chairs, a bowl of mints, and a table with a stack of magazines. The latest issue of People Magazine is on top. Coleman glances at the glossy cover with Senator Oliver Michaels and his wife, Lydia.

"Can I get you a coffee?" Bonnie opens a door with a glass pane.

"A coffee would be great," Coleman says with spirited energy. After the almost three-hour drive from East Chicago, he could use a jolt. It's before noon, almost lunchtime.

Bonnie's red lips move into a smile. She holds the door for him, and he follows her into what is clearly the inner workings of a busy office despite the lack of other employees. There is another office with a closed door and Grayson's name on a black and gold name plate. Kitty-corner to his office door is a desk stacked with Bankers Boxes and manilla file folders. The name plate at the front of the desk reads "Bonnie Dobson." There's a neatly cleared space in front of a paper calendar and her chair is rolled into place. A clear container of something green and thick with a reusable straw plunged into it sits beside the paper calendar.

Bonnie moves to the corner of the office to the small break area containing a coffee maker, sink, microwave, and minifridge. "Sugar? Creamer?" she offers.

"No, straight black," Coleman takes a seat in one of the vacant leather chairs across from Bonnie's desk.

The cup starts to brew and the smell of warm coffee tantalizes Coleman's nose almost as much as Bonnie in those jeans. She drops the pod in a blue bin marked "recycling."

She hands Coleman a paper cup with the recycled label on the side. "One minute."

"Thank you."

Bonnie knocks on Grayson's door.

"Come in," a voice responds. Bonnie slips inside and closes the door behind her, leaving Coleman alone, observing the office suite.

The door swings open moments later, and Bonnie is trailed by a man almost the same height she is, in a dark gray suit vest and matching slacks with a custom, pale blue button-down. His sleeves are rolled up to his elbows.

"Coleman. Grayson Dwyer." He sticks his hand out.

Coleman stands, gingerly cupping the coffee in one hand and extends his other. As he shakes Grayson's hand, he notices the tattoos of individual letters on each of his fingers.

"Thank you for meeting with me," Coleman replies.

"Absolutely. I see Bonnie got you set up with a coffee. Can I get you anything else? Bonnie, did you already put in a lunch order?"

"Deli sandwiches in the fridge." Bonnie moves around her desk and takes a seat.

Grayson's shoulders slump with childlike disappointment. "I wanted a burger from Five Guys."

"Yes," Bonnie says, pulling her lips upward, "and I got you a deli sandwich. Coleman, there's one for you too if you are hungry." She grabs and opens a file with her brace-bound hand.

Grayson grumbles. "Sometimes I forget whose name is on the door."

"Yeah. Me too."

"Might as well move you from paralegal to partner." He heads to the fridge and pulls out two white bags before walking back into his office. "Let's have a chat, Coleman." Grayson closes the door.

"She seems tough."

"She's my lifeline. Couldn't handle even one case without her."

Grayson's office is surprisingly cozy, decorated and furnished in a manner you might find in Better Homes and Gardens. An antique roll-top desk of walnut wood is pushed against one wall. The top is stacked with a brass-plated scales of justice, a carving of a mallard duck, and vintage, gilded leather legal books in navy blue, brown, burgundy, and amber.

A maroon leather desk chair is rolled under the desk, a few closed files on the seat, and a matching burgundy Winchester chesterfield leather sofa is under the front office window. Coleman can see his silver rental car in the lot. Grayson closes the blinds.

He places the sandwich bags on a table and motions for Coleman to have a seat at one of the two wooden chairs placed around it. As he does, he examines a wall with framed papers: an undergraduate degree in pre-law from Michigan State, a law degree from University of Chicago, and board certified and sealed certificate from the state bar in Indiana.

More volumes of law and a few golf trophies are enclosed in a glass shelf behind him.

"Nice office."

"It's a goddamn nightmare. I'm wedged between a chiropractor and a dentist. I hate the dentist. I swear it. Some days, I can hear the drill." He peeks inside the sandwich bags. "Both turkey. That all right by you?"

"I could eat the ass end of a dead horse right now to be honest." Coleman laughs and sips his coffee. This draws a big smile from Grayson.

"Want more than the coffee? Water? Pop?"

"No, I'm good, thank you though."

Grayson pulls out the chair across from Coleman and takes a seat as he pushes the bag towards the reporter. They get settled with the lunch and Grayson digs in, food wedged in the corner of his cheek as he holds the turkey sandwich.

"So." He chews, and Coleman's eyes again move to the tattoos on his knuckles. Grayson's light brown hair, streaked with lines of silver, is muffed. His goatee is also graying. "Bonnie says you're looking into those sons of bitches at Takestrom?"

Coleman pauses from eating long enough to swallow and respond. "Yeah. Thanks for taking the time to meet with me. I met with Aubrey Fischer."

"God, that woman is a fighter. You hear me? Good thing the doctors caught her leukemia when they did; otherwise, she'd be another buried body of evidence."

"She said you are attempting to represent her and a few other Take-strom employees in a mass tort?"

"Yes." Grayson uses the tip of his tongue to pluck mayo from the corner of his lip. He rakes his fingers through his hair and scratches at his scalp. "The thing with Takestrom workers and the people in Marktown is that we saw lots of different types of illness. People were sick, but there wasn't a commonality to it. Yes, a few of the same diagnoses, but it was so vast. It wasn't the same sickness across the board. Some people had cancer; some people had respiratory illnesses. One client had even gotten dizzy and fainted and hit his head."

"From the benzene?"

"From the benzene. Damn," he says, looking away for a minute, "we had good causation."

"Aubrey said her case got to pretrial but not beyond that?"

"She's right. Neither her case nor six of my other clients."

"Why not?"

"Judge Caroline Skinner."

"A judge stopped it?"

"Yup." Grayson pops his lips for emphasis and then folds his arms. "I file the lawsuits. We've got sick patients with medical bills and a common link in that they either worked for Takestrom or live in Marktown. Skinner puts up a good front in the beginning. Seems like she's going to be open to this all moving forward. Then, I'm stopped at every turn."

"How so?"

"First, it was refusing to grant some of my requests during discovery. According to Skinner, Takestrom's defense didn't have to turn over some of the discoverable evidence. I filed a motion to compel but she only granted it for things that wouldn't bear any fruit. It was like pulling up a tomato plant that hadn't produced any tomatoes yet. Pointless if you want to eat tomatoes, right?"

Coleman nods, listening intently.

"I think, all right, screw it; I'll just file for a site inspection. She refuses."

"Why?"

"I'm still trying to figure that out myself, Coleman. I finally think we have a chance to move forward with some of my expert witnesses weighing in on benzene, and I have my plaintiff testimony. Defense brings up a motion to exclude every single one of my expert witnesses. Skinner granted them all and on top of that denied my motion for continuance so I could designate new experts, meaning I can't prove causation. I had no choice but to nonsuit the lawsuit without prejudice before we got a ruling on the merits, so we could bring it again in the future before the statute of limitations runs out. Fortunately, Takestrom never asserted any counterclaims."

"You believe Skinner is in with Takestrom?"

"That was the first thing I checked, and it seems like the obvious choice for her decision. But if there is money going in or some former campaign donors she doesn't want to piss off, it's not on the books. Could be another tie to this whole thing, but if there is, it's buried deep."

"Why would Skinner care and fight so hard to stop you?"

"I've been doing this damn near thirty years. In my experience, most judges want things resolved. I've had maybe a pair in all that time that have said to me, 'Make the case go away or I'm going to make it go away.' In those situations, we settled the case, like with a lumber company once. I was solely personal injury back then. I moved into environmental and toxic exposure seventeen years ago."

"Why the switch?"

"I wanted to do more. I grew up in Michigan. My dad was blue collar, worked at the docks. I saw how broken down he was before he passed.

How all those years of lifting and being out in the elements had just whooped him."

Grayson's eyebrows gather in. He picks up what's left of his sandwich but puts it down again without taking a bite. "He was the strongest man I knew, and he developed Osteoporosis. Can't say it was because of the job but can't say it wasn't either. I got tired of chasing ambulances and car wreck victims and wanted to help people like my father."

"Any negative relationship with Skinner before the Takestrom cases?"

"Had never worked with her. Knew nothing of the woman. Now, Bonnie and I think she's Satan in a black robe with a gavel."

"So, after she shut you down ... you just ..." Coleman trails off.

"Gave up?" Grayson finishes. "No. I haven't given up entirely. I plan to appeal the discovery rulings. I've invested too much bandwidth and finances into bringing on these lawsuits. I am not walking away from the investment. Restructuring. So, none of this Coleman, is on the record." Grayson's pointed stare changes the energy in the room.

"I understand, just as I told Bonnie on the phone. Appreciate the tips."

"I can't walk away from this one," Grayson stresses. "For any reason. I check in with Aubrey from time to time. Did you meet the kid?"

"I did."

"Cute as a button."

"We need to look into Skinner's connections," Coleman says, almost to himself.

"The way I see it," Grayson interjects, "judges face immense social and political pressure. Let's say Skinner is buddy-buddy with Takestrom. What does it matter if she rocks the boat with them? They are one of the town's largest employers, so there's that implication. She is an elected official and if people are without a job, she could be without a job. Jobs and income are votes. There's got to be more than that. I never could find out what. Eventually, I stopped digging and most people seemed to stop caring."

"Aubrey cares."

"Aubrey's special. You know how many of the townspeople accept what's going on? Hell, the local news media knows Takestrom poisons people, and you won't read a headline or see a lower third on your TV screen about it."

"The media knows?"

"Yes. Takestrom is the biggest employer near town. Who wants to piss them off? EPA releases reports every year on companies with violations. Any reporter in the area worth their salt would take twenty minutes to flip through the report and see who's on the up and up and who's not. Not a whisper about Takestrom. You might see the occasional Facebook post about them or a crowdsource fundraiser to help someone with medical bills, but nobody's talking. Oh, and Skinner? She's covering her ass in every way possible, whatever her reason is. Spotless."

"My colleague and I are going to change that."

Grayson gives a soft humph, face conveying disbelief. "If you do, then you're not just a reporter. You're Houdini."

Coleman taps the Bluetooth connection on the rental car's dashboard and selects Alex's number. The rumble of rubber tires on tarmac is his reflective soundtrack.

He'd left Grayson's office to return to Marktown. Speeding across I-30 West, he passes denuded trees and muddy, grassless medians that have not sprung back from the winter freezes yet.

Alex picks up after two rings. "Hey."

"You at the office?"

"Yeah, what's up?"

"Need you to look up some info on Judge Caroline Skinner of Lake County, Indiana. She'd be over in the Superior Court, Civil Division now. She was a circuit court judge for a few years."

"Got it. What are we looking for?"

"Any connection between her and Takestrom Chemicals, Ingelman, Eisenhower, or Chickman. That attorney I told you that I was going to meet with today?" Coleman harkens back to their brief phone conversation from the night before.

"Yes? Did that pan out with anything?"

"Tons!" Coleman grips the steering wheel and checks his speed, easing off the accelerator just a bit. "Gave me great stuff off the record. Confirmed he represented Aubrey Fischer and a few others. Seems like they all had cut and dry cases, but this Judge Skinner made it difficult for Dwyer to get any kind of testimony on the stand or experts to verify the medical implications and environmental impact. Not a single case got beyond pretrial."

"You're kidding?"

"No. Something's up with her. See if you can shake a few trees to see if something drops."

"Campaign donations in her circuit days?" Alex suggests.

"Dwyer said he got suspicious, and that was the first thing he checked. So far, she's clean. Maybe get our guys on it. There's got to be a stone unturned somewhere."

"I need to follow up with Ezrah on the travel and phone records. I'll see if they can do some digging on Skinner as well. I'll also see if I can get some leads on her."

"Thanks, Alex. How are you otherwise?"

"I'm good. What about you? You minding your six?"

"I don't think anyone's too suspicious just yet, but when I went to the municipal office the other day, I got a few stares. Outside of all that, I'm fired up." He glances at the speed—twenty miles over it again. He lifts his foot and hovers it over the accelerator. "The family I talked to, the attorney, whatever is going on with this judge, there's a lot of side dishes here. We've just got to find the meat and potatoes."

Alex chuckles. "I know you're into a story when you start using food metaphors."

"I'm also hungry. I had a dry turkey sandwich for lunch and about two more hours till I make it back to Marktown. The Fischer family invited me to dinner at their place tonight. I'm going to head to the factory, see what I can see, and then stop by."

"Be safe out there."

"Always. I'll check-in with you tonight. Take care."

"You too," she says.

Alex places her desk phone back on the base. She scrubs her hand over her face, weary from lying to Coleman. She was not "good." She still hadn't been able to slip in more than two hours of consistent sleep. Not with the nightmares, Oliver, and this story on her mind.

134

She takes the elevator two floors down to the investigative unit research department.

The rows of white cubicles are decorated with all sorts of oddities. One cubicle is lined with rubber dinosaurs and a Jurassic Park poster. Another is decorated with vintage Marilyn Monroe photos. She waves to a few of the guys as they lift their heads. A woman sits at a desk in the corner, headphones in and typing feverishly on her keyboard.

Alex spots Ezrah leaning back in a chair, twirling a pencil around on the tops of his fingers. He sits up straight when he sees her.

"Hey! I've been looking over the records you gave us earlier."

"Tell me something good, E?" Alex sits on the edge of his desk. Ezrah's floppy black hair cascades over his eyes, and he flips it back.

"Nothing yet. But I'm sure we will find something. To what do I owe the pleasure of a second visit in as many days?" He gives a cheeky smile.

Alex hands him the Post-it note first.

"A judge?"

"Coleman's source thinks she is in with these guys somehow, but none of the conventional records has shown anything. No campaign donations or fundraising events. Still, I plan to look into it. I also want you guys to research anything you can find on her."

Ezrah places the pencil sideways between his thin pink lips and starts typing on his keyboard. "Hmm." Eyes narrowing, he clicks on a few links. "Standard stuff. A public webpage. Looks like she had a Facebook campaign page. Not seeing much in the way of social. Not much on her in the news, either."

Alex turns her head and watches as Ezrah scrolls and clicks, scrolls and clicks. Caroline Skinner's short, all-white hair is parted with bangs concealing part of her large forehead. A pair of pearl stud earrings adorn her ears in the posed portrait of her in her black judicial robe, seated in front of the US flag.

"Judge Caroline Skinner … studied law at Valparaiso, practiced for twenty-two years before running for office, blah blah blah." Ezrah feigns an exaggerated yawn as he sings out her bio. "Boring, boring, boring, mother of four, married to husband Ed for twenty-three years. Yada, yada, yada." Ezrah stops and rolls his fatigued eyes towards the ceiling. "This could take a while."

"There's something else."

"Oh! I hope it's something juicy!"

Alex slides a folded color copy of one of the photos from her pocket and hands it to Ezrah. As he unfolds it, she points to the mystery man with dark hair.

"This guy. Nothing returned from my image search and not even after looking at Lord knows how many photos of Eisenhower, Ingelman, and Chickman did he pop up. I tried looking through crowd shots, but my eyes glazed over. Maybe you guys have a better way?"

"Always." Ezrah winks. "Plus, I love a challenge."

"That's why you're the best! I'll get to work upstairs on finding anything I can on Skinner. Priority for you guys remains the travel and phone logs. If you come across any connection with Skinner, though, please let me know. By some miracle, if you find our Mr. X, please let me know ASAP."

"Anything for you." Ezrah puts a hand to his heart.

"I owe you."

"Every reporter that comes down here says that. Then we don't see you until the next time you need something."

"How about a latte from up the street?"

THE SENATOR

"Make it a cappuccino and we're good."

CHAPTER 13

Washington DC is aglow with street headlights. It's almost midnight but the nation's capital is bustling. On the edge of town, Alex sits on a couch in Oliver's apartment.

"I need to interview Ingleman." Alex turns and raises her knee, resting it on the sofa cushion between her and Oliver.

"Do you think that's wise? It could raise suspicions."

"Not if I frame it the right way. I got a sit-down interview with Clara Goransson when I attended the gala two weeks ago. The profile piece on her isn't written yet. I can add Ingelman to it. A look at what the US is currently doing to keep up with the climate crisis. Those stories run all the time. But since Ingleman was there that night to hear Clara, it's a chance to get into his office and question him directly. I can position it as a look at how the nation's leaders respond to the calls made by the next generation to save our planet."

Oliver grimaces. "I don't know, Alex."

"You don't have to know. I do. I know that we need to start connecting the dots here. The clock is ticking. I need to get in front of at least one of these guys. You've got a better in with Chickman and Eisenhower. Ingelman is my mark."

Oliver's unabashed staring makes Alex shift her position on the sofa, placing her feet on the floor and her hands on her lap. Goosebumps slide along the back of her neck.

"You're fearless, you know that?" His voice is soft.

"I wish that was true. The world terrifies me. I have to push through the fear. Otherwise, why call myself a reporter?"

"I wish I had that same persistence. Maybe I shouldn't be a senator anymore."

"You have a strong will." Alex's stare fixes on Oliver's unwavering gaze. "You have been a fighter and sometimes the underdog throughout your life. You've overcome one obstacle after another. The senate is just another obstacle."

"Thank you. I forgot how good you are at pep talks." A slow smile builds on his lips.

Montana trots across the living room to his water bowl in the kitchen. The wet lapping fills the few seconds of silence.

Alex had returned to DC that evening with an update on Coleman's interview with the Fischer family and where the investigative unit at *The Times* stood with their research.

"Do you ever ..." Oliver's tongue darts out to lick his lips. "Do you ever wonder how different our lives would be if we'd stayed together?"

"All the time."

"Whenever I'm near you, Alex, I wonder if I made the right choice. I know, in my heart, that I didn't. I've never had a feeling of peace in my life since what happened between us and then getting with Lydia. It's like that night at the after-party is haunting me. I think about it often."

Alex puts her hand out, resting it on top of his on the sofa, running her thumb over his knuckles.

"Alex." Oliver's exhale makes his shoulders slump. His grip on her hand tightens. "Lydia is still my wife. Despite everything, I'm still married to her."

"I know," she whispers, "and I know you wouldn't do anything to break your vow to her, whether things are good or not. That's the man you are." Alex feels the sinking sadness in her heart drop down to her stomach.

"I want her to file for a divorce. I've asked her to do it once before, but she still believes we can work through this. There's just so much going on with her. She's drunk half the time. She wants kids together, and I think that's one of the worst things we could do. A few weeks ago, her dad filed for bankruptcy after some bad business deals, and she's been asking me to funnel money to him. I'm not in the NFL anymore. We don't have unlimited funds, but I try to do what I can to make her happy, keep her living comfortably."

"I'm sorry." Alex plays with his fingers. "I'm sorry for what you're dealing with. But ... I can't let a personal situation between us jeopardize this story. If we crossed a line and that came out later, it could easily discredit all the work we are putting into this."

He studies their intertwined fingers, and Alex slowly pulls her hand from his.

"I think ..." she stammers. "I think I should probably go to bed. It's late and I don't know how much more we will really get accomplished tonight."

Oliver does not object.

The digital alarm clock on the nightstand flips to 3:03 a.m. Oliver lies in his own bed now with Alex curled up in the crook of his arm, resting her head on his bare chest. The warmth of her soft exhales tickles over his skin. He envies her ability to find solace in his embrace tonight and slumber. He has daydreamed numerous times since college about a scenario much like this: Alex returning to him, spent, and exhausted in bed together after making love. He never imagined he was still a married man in any of those scenarios.

She was like a dose of caffeine ingested way too close to bedtime. His mind could find no tranquility, no rest from the anxious thoughts that attacked his consciousness like a predator hunting him. Each time he attempted to close his eyes; he relived the moment he had given in to temptation.

He untucks the arm behind his head to reach down and move her hair gently back from her face. She does not stir. His eyes trace down from the hair messily swirled around her head and down her exposed back. The sheets cross their bodies low, giving him a tantalizing peek of the curves below. He caresses the path of her spine. Still in her sleep, her body shifts, and she lets out a barely detectable moan.

Oliver stops and exhales. Reaching up, he pinches the bridge of his nose, His mouth feels dry. His body feels hot and uncomfortable on a frosty night.

Alex sits down on a stool at the bar in Oliver's small apartment kitchen. "I think I should head back to New York," she says.

His back is to her, but she sees him freeze, sees his muscles stiffen through his white T-shirt and basketball shorts. He stops his work of scrambling eggs for their breakfast and turns back to look at her then slides the skillet off the burner, turning it off and dimming its red glow.

"Why right now?"

When Alex woke and found the spot on the bed beside her empty, she knew without need for confirmation that Oliver was dealing with his own misgivings about what had happened. She had said it herself: he had made a vow to Lydia and committed to be faithful because that is the man he is.

Alex felt the pangs of regret as she freshened up in the bathroom following their intimate encounter. She looked at herself in the mirror, shaking her head at her reflection. She loved Oliver. She always had. He'd always been something more than just a friend to her, and they both knew it. The attraction she'd felt toward him only intensified when she laid eyes on him at The Mall three weeks before.

She wanted to believe they had gone too far. She wanted to yell at herself that it was wrong. Still, everything about his touch, his kiss, and the way he moved inside her had felt so right.

Her eyes fall to the countertop where she traces figure eights over the granite.

"A few reasons. I want to follow up on the documents given to our tech guys. Also, I need to line up the interview with Ingelman."

"Any other reason?" He leans back against the counter and grips its edges.

Alex doesn't look him in the eye. "I'm sorry."

Oliver steps away from the counter and nears the sink. She sits on the other side of the barrier, but he draws as close to her as he can. "Don't blame yourself for what happened. I didn't have to keep it going. I didn't have to at all. I don't know what to do here. What feels right is wrong and what feels wrong is the right thing to do for Lydia's sake."

He walks around the counter and stands beside her. "I'll figure this out. I promise you; I will figure something out."

She turns her face to him, and he opens his arms as she leans against him, resting her head on his chest. He rubs her back in small circles as he holds her.

"Are you still okay with helping me with this story? I don't want to continue to put you in this situation if it's going to make things more difficult for both of us. If someone finds out that we slept—"

"I said I would help, and I will."

Alex turns her body on the stool, angling at him directly. Oliver's strong arms are around her again.

At his touch, something inside her grows from a tingle to an ache. She reaches out, her hand inching towards him like a moth fluttering around a light and runs her fingers over his forearm up his bicep. She lifts her eyes slowly but when they find his, the anxiousness is gone and veiled with something much more desirous.

"Alex." His voice is low, and if she was not so close, she would not have heard it.

She closes her eyes before his lips meet hers. He takes her upper lip gently between his before dropping his mouth lower and pulling at her bottom lip with his teeth.

Then, it stops.

He lets go of her, dropping his hands and freeing his body from between her thighs. He runs a hand through his brown hair and turns his back to her as he paces to the other side of the room. He covers his face as he tries to steady his breath, silently berating himself. He grumbles.

"I should get going," she says after several slow breaths.

"Yeah." His back is still to her. "You should."

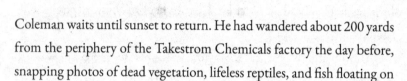

Coleman waits until sunset to return. He had wandered about 200 yards from the periphery of the Takestrom Chemicals factory the day before, snapping photos of dead vegetation, lifeless reptiles, and fish floating on the surface of the nearby creek. The smell of death and decay made his belly lurch.

He'd counted exactly four surveillance cameras on the twelve-foot brick fence that closed off the factory from the rest of the town. He'd used the rotting base of wide tree trunks and worn dark clothes to conceal his body.

Tonight, Coleman gingerly crouches behind a tree opposite the main entrance of the chemical factory. He lifts his camera to his face, the long zoom lens in place as he twists it manually to focus. As he staked out the factory the day before, he quickly learned that around this time each day, trucks with large barrels on the back and tankers begin to leave in droves. Each truck bears no markings, no Takestrom labels, something Coleman found curious. The black barrels were also not marked.

He had gotten close enough the day before to scoop up some soil samples and put a little of the water in a mason jar purchased at a local store. He would get the biology and geology team at NYU to help him detect what chemicals were traceable in both. They had done him several favors in the past.

Coleman is invested in this story. Not because of the national exposure or the massive political impact, but because of the people. Marktown, Indiana deserves better. He owed his very best effort to this story—to Aubrey and Felicity Fischer.

He feels a steadfast determination to shut down the place so Felicity can someday play outside like a healthy child. He shuddered to think of her life being cut short because a few people wanted to grease their palms and cut corners.

He wants to snap a few pictures this evening of the suspicious barrels and tanker trucks being moved out of the facility.

Looking through the viewfinder, he readies his shot as the electric fence to the factory slowly opens. He hears the motor of a large truck starting up and shifts his position.

The snapping of twigs and rustling of leaves is quick. As he turns to look over his shoulder, there is a sudden blackness.

The camera drops to the ground.

Alex leaves her Manhattan apartment building and heads up the sidewalk towards the New York Times Building in midtown.

Cell phone to her ear, she frowns. This is the third time she has called Coleman, and he has not answered. The ringing phone stops, and for a second her pulse quickens, eager to hear his voice. "You've reached Coleman Chester, please leave your name, number, and the reason for your call, and I will get back to you as soon as possible."

She huffs before hearing the tone.

"Coleman! It's Alex. Look, I'm starting to worry. Please call as soon as you get my messages." She shoves her cell phone down into her messenger bag and continues up the bustling sidewalk.

Taxis honk and bus brakes squeal as morning commuters head to the office. Steam rises from underground vents, and she dodges them as she hugs her coat around her body.

Coleman is always swift in reply or, at the very least, sending a text to confirm he will call back later.

She passes a few shops on her route and glances over at the newsstand where she normally stops to purchase several copies of other publications to keep up with the latest news.

She feels her heart hit the ground, along with every liter of blood in her body. On the stands, front and center, Oliver and Lydia Michaels grace the cover of People Magazine.

PART IV

THE NARRATIVE

CHAPTER 14

A lex shuffles her body sideways through the men and women seated in the press stakeout on the second floor of the United Nations Secretariat Building. The backs of her knees hit the bony kneecaps of reporters, her messenger bag bouncing against her hip, before she sinks into a cushioned green chair. Her forehead is damp with sweat. She tucks a wet tendril behind her ear before dropping her messenger bag on the floor between her and the seat in front and fishing out her notepad and pen.

A wooden podium is the focus of overhead omni lights, sitting in front of an electric blue step and repeat with the UN logo of a map of the world flanked by two olive branches. Alex always thought the azimuthal projection of the continents looked like a gun range target, as if Mother Nature had her sight set on humans.

The room, which can seat 127, is at half capacity now, others filing in as a large monitor is rolled in on a cart. The arrangement isn't ideal, but it may provide the level of protection she needs on the job that is causing Oliver so much concern.

Rupert Ingelman's office told *The Times* reporter that his schedule was overwhelmed with site visits, inspections, and meetings with global leaders. However, a limited chance to ask him a few questions during a presser would be available, after his address to the UN General Assembly the following day. After that, he would board a jet back to France.

The growling of her stomach had ceased sometime during her sleepless night. Her body gave up its demand for sustenance as her brain revisited a familiar feeling; the last time someone she deeply cared for had not been heard from in days, he was dead.

The hazelnut skin of her face had faded into purple half circles under her eyes. She'd dabbed on concealer to blend in with a light foundation, but the masking did not cloak her worry for Coleman. Every tick of the second hand on the clock was like a barometer reading of her increasing trepidation.

She was up and moving around her apartment before dawn reflected on the East River. She met a *Times* photographer, Kendrix, at the entrance of the UN Headquarters at 46th Street. It was an arduous push through the line for her UN Media ID Card and for Kendrix' tripods and gear to be tagged with UN labels during a security check. They parted ways, Kendrix heading to the media booth of the general assembly room while Alex jogged to the stakeout for a good seat close to the podium. Ingelman would address the media there after his speech.

Alex reaches into her bag and pulls out her phone, giving it one more check before powering it off. Still no text or call from Coleman. She adjusts the lanyard with her media ID around her neck and presses her shoulder blades to the seat back. A deep exhale an hour in the making escapes her mouth, but her heart is still thumping like a double-bass drum.

A man in a white button-down with a black tie and slacks uses a remote to start the monitor on the stage. The UN logo fills the screen before it fades into a shot of the seal over a podium and below it the speakers' rostrum. Seats begin to fill on the screen; the President of the General Assembly Genevieve Laurent of Liberia, the Secretary-General, the Under-Secretary General and moving into the rostrum, EPA Administrator Rupert Ingelman.

Alex's back leaves the chair cushion as she clicks her pen and watches the screen.

President Laurent bangs the gavel and the commotion inside the assembly and in the stakeout quiets.

"Good morning, delegates," Laurent says, her words tinged with a hint of French accent. "The meeting this nineteenth day of April is officially open. Today, we will hear from the United States Administrator of the Environmental Protection Agency Rupert Ingelman. Following Mr. Ingelman's address, we will hear presentations on cutting emissions. Mr. Ingelman, welcome. If you would please begin."

Ingelman tilts the microphone towards his mouth. He takes a sip of water from a glass on the rostrum. Alex presses the end of her pen to her notepad as she watches the monitor. Rupert Ingelman is svelte with black hair and two thick eyebrows above coal black eyes. Even seated, he still appears tall.

"Thank you, Madame President and good morning to our allies and members of the UN. I appreciate the opportunity to speak to you today in regards to the warming trend of global temperatures and its impact on commerce, in particular fishing industries such as oysters, lobsters, and crabs. This is not a US problem but an earth problem. Our industries and markets are losing millions of dollars—along with jobs—because of overharvesting, scarcity, and extreme weather events. Droughts and heavy rainfalls over the past decade are creating a decline in supply for fishing industries. We are not beyond the point of positive change, but we are lethally close."

As Ingleman speaks, Alex examines the measure of each word, the conviction of his micro-expressions, including the way his thick brows meet as he continues to discuss the dredging of underwater habitats and its long-term implications.

"We see it with the salmon industries in the pacific northwest, the oyster industries in the gulf, and the king and snow crab industries near Alaska and Russia."

If it were not for the photo proof that had come across her desk, she would believe he subscribed to the dogma he was preaching. From her research of Ingelman, she'd learned he'd received a degree in environmental science from Rice University. He'd worked as a specialist in oil and gas in the Houston area for several years before adding air quality to his specifications prior to working for FEMA. Ingelman was appointed to his position with the EPA three years ago.

"With ecological changes, we can improve the health and preservation of reefs. By regulating fossil fuels and emissions, we hope to stabilize the weather extremes and temperatures, and to restore a healthy supply for commerce, nutrition, and a better planet," Ingelman wrapped up a fifteen-minute address to applause from the general assembly. He left the rostrum with a security escort.

Alex's gaze affixes to the side door of the press stakeout. When a security guard opens it, a team of suits walk in ahead of Ingelman. He buttons his jacket and steps behind the podium, a lift in his chin as he inventories the room.

"Mr. Ingelman will now take questions," a woman announces from the corner of the room.

Alex's hand shoots up but the political reporter from the *NY Post* is a quicker draw. Alex suppresses an eye roll as he asks Ingelman about his favorite seafood restaurant in NYC, meant to be a subtle jab at his remarks.

Ingelman's countenance shows patience despite what Alex feels is wasted time with the question.

"I eat a plant-based diet. I'm vegan." Ingelman gives a saccharine smile and the room chuckles.

Alex's hand is up before the laughter subsides.

"Mr. Ingelman, Alex Broussard with *The New York Times*. You mentioned during your speech the need for stricter regulations on emissions to ease temperature extremes. In a recent report from your agency, the EPA, it was found that many companies across the US are still putting out emissions that violate these regulations. Would you say stronger enforcement is needed?"

Ingelman draws his lean body up to his full height before placing a palm on the podium. "Yes, absolutely. We have to send a message that our planet is in peril and though there is a grace period to get up to current standards, we must make sure that by the time that period ends, every corporation, factory and plant in this country is doing its part to limit harmful emissions."

Refusing to break eye contact, Alex continues her line of questioning. "If you believe stronger enforcement is needed, is it not the job of the EPA to enforce these policies and take action against violators? Do you think the EPA needs to do a better job?"

Ingelman takes a moment to answer, his stare challenging Alex's. A smile curls on his lips. "We can all do better. As a government, as an agency, as individuals. We all are responsible for the world we live in. Yes, there is room for improvement in enforcement, and I take responsibility to lead that effort."

"What would you suggest be done to violators? Harsher penalties? Longer suspensions of employment licenses? What about extending their ineligibility to apply for things like government contracts?"

Ingelman claps his chin. "I think those are all fantastic suggestions." It's almost indiscernible, but Ingleman shifts from one foot to another.

Alex nods. "A couple of weeks ago, you attended the DEED's gala with Clara Goransson—"

"Ah, yes." Ingelman wears the grin of a megachurch televangelist. "Such a dynamic and inspiring speaker."

"Yes," Alex continues, not deterred. "What do you have to say to those like Clara, the next generation, that feels there is hypocrisy in environmental protection, and that transparency from policy makers and enforcement agencies is a needed change if there is any hope for their futures?"

The squeaking of chair seats and the squirming of restless reporters beside her, is Alex's cue that her colleagues are displeased with her monopolizing the press conference. Her concern was on her story, not their time allotment. She may not have another shot at questioning Ingelman again.

Ingelman adjusts his tie. "It's easy to understand their frustrations. Environmental protections are seen as lacking by some and too woke by others. The thing to keep in mind is that we are making efforts. We can do better, of course. The loss of hope does not help. We must try. Where there are violations and flaws in the system, the United Nations and the American government will work to do better for the next generations."

A woman raises her hand and asks about commerce and the oceanic atmosphere. Alex sits back in her chair. She underlines the word "enforcement" on her notepad, recalling Ingelman's promise for improvements. *Oh Rupert, if only that were true.*

CHAPTER 15

Her flat shoes slap over the thin office carpet, her messenger bag jostles at her side. The polyphonic sounds of desk phones ringing, and the jumble of dozens of conversations fill the newsroom, but Alex can only hear her own breaths as she rushes towards the office in the corner.

A tang meets her mouth as sweat rolls down from over her lips. Short of sprinting at Olympian speed, Alex's hurried steps still feel as if she is moving through molasses. She doesn't want to run and raise an alarm, nor does she want to wait another second to speak to her boss.

She throws the glass door open. Pat flinches from the stark interruption, spinning frantically around in his desk chair, away from the keyboard he had been typing on. His startled eyes bulge as he stares back at her. The chomping of his gum stops.

"Pat!" Her bag drops off her shoulder and onto the floor.

"Alex?" Concern is etched into the deep creases in his forehead.

"Coleman." She licks her lips, her chest rising and falling rapidly; the word shakes as it leaves her mouth. A lump in her throat burns.

Pat holds a hand up to silence her momentarily as he stands and moves swiftly around his desk. He closes the glass door to his office, then turns to face her.

"Something's wrong." Alex gulps, trying to regain her breath. "I haven't been able to get a hold of him for two days. Then, a few minutes ago, my phone rang from his number."

She'd been exiting the United Nations Headquarters with Kendrix when her phone rang. As soon as she saw "Coleman Chester" on the caller ID, she hit accept, waving Kendrix to go on without her.

"Coleman! Thank God! I have been worried sick about you!" The departure of her anguish returned seconds later with a deeper dread.

She was met with silence.

"Coleman? Coleman, are you there?" Alex pressed her finger into her other ear, the warmth of her screen crushing against her other lobe.

The unnerving silence followed again. She glanced down at her phone to make sure the call hadn't ended. She saw the time continuing to count upwards.

"Coleman, if you're there, I can't hear you! Hang on."

She left the call going but sent a text: <<*Can't hear you*>>

When she pressed the phone against her ear again, there was no distorted voice, no breaks in the connection, only silence.

"Hello? Who is this?" she demanded.

There was a rustling, the sound of a hand fumbling with the device controls, and then a beep as the call ended.

Alex flagged down a cab and began the 20-minute ride back to the office. She'd tried calling Pat's office and cell numbers, and neither was answered. Likely on a smoke break this close to lunchtime.

After an elevator ride that seemed to last years, she reached the newsroom floor, fear coursing through her veins as she made her way to Pat's office.

"We need to call the police," Alex says. She watches her boss, who scratches at the spiky hairs of his short gray beard and then moves around his desk.

Pat's tongue flutters over his teeth. Then he gives a slow nod.

"Wait ... you know?"

"I received a voicemail here this morning. Someone had contacted the subscriber support number late last night, but the office forwarded the call to me. I'd already gone home. Message from a woman named Aubrey Fischer." Pat freezes and Alex goes pale and her jaw slackens.

"Familiar?"

"Y-yes."

"Her message said Coleman was supposed to have shown up for dinner at their home the other night, but he didn't arrive. She said when she called his cell, she got no answer. She was wondering if he'd come back to New York, but she said she had quote, 'a bad feeling about all this.'"

"Did you call the cops?" Alex pleads. "Did you call Aubrey? Did they file a missing person's report?"

"We don't know that Coleman is missing," Pat interjects.

Alex lunges over Pat's desk. "Something is wrong! Did you hear what I said about the phone call? He didn't show up at the Fischer's! You know that's not like him. Call the police right now!"

"This is across state lines. He was on business for us. We need to contact the FBI."

A tightness in her chest forces a gasp from her, and she places a hand on his desk to balance herself. "Coleman."

"Don't think the worst. There could be a number of reasons he hasn't responded. Maybe that was him on the phone earlier, and you couldn't hear him, but he was trying to get through. Something could have happened to his phone or the reception out there ..." Pat doesn't sound convinced of his own words one bit.

There is something ominous in the room, something that makes the hairs on the back of Alex's neck stand up.

"I've got a contact at the FBI. I'll get him on the phone now," Pat says and rounds his desk, reaching for the phone receiver.

"Can we trust the FBI? I mean, really? We are going after two senators and the head of the EPA. You don't think they've got eyes and ears in the FBI looking out for them, too?"

Pat's hand hovers over the phone. "Alex. I don't know the answer to that. But, for Coleman's sake, we have to make this call."

She sighs as he picks up the receiver and flips through his relic of a rolodex.

A lukewarm cup of tea sits next to her computer monitor. Alex rests her elbows on the edge of her desk and closes her eyes, rolling her head in circles.

Four cups of tea had been made over the course of the afternoon and late into the evening. All met the same fate. They were discarded only to be replaced by another untouched brew.

Alex's vision begins to blur as she stares at the words in black on her computer screen. Her knee bounces rapidly and her lower lip is numb from the clenching of her jaw.

She did what she always did when she felt helpless. She put herself into the distraction of storytelling.

She'd waited in Pat's office as he made a call to his friend at the FBI, relaying the details of Coleman's disappearance. That had been seven hours earlier. Her stomach is empty but in tangles.

She and Pat discussed the story. Guilted racked Alex; she was responsible for whatever Coleman's fate was in Marktown. Attempting to honor him by continuing the pursuit of the story, she pecks away at her keyboard, putting together the profile on Clara with Ingelman's response. She works with determination and urgency, putting the utmost attention into every word. Coleman may never read another story of hers, and she may never read another of his.

Pat had ordered her to go home. She refused. She would stay and write because it was the only thing that felt sane to do.

The suits walking into the newsroom did not go unnoticed by the overnight crew. FBI agents Thomas and Sinclaire were about as inconspicuous as a pair of giraffes at a Victorian tea party. Walking side by side in their basic black and navy suits with a military pace to their walk, a silence fell over the newsroom as building security ushered them to Pat's office minutes before 10:00 p.m.

Alex leaps up from her cubicle and rushes towards Pat's door before the security guard can close it. He holds up a hand to Alex before looking at Pat. Alex balls her hands into fists at her sides as her chest heaves.

Pat signals for security to let Alex through.

The woman makes a quick introduction as Agent Thomas, the man, Agent Sinclaire.

"What have you found? Any news?" Alex's tongue can barely keep up with the speed of her words.

"A man fitting Coleman's description was admitted to St. Catherine Hospital in East Chicago, Indiana, early this morning," Agent Sinclaire says.

"Hospital?" Alex utters.

"Yes," Sinclaire continues. "He had no identification on him. The hospital notified the local authorities in hopes there might be a missing person's report. When our director got Pat's call this morning, it was immediately flagged in the system. White male, early thirties, blonde hair, tall, brown eyes."

"But if it is Coleman, is he okay?"

Thomas steps forward. "We were told he had a head injury that appeared to be from some type of blow to the head with a blunt object. He has a skull fracture and also a broken arm."

Alex closes her eyes as her shoulders slump. "Will he be okay?"

"He has a concussion. He was not familiar with his surroundings early on from the report we were provided, but that's not uncommon with a head injury. He was unresponsive when he was brought in but has since woken up," Thomas's words are efficient, as if any emotion was an unnecessary detail and did not fit the job description either.

"Who brought him to the hospital?" Pat questions.

"A local found him. He was lying on the side of the highway. We don't know how he got there or if that is where he may have been attacked, but the report says a man was driving when his headlights shone on a human body lying near a ditch. He pulled over and called 911. Fire and ambulance showed up and took him in."

Alex takes a seat, putting her head in her hands, elbows on her knees. She gulps down waves of nausea.

"Some fishermen also found a silver car half submerged in a canal before dawn about twenty miles away from where the John Doe was picked up. Ran the plates and found it was a rental. Traced it back to a purchase order and company link to The Times," Thomas adds.

"If the guy at the hospital is in fact Coleman, we need to find out who did this to him," Agent Sinclaire stipulates. He steps directly in front of Alex, looking down at her. Alex lifts her head when Sinclaire's shoes come into her line of sight. He looms over her.

"He had no ID on him?" Alex asks.

"Nothing. No phone either."

"Can you trace where the phone is now?" Alex asks.

"We tried. Whoever had it shut it off. Last call reflected was from Marktown, which means nothing to us right now."

"What about his camera?" Alex asks. "He always has it with him."

"Camera?" Sinclaire's eyes narrow as he tosses his head back. "No mention of any camera."

Alex glances at Pat before she gives a furtive stare towards Agent Sinclaire.

"Miss, if he was there working on a story, we need to know the details of the story. Who would have the motive to cause him harm?"

Alex stares up at the tall, slender FBI agent. His skin is like a cowboy's, thick and rubbery. His eyes are lifeless and melancholy, void of emotion.

Alex's posture straightens. She glances at Pat again as she squares her shoulders. When her challenging glare returns to Agent Sinclaire, his lips are pressed into a straight, immovable line.

CHAPTER 16

Alex could feel the vein in her throat pulsing beneath her skin, bulging with adrenaline, as she returns to Pat's office two hours later.

"You have to hear this," she announces.

Pat pinches at the skin of his own throat before standing quickly with a labored groan. Alex spins on her heels with the efficiency of a bellhop. Pat follows so closely she can smell burnt tobacco wafting from his skin and clothes.

Alex ignores the curious stares of the handful of colleagues lingering in the quiet newsroom and picks up her desk phone receiver, handing it to Pat. When he presses it to his ear, she taps a button and enters her voicemail. She stands close to him listening intently as the deep voice with an unfamiliar accent, muffled slightly by Pat's ear, is heard for a second time. A new fear grips her.

"Alex Broussard. You listen up, you Creole bitch. You keep poking your nose into business that don't concern you, it's gonna get clipped off. You think we're playing? We will come for you. You hear me? We're coming for you."

Pat's nostrils flare. He stops chewing his gum. Alex hadn't eaten that day and still she felt like a fifteen-pound dumbbell sat in her stomach. Pat hands the phone back to her and she hangs it up.

"Don't delete it," Pat whispers calmly.

"Of course not."

"Caller ID?"

"Says 'Unknown' on the most recent call."

"Cowards," Pat croaks.

Pain in Alex's left side radiates like growing tree roots, thick, strong, and slow against her spine. She'd needed to pee for at least two hours but had suppressed the urge while writing the Ingelman story and waiting for any update on Coleman. She'd finally left her desk after the pain in her body began signaling it could hold no more. Alex returned from the bathroom to find her phone blinking with a new message.

Pat rubs at his jaw as he thinks for a moment. "Research all gone home for the day?"

"Not yet." Alex folds her arms across her chest and leans back on the edge of her desk. Her lower back pain was relenting as her head was starting to ache. She glances at her desk phone, expecting to see the red light flashing again. It's dark.

"Maybe try to get them to trace it." She finds Pat's gaze on the phone as well.

"They are doing research for me right now. I don't really want to pull it for ..." She wags a finger up and down at the phone. "This."

"Any other threats come in?"

"Nothing on email." Alex takes a seat, logging into one of her social media accounts. She rarely looks at it, possessing it more to protect her name and for work purposes than for any real interactions with readers.

Pat hovers over her shoulder, a slight wheezing near her ears, as she opens her profile page. A "12" is circled in red on her notifications and she opens her direct messages. The most recent, time stamped almost an hour ago, is from an account with no profile picture, a gray faceless icon in the space.

Alex finds herself facing a preview of the profane message. Pat places a hand on her shoulder. "You want me to open it?"

"No, I got it." Alex sets her jaw and clicks.

STUPID BITCH STAY OUT U R NEXT

Alex's lips curl back in disgust, but she clicks the profile of ABReader1111. The new user account had been created that month. There were no posts or likes but the pin dropped location showed as Chicago, Illinois.

"They aren't nearly as clever as they'd like to think they are," Alex remarks. "Forgot to turn off the location when creating this bogus profile."

"What do you mean?"

"Chicago? That's where MacAllen Industries headquarters is located."

"Screenshot that, will you?" Pat says and pulls out his phone.

"Sure—Wait. What are you doing?"

"I'm notifying the FBI."

Alex springs up, her chair rolling back before hitting her desk with a whack. The pain in her back fires up again and she grimaces. "Pat, you can't!"

"Alex, you have received two very real threats tonight. I'm not taking any chances."

"It means I'm getting close to something. If the FBI gets in on this, too, it may ruin everything! Looking for Coleman was one thing. I don't want them getting too deep into my work."

Pat puts a hand up, warding off whatever protest Alex is about to make next. "Coleman has already been through God knows what. I am not going to risk another reporter getting hurt."

"I know, I understand, I do," Alex says. "But Pat, do you really trust other people to get involved with this?"

Pat's eyebrows draw close together. Still gripping the phone, his finger hovers over the call icon. "Being in a bubble is not a luxury we have on this. Your life is worth more than a story. I hope you do realize that?"

Alex doesn't reply. She closes her eyes and lets out a resigned sigh.

"I don't want you staying at your apartment tonight. If they have Coleman's phone and know you are involved, it might not be safe there either. We can put you up in a hotel for a while, some place discreet. I'd prefer that rather than staying with friends or anyone else. If someone were following you—"

"You really think they'd go that far?"

"After Coleman, I'm not taking any chances. We may have to get NYPD in for security."

"No cops! Who knows who all these guys have in their back pockets."

Pat's raised voice brings the newsroom to a halt. "This is not even remotely up for a debate, Alex. Stop being so mule-headed! Lives are at stake here. If you don't care about your own safety, that's one thing. I *am* responsible for you and you're going to have to accept the help and get over it."

Across the way, Alex meets the wide eyes of Pierce Valentine, an arts and entertainment reporter working on a show review.

"Pat—"

He lifts his hand and walks back to his office to make arrangements.

———————————•◊ — ◊•———————————

Senator Chickman pours himself a scotch from the decanter on the buffet in front of the bay window before he sits down on the uncomfortable, antique Revolutionary-era sofa his wife purchased for their living room. The old springs and diminished stuffing underneath his back and ass creak as he sinks down onto it. Soon enough, he will be too buzzed to feel the prick of the old, rusted coils in the back cushion.

Lena had bought it for the "aesthetics" she had explained. They were in DC, the land the Founding Fathers had selected as the home seat for all governing decisions. The dark wood paneling of the renovated eighteenth-century home they had bought needed the furniture to match. Chickman would swear Washington himself may have planted his butt on this thorny sofa.

He swirls the scotch around, spreading his knees before he takes a sip. The ice makes the liquor both burn and cool his mouth with satisfaction. He works his jaw at the bite of the drink. Holding his glass in one hand, he stretches his other arm out against the back of the blue, velvet sofa. The circling of the glass in his hand clinks the ice cubes in it as his eyes drift off with his thoughts. A soft lamp light glows from the corner of the otherwise dark room.

"Dad! You're home," a voice calls from the doorway.

He turns his head and smiles at his only child. Charlotte Chickman has black hair like her mother did when he first met her. She looks more and more like her mother as time passes. The influence of his genes is weak in his offspring. She has her mother's looks and mostly good nature.

"Hey pumpkin." He smiles at one of the only people in the world he is ever truly happy to see. He puts his glass down on the coffee table and opens his arms out to her. She doesn't give hugs as frequently anymore, now that she's nearing double digits in age, but it's so rare for her to see him before bedtime that she rushes from the doorway and almost stumbles onto him as she hugs him back.

He chuckles softly. "Homework all done?"

She takes a seat next to him. "Um, kinda." She winces. When she opens her mouth, her front two teeth are much larger than the rest. Her brown eyes plead with him to not lecture her.

"Hmmm." Chickman pretends to scowl. "What are you working on?"

"We're studying the Conquistadors and Aztecs. Super boring." Charlotte rolls her eyes.

Chickman laughs before he smooths her hair. He had been forty-three when Charlotte was born. He and Lena had tried for years, and Lena had been surprised to learn she was pregnant at forty. She carried Charlotte to term and Travis had always called her his little miracle, their rainbow baby.

Charlotte's bug-eyed stare spots the drink on the table. "You better put a coaster under that or Mom's gonna flip," she warns.

Chickman holds his finger up to his lip and winks at her. "You don't mention the drink, and I won't mention the homework?"

Charlotte gives a mischievous laugh. "Deal."

"Travis!" At the sudden calling of his name, both Charlotte and the Kentucky congressman jump. Lena's heavy accent pronounces it more like "Trahv-ass." He wondered sometimes if this wasn't dialect, but intentional.

He quickly reaches for the glass on the table as Lena's footsteps approach on the hardwood floors.

She enters the room wearing a beige sweater dress and slouchy white socks, her black and silver hair in a tightly pulled bun. Her pale face is free of makeup. She spots the drink in his hand immediately.

"Charlotte, hun, did you finish your homework?" Lena's pointed stare falls to her daughter.

"Dad said I didn't have to," Charlotte offers.

"Traitor," Chickman breathes out, and Charlotte fights back a grin.

"Upstairs. Finish it, now," Lena commands.

"Yes ma'am," Charlotte rises dejectedly from the sofa. "Will you come say goodnight?" she asks her father expectantly.

"Absolutely." He nods. Charlotte smiles at her dad, then turns and eases past her mother, careful not to let any part of her body brush against her as she moves through the doorway and takes the stairs up to her room.

"Telling her she doesn't have to finish her homework? Really?" Lena scoffs. "You know the slightest slip at that school and she's out. Their standards are—"

"I know what their damn standards are, Lena. I pay the goddamn bill every month for that hoity toity school." Chickman sighs and doesn't care about her glare; he drinks his scotch and plays with the end of his tie.

"What's going on with you?" Lena interrogates. She moves around to stand in front of the coffee table to look down at him.

He presses his lips flatly together before giving an audible sigh.

"The nights you are home, you barely sleep. You are moody, barely talk to me, and you look worn out."

Chickman spreads his arms wide in a grand, sweeping display. The scotch sloshes dangerously close to the rim of the glass when he does. "The life of a US Congressman, baby. Plus, trying to take care of you and Charlotte." He sips his drink, this time emptying the glass until the remains of the unmelted ice cubes touch his lips.

Lena shakes her head. "You keep all this stress on you, you won't be a congressman for too much longer."

Martin Eisenhower pulls out the center drawer of his desk in his home office. He can smell the lingering chemical scent of paint from the touchups the painters did to the walls the week before. The wood of the desk drawer scrapes and strikes his legs. He checks to make sure the door is still closed to his home office. Staples, loose paper clips, some Post-it Notes, and a calculator are at the front of the drawer. He tries to flatten his hand to reach the envelope at the back. His fingers fumble, his knuckles scrape, and the skin tears against the wood before he pulls the envelope out.

On his desk is a picture of his oldest son, Bradley, in his third year at Yale, and his daughter, Lila, a freshman at Duke, that serves as a reminder of the fishing excursion they took last summer near Hyannis Port. Senator Eisenhower stands between his two college students. Their mother, his wife of twenty-seven years, Vivian, had snapped the photo as they stood at the bow of a sailboat. He surveys the smiling face of each of his children and then turns away from the photo.

He reaches into the envelope and pulls out a small slip of paper. Gray lead was scribbled on the torn shard of parchment in a series of letters, numbers and symbols. To the common eye, it didn't mean much. To Martin Eisenhower, it means access. Ingelman had given him the updated information at the fundraising gala last Saturday night with a warning to destroy it once he was logged in.

He flips open the laptop on his desk and presses the power button. His fingers clumsily plunk in a password before reaching the home screen. His kids always joke that he is "technologically incompetent." Every new update for the streaming services on their TV led to a phone call from dad on how to get back into the family account. That's why he'd had to write the login information down. The gibberish was too much for him to keep in his mental storage shed. How his kids would marvel at his use of the VPN software now. He makes sure it is turned on before he enters the web address. He studies the piece of paper and types its match into the encrypted website.

After the veneer of Washington had eroded for Eisenhower during his second term twenty-two years ago, the payouts back then were all cash. Crisp bills in thick stacks, with non-numerical numbers. Nowadays, accepting cash under the table was passé.

Things today are much more sophisticated with Bitcoin and other cryptocurrency. Eisenhower doesn't entirely understand how it works but he could care less about that part as long as the end result is the same. The transactions on the ledger on the screen are mostly deposits, with the occasional withdrawal. Those came at the start of the new school semester or when he wanted to surprise his wife with something sparkly to wear to one of those high fashion events they were always having to attend. The updated total sum is approaching seven figures. He will need to make another withdrawal soon. The money is transferred to offshore accounts and buried under the name of a limited liability corporation that Eisenhower had ensured was hard to trace back to him.

He logs out and clicks a few buttons to delete his history and the cookies. *Technologically incompetent.* Martin Eisenhower had become the jolly old grandfather of the Senate. Most people believe he is good-natured and harmless.

The payments have been the same every six weeks for the last year. He can't remember exactly how long the transactions had been taking place, but they are consistent enough to keep Bradley and Lila comfortable in two private universities at the same time.

They don't have to work two jobs and try to juggle a full class schedule like he had to do as a student at the University of South Carolina. His kids can focus on their studies. Once Lila is a college graduate, he intends to retire. No more politics for him. He swings his gaze to the picture in the brass frame again.

A soft knock comes at the door before the knob twists. Vivian peers around the door just as the drawer closes.

"Dinner's ready," she announces. He eyes his bride, which is what he still calls her. She'd stuck by his side for three decades, during the good times and the lean times. She had given him Bradley and Lila. Her face had lines etched into the corners of her eyes and around her lips. She had always had big breasts and hips; it was what had attracted him to her in the first place. Plus, her eyes. She had the kindest eyes of anyone he had ever known, even his dear mother, who had passed six years ago. Now

Vivian's breasts met the same spot as her hips. Her hair had been fully gray for two of the decades they had been together. She was still his bride.

"Be there in just a minute." Eisenhower jerks his lips up in an anxious smile.

"I was thinking earlier," Vivian says. She opens the door wider and leans her body against the white trim of the door frame. Eisenhower double checks the drawer and places the bronze key that unlocks it under his hand and out of her sight on the paper calendar in front of him.

"What's that now?" he asks and continues to smile.

"When this next session is over, we ought to go on a trip. Somewhere nice. As much as I love traveling with the kids, I think we need some me and you time. It's been years, and they are older. They want to party with their college friends, not their stuffy old mom and dad." Vivian sighs.

"Time changes things," Eisenhower replies. "You can look at my hair and tell as much."

"What hair?" Vivian snorts. They laugh in the teasing way an old married couple could, immune to most insults and taunts.

"I've still got a few pieces." Eisenhower reaches up with his free hand and touches the thin strands swirled on his head, causing Vivian to laugh harder.

As the chuckle in her chest subsides, she tilts her head. "Really. Let's get away. These long days and nights are getting the better of you."

Eisenhower thinks about the envelope in the drawer and the next payment in a month.

"Where in the world would you like to go, my bride?"

Chapter 17

"Yes, I'm trying to reach my brother," Alex says into the phone politely. She sits in her cubicle and watches to make sure the desks around her remain vacant. Coleman is normally planted on the opposite side of her. A knot of sadness tightens her stomach.

"I was told by the police that they had located him," she says quickly. "We have been so worried; my mother is beside herself. We are about to leave for Indiana, but I wondered if someone might be able to make sure he answers the phone in his room?

"I am sure it's not exactly protocol, but you can understand our situation," Alex pleads. "To find out he was attacked and then found in some hospital thousands of miles away, I need to hear his voice. Please, if a nurse or someone could make sure he receives this call, I will make it brief. I'm his little sister, Sarah." She has no idea if Coleman has a little sister and if so, what her name is.

The person on the other end of the line decides to show some compassion. "I'll call the nurses station," the motherly voice on the other end of the line responds.

"Oh, God bless you!" Alex rejoices and part of it is genuine. "Thank you so much!"

"No problem honey, hold on."

She listens to the boring drone of Muzak for five minutes. She watches the phone and the clock on her desk, tapping her pen and swaying in her chair.

The music stops and even though it is heavily laden with grogginess, she recognizes the voice that replaces it.

"Hello?"

Alex breathes out a loud sigh of relief as tears spill suddenly from her eyes in a sob of joy.

"Coleman," she exclaims then lowers her voice. "Oh my God."

"I'm on some really good drugs right now, I cannot be held accountable for what I say," Coleman replies, and Alex chuckles through her tears. "I don't have a sister Sarah. Thought this might be you."

"I'm so glad to hear your voice. I have been scared to death! How are you feeling?"

"Like I got hit in the head with a brick … or a two-by-four … or a bat, not sure which, but all would deliver this level of suck that I'm feeling." He groans.

"I'm so sorry. I'm so, so sorry. This is all my fault." She wipes at her eyes.

"Don't apologize. We're getting to them. That means this is a big fucking deal. We aren't taking our foot off the gas. As soon as the doctors say I can, I'm heading back to New York, and we are exposing this whole thing."

Alex feels a pang of hesitation. She does not want to worry Coleman by letting him know about the threats she's received.

"I'm coming to see you," Alex says. "Tonight. I wasn't sure if you were awake and talking yet. I'll book a flight."

"Alex, no," Coleman says emphatically. "Don't."

"I want to be there for you and—"

"Alex!" Coleman interrupts. "Alex, don't. They could be watching the hospital. Waiting to see who comes to check on me. You would be putting yourself in danger. I'll be fine. Do not bring your ass out here, do you hear me?"

Alex grumbles. "Okay, I just would feel better if I could see you."

"Believe me, gorgeous, I'd love to see you. It's not safe."

"They got everything?" Alex asks him.

"Not quite." Coleman lets out a chuckle then groans. "Fuck, my head." There is a rustling and Alex hears another voice. "Nurse says time is up, I got to rest."

"Okay, I'll check in again tomorrow."

"Don't. I'll be fine."

"I'm so sorry, Coleman. I can't say that enough."

"Don't be sorry."

"Get some rest, okay?"

"I will. Oh, and Sarah? I always keep backups to my backups."

"Alex?" Pat's deep voice resonates across the room from the door of his office. She looks up from her cubicle before she hangs up the phone.

She walks the same path she spent the vast portion of the day pacing. He closes the door behind her.

"How are you feeling now?" Pat questions.

"I talked to Coleman," she announces proudly. "I pretended to be family to get the call in."

"How is he? I need to get in touch with him, bring him home."

"He sounded okay, but he's in pain. It helped hearing his voice."

"Good. Stop blaming yourself. This is the world we live in and any time you go after men in power, there's the potential for casualties." Pat reaches into his desk drawer and pulls out a pack of Doublemint. He unfolds the silver wrapping and slides another stick of gum into his mouth. With the situation in Indiana and trying to calm his ace reporter's nerves, Alex knows he's been unable to take a single smoke break today.

"I've been doing this for more than ten years and never once have I gotten a death threat." Alex takes a moment. "I've been bullied, yelled at by a few pissed off public officials but no one has ever threatened to hurt me over a story."

She'd never considered her own safety through this entire ordeal. Coleman's warning about coming to the hospital and now Pat's caution in her venturing home have raised the red flag in her mind to full trim.

"They can't scare me into silence. Coleman says we don't let up. He's right. I'm going down to research. Going to see what Ezrah and the guys have uncovered. I'll get the hotel info before I head out."

Alex exits his office and heads downstairs to tech.

Ezrah slaps his desk with excitement when he sees her. "Just the woman I was going to call!"

"Oh, really?"

"We've got some connections here! These bastards have been careful, but I did find one number we can link to Eisenhower and three calls on here we can link to Chickman. Also, several calls between Ingelman and Lonnie Colbert with Takestrom. Plus, we ID'd our Mr. X, this guy." Ezrah slides over a printout of a blurred image.

Alex grasps it, squinting at the enhanced image. The dark-haired man is getting out of a luxury car. "Who is this?"

"That, deary, is someone who it took a whole hell of a lot of work to find but we did it. That is Peter Vitale."

Alex peers over the top of the paper at Ezrah, the name not jogging a memory.

"Peter Vitale is the boss of the Insigne clan, operating out of Chicago."

Alex's shoulders curl forward. "The mob?"

"Afraid so. Lesser known, young, organized crime syndicate in the Midwest. Vitale is considered new money. We found some birth records and property appraisal details. He's 48 and lives in a swanky suburb outside of Chicago. The guy holding the car door for him is believed to be the under-don, his brother Roberto."

Alex rolls her neck. "I ... what are they doing with Takestrom?"

"My guess is Skinner. We looked into Vitale's known associates. Guys from the Insigne clan have faced money laundering, fraud, drug trafficking and holding illegal weapons to name a few. Their sentences have amounted to slaps on the wrists or no sentences at all."

"Ezrah, how in God's name did you manage all of this?"

"We had to do some tracking, and VPN breakthrough, and some decryption, but it's for sure between him and Ingelman."

"Is that legal?"

"Is what they are doing legal?" Ezrah counters.

Alex concedes.

"We also got the names from a few numbers and found they are, in fact, Takestrom employees."

"You are a genius!"

"I know." He shakes his head rapidly. "There's a part two and a part three to this little breakthrough."

"You've got more?"

"Yeah, on that judge. Skinner." Ezrah points over the top of his cubicle at a man in a Slayer T-shirt. "My man JB went to work on her while I kept up with the logs and Vitale."

Alex folds her arms and turns to look at Ezrah's co-worker. When he begins to speak, it turns out he has a thick accent, possibly Texan. He wears his hair in locs that hang down to his tree trunk of a neck.

"Her bio said she had four kids, right?" JB motions, moving his hand through the air like there's an imaginary serving platter on it. "Judge only has Facebook for old campaign purposes. No way in this day and age that at least one of her kids doesn't have social media. Maybe even without her knowing."

Alex moves around to the rows of cubicles and stands behind JB, looking over his shoulder. He pulls up an Instagram page.

"Her youngest, Amanda Skinner. Sixteen." JB slides over to allow Alex a closer look. "Attends Forest Hills Academy in Chicago, a sixty-two grand a year boarding school."

Alex whistles. "On a judge's salary?"

"Oh, but it gets better," Ezrah chimes in.

"Amanda posts the usual selfies, a few dance videos, and some snaps with classmates. In this case—" JB clicks on one of the photos "—Amanda tagged a classmate."

He clicks so that the picture tags pop up.

"You're kidding me!" Alex's voice causes everyone to look up.

"Nope! Isn't it great?" Ezra squeezes his fist and wiggles his shoulders in delight.

"One of her classmates is Vitale's kid?" Alex shrieks.

"I tried to click on the page for Marcu Vitale, but his page is private." JB demonstrates for Alex, showing the profile and the locked message below it. "That might be enough of a connection we need, though. Social, maybe not so strong politically, but there's something. Skinner's daughter is close pals with Vitale's kid. There's more than one photo of them in groups together on her page. If she's close to the son, mom may be close to the dad. At the very least, they have probably interacted together at school events and moved in shared spaces."

She puts her hands on JB's shoulders and gives them a squeeze. "Thank you! It's a fantastic lead. This is the second-best news I've gotten all day."

"Only the second best?" Ezrah puts a hand to his heart. "That wounds me. Anyways, don't thank us yet. There's a part three." Ezrah lets his statement hang in the air.

"Oh my God. What is it?" Alex raises her voice.

"I may have found the financial link you were looking for." Ezrah wiggles his eyebrows. "Don't know if you are ready for this much sexy," he teases.

"Tell me."

"There's a number on here that shows up a few times. You didn't highlight it and if I hadn't been going over these so many times, I probably wouldn't have noticed myself. It's a California number. I looked it up and traced it back to a broker. A guy by the name of Jamison Ainsworth."

Alex freezes. Her breath catches. Her heart stops beating. "Ainsworth?" She repeats, wondering if she misheard.

"Yeah. Out of Del Mar, California."

THE SENATOR

Alex's hands tremble as she covers her open mouth. She tears her body away from the cubicle and runs towards the elevator, frantically pushing the up button.

CHAPTER 18

He keeps strict business hours. He is not to be disturbed during breakfast or dinner. Those times are reserved for his family.

Peter Vitale knows when his brother Roberto walks into the breakfast area that morning, signaling to him that he had a call, that it meant trouble. Golden light is beaming in through the large windows of the nook and dew covers the manicured lawn outside the Oak Brook mansion, forty minutes outside of Chicago. The Vitale family is biting into flaky, warm croissants, poached eggs and fresh cut fruit prepared by their chef when Roberto enters. Peter veils a scowl, pushing his chair back. He kisses his wife, Laura, on the temple.

"No phones at the table and no calls during breakfast, Daddy," his youngest child and only daughter, Sara, chirps.

"I'm sorry, princess." He checks his smartwatch and then swings his gaze to his sons Marcu and Leo. "You boys get out the door to school on time. Piu is out front to drive you."

"Come on, Dad! Can't I drive?" Marcu pleads.

"Boy, the laminate on that license isn't even cooled off yet. No. Safer if Piu drives." He turns away, letting them know it wasn't up for debate. "Work and study hard today."

Peter leads his younger brother across the marble-floored grand foyer. He opens French doors for his sibling as they step into the east wing of the mansion. When the door to Peter's two-story office with coffered ceiling closes, he lets his scowl manifest.

"What's up?"

"Colbert phoned." Roberto cocks his head to the side.

Peter gestures to the phone. Roberto dials a number before handing it to him.

"Yes?" Peter says. An iPhone rests in the pocket of his custom-made, $3,200 beige suit jacket, tucked away for other professional use. The flip phone and its seemingly dated technology are for brief, more primitive forms of contact.

The gold nugget ring on his pinky finger and his wedding band beside it gleam as he turns on the banker's light on his desk. Diamond encrusted cuff links in the letters P-V sparkle as they catch the dim light and cast prisms onto the desk.

He sits and listens attentively, his body rigid in the plush leather chair. He runs a hand through thick black hair.

"I got another call. We've got more eyes on us," Lonnie Colbert responds, on speakerphone. Wind gusts around Lonnie, creating a whooshing noise in the phone.

"Explain," Vitale snaps.

"Security in Marktown caught a reporter snooping around the factory last night. Found him with a camera. They've taken care of him. Identification in his wallet shows he's Coleman Chester with *The New*

York Times. They took the SD card from the camera. Turns out there were hundreds of pictures he took outside the factory. Also, they found a notepad on him. Seems he talked to a few of the town's folks. Got some names. A doctor and a family."

"You said he was taken care of?" Vitale asks. "Permanently?"

"... Well, no." Colbert sounds confused by the gravity of the question. Vitale balances the phone on his shoulder. "So, he is still a threat?"

"He's incapacitated. "But ..."

"Goddammit, what?"

"He's working with that female reporter. Phone messages showed he was in fact talking to the lady reporter I spoke to a few days ago. The one I told you about: Alex Broussard. He was in contact with her, discussing Marktown in the texts. She's listed in the phone contact list as AB. There were several calls made to her in the last week. She's definitely still snooping and digging too deep. Plus, there's her latest report."

"What are you talking about?" Vitale challenges.

"You seen *The Times* this morning?" Colbert asks.

"No."

"Might want to give it a read. This Broussard chick talked to Ingelman."

Peter snaps his fingers at Roberto and points to a tablet on a bookshelf. He brings it to him and powers it on.

"Did Ingelman say anything?"

"You might find it interesting. I got a bad feeling about this, Pete."

Peter takes a deep breath. When he speaks, his voice is eerily calm. "Then we make sure to fix this. We make sure that woman and this Chester fellow don't keep poking around. She didn't seem to get the hint the first few times, so we send her a very clear message now. You said the photos and card were destroyed?"

"Yes."

"I'll get my guys on it. Maybe use the name of the family and the doctor and pay them a little visit. Make sure they don't do anymore talking."

Colbert falls silent. "There's a kid."

"More reason for them to keep quiet." Peter runs a hand over his face impatiently. "Where is Chester now?"

"Hospital in East Chicago."

"We will handle it," Peter assures. "We won't let him get any further. I handled it with the judge, didn't I? We didn't have to move mountains. All we had to do was lean on one tree. Our assets are safe."

"What about Ingelman? What if they're onto him?" Colbert questions.

"Lonnie, all these are 'what ifs.' You gotta learn how to take out the variables. Don't call me again." Vitale taps a button, and the irritation named Colbert is gone. He presses the top of the phone to his lip as he thinks. Roberto approaches and offers him a glass of brandy. It's 7:47 a.m. He nods as his brother pours.

When the tablet is powered on, Peter types in the passcode and selects the news app. He scrolls through Ingelman's rant about enforcing harsher penalties on companies that violate environmental policies.

He scrolls to the top of the article again and taps the name of the reporter: Alex Broussard. He reads through her bio and presses a few buttons on the flip phone, taking a large sip of the brandy as he waits for Senator Travis Chickman to answer his call.

Her cell phone rings as she swirls the powder brush over her nose and once more over her chin. She inspects her makeup, turning her head from side to side before puckering her lips and studying her pout in the mirror.

Lydia reaches down and looks at her phone. Her head jerks slightly when she sees Oliver's name.

"Hello?" she answers, watching her own curious reflection in the mirror.

"Hey Lydia," he greets solemnly.

"Hi, what's going on?"

When Oliver had shown up at their townhome four days before, she thought he'd seemed open to reconciliation. She was trying to be better. She was trying to be the Lydia who was once full of confidence and bravado, not the crumbling mess to which her own ambition and perfectionism had reduced her.

AA is helping. She is finding her voice. She has not had a drink in six days. It's becoming harder, the temptation greater, but she has emptied the bar, the pantry, and the refrigerator of any traces of alcohol. Her hands tremble here and there from the withdrawal. She struggles to keep her fingers still as she applies eyeliner.

Oliver had shown interest in their magazine spread and had even spent the remainder of the afternoon at the townhome, talking with her and sharing his frustrations about political life with her. She thought they had reconnected.

As soon as Oliver walked out of the door, so walked out the hopes she had for them. He had not called or texted to check on her, and they were back to living separate lives. He was at his apartment, she at the townhome, as if their existences were never meant to cross paths ever again.

She is finally sobering up and showing promise of a happy and healthy life again. Still, if Lydia is getting her life on track, she will have to do so without him. Maybe now that she has a support system and tools for recovery, his request for a divorce will not flatten her. She will have the means to hold it together and keep plugging away.

The timing sucks, but there was never a good time to end a marriage. Lydia is out of tricks up her sleeve, new lingerie in the drawers, or emotional support putty to patch the crumbling of their marriage.

"I wanted to make sure you were home," Oliver begins. "I wanted to come by after I left the office and talk to you."

"Oh, I um, I was just about to go out," Lydia explains. The stoic tone in Oliver's voice lets her know this will not be a pleasant conversation. She feels the inevitability of the talk she has dodged several times. "There's a charity gala tonight. A few of the congressman's wives are attending, and I also RSVPed to represent *us*."

"Oh, okay then. Maybe tomorrow?"

"No, wait." Lydia huffs. She resigns herself to the situation. "It will be over around nine, and I'll be near your part of town. I can come to the apartment. If that's not too late?"

"No, not at all," Oliver replies. "I really need to talk to you and if you can come here, that's fine."

"All right. I'll see you later tonight then."

———— •◦• — •◦• ————

She could not call him. She could not email him. There could be no record of Alex's connection to Oliver, nothing more than old history that they were once suitemates in college. It was her own rule but one for his protection. Eyes and ears were all around Washington, and if she hoped to protect Oliver from the nuclear fallout of her and Coleman's story, she had to make sure there were no records to connect their dots.

The four-hour drive was the safest option. She talked to Pat and explained that she needed to get to DC and her contact that night. He did not question her, working with Rubyth to make the arrangements. He cautioned her to be safe before she was out the door. She hadn't bothered with luggage, and had taken one of the unmarked company vehicles, parking it a mile from Oliver's apartment.

She took a cab, paying the driver in cash and had him stop two blocks up the road from Oliver's place.

The pounding of a fist on his front door startles Oliver. He settles his nerves with a deep breath to confront Lydia.

Their faces are on the cover of a magazine as happy and they appear to be in love. Oliver knows a public uproar will ensue, but he can't let that stop him from doing what is best in his life any longer.

The gentleman in him had chosen to be polite to support her recovery but he knows in his heart it's over. Alex is all he can think about. On the floors of the Senate Chamber, seated at his desk, he found his mind constantly drifting to their night together. When he tried to listen to a bill proposal, he drowned out the incessant monotone droning of his colleagues and thought of her kiss. Alex had always been the one. It was his fault his life had been a mess and now it was his responsibility to fix it.

He rises to his feet, peering through the peephole. He is astounded and rendered breathless when he sees Alex. He unlatches the chain at the top of the door, dragging it back before cracking open the door and looking back at her.

"Alex?"

"Oliver I—" She pushes past him and races inside.

Her steps halt and she almost topples over. Regaining her balance, she peers at the neatly dressed blonde on the sofa wearing pearls and an immaculate blue dress.

Oliver stands stupefied and speechless.

Montana barks twice, wagging his tail as he approaches the familiar face. He licks her hand happily as she stares silently back at the woman with the unrelenting glare.

Lydia's eyes drop to Montana as he bounces on his paws, tail continuing to wag happily. Clearly, she recognizes the dog is greeting a friend.

PART V

THE DEADLINE

CHAPTER 19

The pressure of Montana's cold, wet nose and eager tongue are the only reminders to Alex in that moment that she is alive. Lydia rises with painstaking slowness to her feet. Her gaze is locked with Alex's, the contempt in her eyes invoking the power of Medusa, rendering Alex frozen.

Alex can hear the low hum of the heater. It strikes her as odd that she would fixate on that sound, but it is the only other noise in the room besides Montana's panting. Silence falls upon the three humans. Seconds tick by, drawn out into torturous minutes of unspoken words.

Lydia's perfume fills the apartment like a burning candle, powerfully strong and almost abrasive.

Montana moves away from Alex, whining as he trots, tail wagging, back to his bed. He curls up, resting his snout between his paws.

"Is this why you want a divorce?" Lydia's voice is not much higher than a whisper, but after the menacing silence of the last few moments, it jars Alex like a scream.

Oliver's shoulders roll as if he is trying to disappear inside himself. Alex sees the hen-pecked husband he had become over the last few years return as he guiltily stares down at the floor and away from Lydia.

"Is it?" Lydia repeats her question, her voice rising this time.

"Lydia," Oliver begins. When he lifts his head, his eyes tracking to hers, there is shame in his retreating glance.

"Is it!" The shout vibrates off the walls, a slight echo in the sparsely furnished apartment. Alex watches as Lydia's entire torso begins to move with the heavy, restrained breaths she is taking.

"You and I discussed separation and divorce a long time ago ..." Oliver can't finish his sentence, withering under Lydia's laser-like stare.

"But tonight," Lydia seethes, jabbing a finger down towards the floor as she stomps her foot, "right here, you just told me you were going to file for divorce. End of story, no chance of reconciliation. Now, *she's* here! She's here at the apartment no one is supposed to even know you have, Oliver! Tell me, how is that possible?" Lydia folds her arms over her chest, her chin angling upwards almost regally. She cocks an eyebrow.

Alex steps forward. "I can explain."

Lydia's head whips from Oliver to Alex.

"Alex. Let me." He takes a deep breath.

Lydia's brows rise towards her hairline.

"She needs to hear it from me."

Alex's eyes dart back and forth between the married couple.

"You know that you and I have been having problems for years," Oliver begins, turning his head and staring directly into Lydia's eyes. She frowns deeply. "Months ago, I talked to you about a divorce but you wouldn't listen. I asked you to file and I realize, now, I was doing that to protect myself. That was wrong of me. I didn't want to hurt you. So, I wanted to put the ball in your court, let you be the one to pull the trigger on us. It wasn't right, but Lydia, you also have to be real about us. We've both been miserable for so long, we've both forgotten what feeling good was like."

Lydia holds her hands up, and Oliver stops, tilting his head to the side.

"Are we really going to do this with *her* standing right here?" she asks.

The muscle in Oliver's jaw flexes as he gulps. "Yes. Because what I have to say, she needs to hear too. I need you to understand something," Oliver continues. "When we separated, when I moved into this place, it really was my own doing. There was no other motivation. There was no one else. A couple weeks ago, Alex needed some help with a story. She reached out to me and that's how we reconnected. I swear to you, Lydia, there was nothing going on with her then."

"Reconnected? Then?" Lydia's eyes become narrowed slits of disapproval. "I'm not one of your constituents Oliver, don't play vocabulary games with me to try and clear your own conscience. You think how long this has been going on makes any difference to me? If you fucked her yesterday, a month ago, a year ago, I am still your wife!" Lydia slaps at her thighs as the words leave her mouth. She lets out a pained gasp and turns her back to them both, putting a hand to her forehead.

Oliver pauses.

"You are having an affair. You, Oliver! I never thought that you of all people ..." She is unable to finish. "If Alex hadn't shown up here tonight, would you have ever told me about what was going on with her?"

"Yes," Oliver admits. "You've been doing good lately. I didn't want to set you back. I'd hoped that a divorce wouldn't cause you relapse. Eventually, I would have told you."

Her laugh is a sardonic opera for several breaths.

"Lydia, it was never Oliver's intention to hurt you," Alex says earnestly. "If you want someone to blame, then blame me."

Lydia whirls around to face her. "Oh, that's not a problem for me to do at all. You've been nothing but a pain in my ass since the first day I met you. At the first sign of trouble between me and him, you slithered right back into his life like the low-life snake you are."

"I—" Alex licks her dry lips and exhales. "I deserve that."

"You deserve a broken jaw!"

Oliver steps forward, putting himself between them.

"This is my husband, Alex!" Lydia shouts, her voice cracking as a gap breaks in the dam of her emotions. She peers around Oliver at Alex as she shouts at her. "Did you not have any respect for that? That we are married? That he is mine!"

Oliver puts his hands on Lydia's shoulders, guiding her to take a step back as she pushes towards Alex.

Lydia's lip trembles. "Or at least he was! Get off me." She throws Oliver's arms off her. She paces to the other side of the room, hugging her arms around herself. She weeps, her body trembling with each wave of sorrow.

Alex and Oliver exchange repentant glances. They let Lydia have a minute to compose herself. She wipes at her eyes with the back of her hand and sniffles.

"I'll sign whatever you want. There's no point in fighting it anymore. No point in pretending." Her voice is thick with pain. "You win, Alex."

Alex opens her mouth, stammering silently, unsure if now is the time. Lydia's presence was unexpected, but she was still on a mission when she arrived at Oliver's apartment. She had something very important to share with him. Lydia needs to hear it too, and Alex's chest tightens before she speaks.

"There's something," Alex says meekly. "Something else that, Lydia, you really need to know. I know now isn't the best time."

Lydia turns her head slightly, letting Alex know she is listening, but does not look at her.

"It's why I'm here tonight," she explains to Oliver. "I came as soon as I knew the truth. I came here to warn Oliver."

"Warn me? Alex, what's going on?"

"The story I'm working on, Lydia, it's an investigation into the EPA head and a few senators; that's why I asked for Oliver's help in the first place. Well, it seems they are now aware that the paper is looking into them and my colleague, my partner on this story, Coleman Chester, was attacked and left for dead while on assignment last night."

Oliver takes a step back. "Is he all right?"

"Yes, he's in the hospital, but he'll be okay. There's more." Alex stares at Lydia's profile. She turns slowly and faces her. Lydia's tear-stained face is now questioning. Her bloodshot eyes still shimmer with tears, her cheeks splotchy and red, the rims of her eyelids crimson, her mascara and eyeliner smeared.

"What?" Lydia nudges.

"The two senators, they were funneling money through a broker." Alex gulps.

Lydia blinks silently before realization sets in. It starts as a flicker of understanding in her eyes before her mouth opens as her jaw drops. "Oh my God."

Oliver stares at Alex, frowning deeply, searching her face for an answer. "I don't understand."

"Our research guys traced back some of the numbers in the phone records to Jamison Ainsworth."

"What!" Oliver's exclamation could no doubt be heard on the entire floor of the apartment building.

"Daddy?" Lydia covers her face and shakes her head. "I knew he had been having money problems and then he was making all these random trips out here from California, but I didn't think he was involved in anything shady." She drops her hands from her face, her eyes pleading. "You're sure?"

Alex nods slowly. "I'm very sorry, Lydia." Her apology extends well beyond the news about Jamison. Their eyes meet in a temporary truce.

"I want to talk to him," Oliver says adamantly.

"No. We've been trying to keep your name and your association out of this as best we can and if Jamison knows and then tells the others, Coleman may not be the only person to get hurt."

Oliver scratches at the back of his head and huffs. "I know, I know, it's a risk. My name will already be in it now. He's my wife's father." Oliver grunts in frustration. Use of the term "wife" gives all three pause. "If he gets pinned in this deal, and they all go down, he's automatically tied to me."

"Other than the money, though, are things really that bad?" Lydia questions. "I mean, if there's a way to protect my dad then ..."

"Does the name Peter Vitale mean anything to you?" Alex asks.

"No. Should it?" Lydia's eyes shift from Alex to Oliver.

"Have a seat, Lydia, there are some things you need to know." Alex motions towards the sofa. Lydia defiantly remains standing for a moment but gives in and takes a seat. She sits and listens in horror as Alex explains the health risks of the people in Marktown and how Takestrom's factory is responsible for dozens of deaths because of the toxicity of their materials going into the water, soil, and air.

"Chickman, Eisenhower, and Ingelman all know it. Now, Vitale and the mob are tangled up in it and your father is likely connected to one or all of them." Alex gestures. "They know people are dying, but they are getting kickbacks from Takestrom. Your dad," Alex continues, before pausing sympathetically when Lydia looks up at her, "your dad has probably been doing what he can to hide the paper trail for them."

"How? How would he have gotten involved in all of this? That's crazy! His son-in-law is a senator he—" Lydia stops herself. "His son-in-law is a senator." She sighs and clenches her fist. She lifts her eyes sadly to Oliver. "I'm sorry."

"It's not your fault," Oliver offers.

"Knowing Daddy, he probably saw an opportunity when you got to Washington and took it." Lydia places her hands in her lap as she thinks.

"What can I do to help?" she asks.

Alex's lips part and her eyes widen. "Help?"

"With your story. Look, Alex, I don't like you. I never have, and I most certainly never, ever will, especially now," she says flatly. "This entire situation is shit. But," she says, looking up at Oliver, "if Daddy has done this, and babies are sick and he doesn't even care, if he used Oliver's status and manipulated my ties here too, I want to make this right. He can't get away with it just because he's my dad. So, what do you need me to do?"

"Can you get him here? Get him back out to DC? Then if you can get him to go somewhere private, Oliver and I both can question him."

Lydia snorts and laughs. "I can get him out here first thing tomorrow morning."

"How's that?" Oliver questions.

"All I have to do is tell him the truth," Lydia says looking up at him. "I just have to tell Daddy that you left me, and he will be right here."

CHAPTER 20

There is a stirring at Coleman's bedside. Through heavy eyelids, the glow of fluorescent light panels overhead appears as a blur. His brain seems to punch itself as light pierces like shrapnel, setting his skull on fire again.

The pain renders it hard to move his head and limbs even a centimeter, and the slightest bobble and the fault line of agony sends another quake through his muscles. He groans and lifts his hand to his face, shielding his eyes from the light. As he lifts his hand, he realizes there is something taped to it. He attempts to touch it with his other hand, but a tight sling hinders him from moving his arm. He squints and blinks. A tube runs from the back of his hand up to an IV bag hanging on a hook next to the bed.

The hospital, he reminds himself. He is still in the hospital.

He fumbles around trying to reach for the call button. He needs a nurse, a doctor, someone capable of easing this misery.

His hand runs over the blanket, unable to find the remote. He cusses to himself before narrowly opening his eyes again, the blinding light setting off alarms in his nervous system. His hand finds something next to his hip and he grasps it before another eruption between his ears is set off.

"Agh!" Defeated, he lays his head back.

"In pain, Mr. Chester?" a voice asks.

Coleman pauses when he hears the man's voice. Not a single one of his nurses has been a man up to this point. He reaches down to his hip again.

"Need someone to take the pain away?"

Coleman forces his brain and sight to adjust. He can make out a dark-haired man standing a few feet away from his bedside, dressed in scrubs. His scraggly goatee, the vein in his forehead, and the sleeve tattoo that begins at his neck, indicate a hard life, not RN or doctor. A teardrop is tattooed underneath his right eye. Coleman slams his eyes shut, another volcanic explosion in his head.

The man's boots ease from heel to toe, heal to toe, tapping over the linoleum floor as he paces closer and leans over the bed rail. "The pain you feel right now is a warning. You keep snooping around, spending time where you shouldn't, asking too many questions, and that pain will be a hell of a lot worse."

Coleman wills his eyes to open, the pixelated images now forming clear shapes. "Nurse!" he calls out towards the closed door of his room.

The man's hand clamps over Coleman's mouth and nose. A viper tattoo in bright green is close to his line of sight as he kicks his legs. He shoves the man with as much strength as he can muster from his unbound arm. Coleman's cries are muffled, his breath suffocating, as he forces a hand up and under the chin of the assailant. The IV needle in the back of his hand wiggles, causing more fire to spread in his body but he will not stop his fight. Coleman shoves upward against the attacker's nose, the effort leaving him in a daze.

The door to the hospital room swings open. The attacker frees his target and begins to fluff the pillows behind Coleman's head.

"There, there," the man coos. "It was just a nightmare. Do try to rest."

"Mr. Chester?" A chipper blonde nurse questions as she stands near the door. "You pressed the call button?"

Amy. She has been attentive and sweet as he has struggled through the subsequent pain of his first attack. When Alex called earlier, Amy brought him the phone.

"Oh." Her hand rests on the door handle as she stops. "I'm sorry, I didn't realize someone else had responded."

"No, no, please," Coleman begs. "Please stay."

Amy's eyes dart back and forth between Coleman and his current attendant.

"I'd be more comfortable with someone who has already helped me." Coleman's chest heaves. He would shout at the top of his lungs that this devil beside him is trying to take his life, but he fears he would only be putting Amy in danger.

"I've never seen you before. Are you new?" Amy studies the man in green scrubs.

"Uh, yeah," He tries to keep his voice pleasant and his posture open. "Second night, got here early before the shift change." His raspy voice is as hard as his appearance, and his laugh the same.

"Oh." Amy paces to the other side of Coleman's bed. "And your name?"

"Nurse!" Coleman interrupts. He fears any further questioning from Amy will render them both dead. He does not know if this man is carrying weapons on him. "My head! Could you stay here and page the doctor to come, immediately?"

"You're perspiring," Amy notes. Beads of sweat are rolling down his temple, his breath erratic. "Your complexion is flushed."

Amy draws closer and examines Coleman's bandage. "There's blood seeping through this again. Poor thing. You've been suffering all day. Let me get the doctor on call tonight." She reaches for the call button at his hip and lifts it to her mouth as she pages the nurse's station.

Amy pulls the bandage up from Coleman's head to peek at the stitches in his scalp. Coleman holds his breath as the man slinks back from the side of the bed towards the door.

When he is out of sight, Coleman gulps down breaths. "Amy, you are an angel."

She laughs. "I should take your temperature."

"No," Coleman rests back against the pillows. Exhaustion and pain pump in his veins. "You need to call the police."

<hr />

Amy is not sure what is going on with the mysterious blond man that was admitted the previous morning. He'd made a disoriented plea before passing out. *Call the police.* He wasn't making much sense, but head trauma could do that to a person, as well as create paranoia and panic.

When he was admitted, a few detectives had been through to check on his status and see if he was awake and cognitive enough to answer questions. At every one of their arrivals, the patient had been snoozing due to a steady dose of painkillers. The police would likely be back again soon, but something about the haggard-looking fellow in his room earlier isn't sitting right with Amy's spirit. She ventures to his door to inspect his room as he continues to rest.

Amy returns to the nurse's station and grabs her tumbler. She folds a fleece hoodie over her arm as her shift ends. She sips coffee from tumbler's straw as she rounds the desk and approaches her co-worker, Margo.

"Keep an eye on the guy in 520, will you?"

"You got the hots for the dude with no ID?" Margo teases.

"Even with that head injury, he ain't ugly." She pauses. "Can you watch for anything suspicious? There was a guy in there earlier that gave me the creeps. Have you met any new male nurses around here lately?"

"You know this revolving door." Margo shrugs. "Nurses come and go. Hard to keep tabs and it's not like HR asks us for our opinion on hiring."

"Yeah." Amy turns and stares fixedly at the door of room 520. "If you see something odd, report it. A detective left his card earlier. It's there, next to the phone."

"Will do." Margo salutes. "Go home, get some sleep. I'll see you in a few days."

"Take care, girl."

Amy walks up the hall and stops at 520. She peers inside one more time. The EKG machine is bouncing and beeping steadily. The man's eyelashes rest on the apples of his cheeks.

Coleman is jostled awake as his shoulder is lifted off the bed. He groans, a drugged sleep slowing his return to the present world.

"Coleman," a voice says to him. Unlike the ominous sound of being called "Mr. Chester" four hours before, this baritone voice registers with familiarity, not fear. "Coleman, you've got to sit up."

"Pat?" Coleman's head lolls forward.

———————

Pat rang the doorbell of the two-story wood frame home. A porch light was on, highlighting the black shutters and door. A cab waited near the curb.

The door opened to reveal Pat's buddy Steve Vargas, who blinked rapidly, rubbing at his chin. He wore striped boxers and a plain white T-shirt. "Pat?"

"Steve." Pat spun around and gave a smile as his breath made puffs of mist in the Chicago night air. "Hello. How are you?"

"I'm good. We're good. Do you know what time it is? What are you even doing in Chicago?"

"I need your car."

"Is this a joke? Pat, it's after nine o'clock."

"Sorry if I woke you and Cynthia. I need your car." Pat cleared his throat and then waved to the cab driver. The driver lifted a hand and waved back before navigating the yellow cab up the street.

As soon as Alex had left for DC, Pat felt an unnerving concern about both of his star reporters. There was no balm for his anxiety other than action.

His concerns grew when he tried to reach FBI Agents Sinclaire and Thomas on several occasions and neither responded to his calls. His contact at the FBI also had posed some prying questions when he phoned for help.

His secretary booked him a reservation at a journalism conference in Chicago that week as cover. He made sure others at the Society of Professional Journalists knew he was registered, emailing that he'd be in town and putting up a post on LinkedIn. Rubyth booked a flight to Chicago. If the conference was a success, Pat had no idea.

He grew impatient standing in the dark of night as he began to shiver. The neighborhood was settling down for the night, except for the red glow of the retreating brake lights of the cab. A dog barked in a nearby backyard.

Pat's old college newspaper buddy owed him a favor. Pat had been charged with throwing Steve's bachelor party twenty years ago, and to this day, his wife, Cynthia, had no idea what had taken place that night with the party entertainment. Steve is now a copyeditor at *The Chicago Tribune*.

In their quarter century of friendship, Pat's unexpected arrival and request was one of the least odd experiences they've shared.

"Can I ask what for?" Steve stuttered.

"Nope. Give me the keys. Tell Cynthia I owe you both one."

"Why *my* car?" Steve asked as he slid a grouping of copper and silver keys and a remote off the front door key holder. He slid on a pair of house shoes and stepped outside. His shoulders hunched up to his ears when a gust of wind blew. He lifted a shaking arm and pressed the button on the remote. A metallic clanking and motorized pull began as the garage door lifted, the light inside turning on. He led Pat up the sidewalk, past Hollytree bushes, his house shoes flapping against his heels and the pavement.

"Rentals aren't safe." Pat swiped the keys from Steve's hand.

"Safe from what?"

Pat removed his phone from the pocket of his khakis and searched for the hospital in Google Maps. "I'll be back as soon as I can."

Steve waved goodbye as Pat backed the sky-blue sedan out of the driveway. Pat politely pressed the garage door button to close it as he began the thirty-five-minute drive to St. Catherine Hospital.

He pulled into a truck stop and bought some Chicago Cubs sweats and a ball cap.

He arrived at St. Catherine's carrying a plastic bag, pretending to be a local detective. If Coleman's activity was being monitored for visitors, given the nature of his admittance, there was nothing abnormal about a cop showing up with questions. The receptionist gave him the room number, not even bothering to ask for identification. Pat hurried to his reporter's side.

"Coleman, I love you. But you are six foot two, I'm five foot eight, and I'm gonna need you to give me some damn help here, okay?" Pat grunts, lifting Coleman to his feet. "Can you stand on your own?"

"No." Coleman wobbles slightly. He braces his unbound hand on the edge of the bed.

"We'll get you a wheelchair."

Pat hurries out into the hall and past a nurse who is distracted by her phone. He grabs a wheelchair from the many parked in a cubby in the hall and wheels it to Coleman's room.

"Put these on." He opens the plastic bag and places the sweats on the bed besides Coleman. Pat adjusts the snap back on the ball cap and pulls it over his own head.

"I need you to get to the front door."

"And then where are we going?" Coleman's speech is labored. He slides on the pair of sweats underneath his hospital gown with one hand. His feet are covered in the grip bottom socks provided by the hospital.

"Back to New York City."

Coleman tucks the gown into the sweats with one hand before Pat struggles to help him into the wheelchair. Using all the strength both can muster, Coleman falls down into the chair as it wobbles. Pat steadies it as Coleman lifts his sock clad feet into the footrests.

Pat makes good on his promise to Alex to bring Coleman home. He just omitted his plan to do it himself.

CHAPTER 21

L ydia spots her well-dressed father and pulls her car up to the area designated for pick-ups. Jamison steps onto the curb in front of the arrivals section of Washington Dulles International Airport. Lydia hops out and moves around the car as he rolls his luggage towards the trunk.

"How's my princess?" He hugs her.

"I'm okay, Daddy," Lydia answers, feeling the puffy skin under her eyes jiggle as she nods.

She'd broken down when she phoned to tell him Oliver had asked for a divorce. The raw emotion and grief were not an act. However, when she asked if Jamison could come see her right away, she felt betrayal and remorse at her deception. She reminded herself there were people suffering for his financial gain. If Oliver had any influence in her life, it was his desire to care for those who couldn't care for themselves.

Jamison puts his luggage in the car's trunk before Lydia battles her way through departure traffic and leaves the airport. She drives for several minutes on the slow-moving freeway.

"You sure you are holding up okay?" he asks, finally.

She opens and flexes her hands, relieving the tension from her tight grip on the steering wheel. "It's just so much happening all at once."

"He never deserved you." Jamison snorts. "I never really liked him, to be honest. I always thought he didn't treat you well enough and now I'm sure of it. How dare he think he can discard my daughter like—"

"Daddy, please. Oliver and I had our problems. This isn't all on him."

"Of course it is. Don't you say that."

Lydia huffs and takes an exit ramp. The road curves through a manufacturing and office building area near the outskirts of town. Jamison's head swivels.

When she pulls into a parking garage, Jamison's voice is tremulous. "Pit stop?"

"Something like that." Her manicured nails had made indentations in her palms. She drives up a few levels of the parking garage. There are sparse vehicles parked in different locations but there are no patrons around them. They reach the fourth level where she finds Oliver's black truck is backed in and parked. Lydia pulls into a spot beside it. She puts the car in park and cuts the motor.

The door to the truck swings open and Oliver steps out, Alex following his lead.

"Lyd, what is this?"

"Believe me, they've got questions for you too." Lydia purses her lips. She opens the door without another word to her father and climbs out.

Alex, Oliver, and Lydia stand together as Jamison bewildered eyes gawk back at them through the windshield. Finally, he steps out of the car and approaches them.

"Daddy. We already know." Lydia sighs. "We know almost everything. This is your chance to come clean."

Jamison cracks his neck and lets out a humph. His gaze falls to Alex, and she frowns.

"I take it you got the package I sent you." He rubs at his clean-shaven cheek before shoving his hands in his pockets.

"Excuse me?" Alex's head jerks back.

"The package, the photos of Eisenhower, Chickman, Ingelman, Colbert and Vitale. Plus, the note about Takestrom and Marktown."

Jamison Ainsworth stands like a man not on the verge of professional and personal collapse but unassailable confidence. His expression is that of satisfied defiance. Oliver and Lydia both peer back at each other in matched surprise.

"You? You sent that? That's makes no sense! Why?" Alex croaks.

"When Oliver got to Washington last year, business was, well, not doing so hot," Jamison admits. "It was at one of those big black-tie affairs where Oliver was being introduced. You invited me, Lyd. I bumped into Chickman. We got to talking. I told him what I did for a living, and he mentioned some opportunities ahead. Told me it was not to be talked about at a party." Jamison seesaws his head. "Next time I was out here to see Lyd, I had a meeting scheduled with Chickman. I laid it all out there; I'd declared bankruptcy and at this point was looking for something to rebound with. He sets up a meeting with Vitale, all under the table stuff. Eisenhower and Ingelman make sure Takestrom gets a government deal. They want me to wash the money trail. Put some dollars here, some investments over here, all offshore accounts and hard to trace with crypto currency. They tell me I'll get a cut of their dollars, like a commission.

They ensured Takestrom was going to get the federal contract and not have to deal with any of the hassle."

"What hassles?" Alex demands.

"Proper chemical disposal, paying fines for safety violations. All those things cost money and eat up profits."

"So, Takestrom *is* paying off Ingelman, Chickman, and Eisenhower to look the other way?" Oliver confirms. "You've got evidence that links them?"

"Oh absolutely." Jamison gives a precocious smile.

"Where does Vitale fit? Why is the government working with the mob?" Alex asks.

"Oh, honey. You need to study US history again," Jamison replies.

"Why Vitale?"

"He's got his hands in some legitimate businesses, manufacturing being one of them. From what I know, the EPA began looking into Takestrom years ago. That's when Colbert took over as president of the company. I don't have all the facts, but Vitale has the resources to put pressure on officials, make some of the red tape go away."

"Officials like Ingelman?" Oliver interjects.

"And Skinner ..." Alex ventures.

"Judges can also make cases go away. Even cases against organized crime members," Jamison adds.

"So, if you were going to benefit from all this, why throw them under the bus?" Oliver asks.

"Last second, they cut me out of the deal." Jamison rubs his chin. "I moved the money around, lined things up so that it was hard to trace the dollars back to Takestrom, invested in a few things to triple their profits. I didn't see a fourth of what was promised to me."

"They screwed you, so now you are screwing them?" Oliver sniffs. "But they took a risk, didn't they? I mean, you control the money so—"

"I turned over the access information." Jamison sighs. "Before they dropped the hammer that I wasn't getting another dime. I turned over the information they needed to get their money to Ingleman. Lesson learned: you can't trust Washington politicians." He winks at Oliver.

"Why did you send the envelope to me? Out of everybody you could have dropped that to?" Alex steps forward an inch. "Lydia always said you were nosey," Jamison comments. Alex expels all of the breath in her chest. "She had told me a while back that you were a reporter now for *The Times*. From what I knew, if there was any reporter that couldn't resist a story like this and would take the bait, it was you."

Alex stares at him, her lips pressed together as she silently seethes. A car enters the garage on the levels below.

"Look," Jamison addresses Alex. "I'll tell you everything. I'll tell you how the money was moved and where it is. I can show you records and documents from my computer files, as long as you don't print my name with it."

"I can do that, but if the authorities start to question all this, I don't know that I can protect you, Jamison. I would do anything for most of my sources, protect them at all costs. I don't know that I want to do that in your case," Alex quips.

Jamison nods. "Understandable, no harm, no foul. That's where you come in." He points at Oliver.

The senator frowns. "What do you want?"

"Immunity. I fork everything over to you and Alex here, you take it to Congress. I get immunity for my illegal actions. You however, the savior of American politics, can stand before the American people as the champion of all that is good, milk the whole cleaning up Washington thing, and become president someday like you want. It will also be a great way to distract the world from the affair you were having with the reporter on the story and the woman you left my daughter for." Jamison thumbs at Alex.

Oliver opens his mouth to speak when a car moves up the ramp and turns onto the fourth level. They are about to step out of the way, to let it pass, when the engine revs and the tires screech. Smoke billows from the rubber tires, leaving black streaks on the cement as the black Expedition barrels towards them.

For a moment, the party of four stands in frozen terror. Then Oliver and Alex lunge to the right and narrowly out of the way. Lydia lets out a shrill cry and shoves her father as the SUV swerves towards him. As he falls to the ground, Lydia falls awkwardly in the opposite direction, turning her ankle and slamming her shoulder into the cement. Her collarbone snaps from the impact and she lies writhing in pain on the ground.

The SUV halts just before it reaches the turn exit. The taillights flicker and white lights pop on as the SUV is put in reverse.

She tries to lift herself up, her ears ringing from the impact of her fall and the break. Tires screech again as the SUV speeds towards them. Her father crawls away. Lydia lays in the reverse path of the vehicle.

"Lydia!" Oliver shouts. Crawling to his hands and feet, Oliver clambers with as much speed as his pro football days. He lifts her up and shoves her to the side. Lydia rolls on the floor. With a nauseating crunch, the SUV slams against Oliver, launching his body into the air with a sickening twist. Oliver's body collapses onto the ground, motionless, as the SUV turns and takes aim towards Jamison.

Her father moves like a toddler in a frenzy on his hands and knees, wedging himself between two structure beams. He cowers between them; mouth open wide with terror. His body is blockaded by beams, shielding him from the reach of the SUV.

A window lowers. Two muted pops of golden light break through the still air and Jamison Ainsworth recoils with dual impacts. As the SUV peels away, Jamison slumps between the beams, his chin dropping as if he has drifted into a nap. Two crimson circles form on his chest. The back of his suit jacket is torn open from the exit of the projectiles.

"Daddy ..." Lydia calls weakly from the ground.

"Oliver!" Alex shrieks. "Oliver!" She scrambles towards his body. The pavement scrapes her palms and bloodies her knees as she moves over the concrete to her love. She doesn't feel the sting of her injuries.

His broken body is limp, his leg twisted in an inhumane fashion.

"Oliver," Alex repeats.

Lydia slowly sits up. She looks from her father to Oliver, feeling like she is watching a movie and not inside her own body. Alex's hands shake as she turns Oliver over. His head lolls to the side, a trickle of blood rolling from the side of his mouth. There is a gash on the side of his head, crimson streaking down the side of his face.

Alex cradles his bloody head in her hands, her entire body trembling.

"Lydia!" Alex lets out an anguished cry. "Call for help!"

PART VI

THE OUTCUE

CHAPTER 22

Dexter Adkins is in his fifth year of working for the Office of Public Affairs at the US Department of Justice. His job title was Principal Deputy Director, but by all accounts, the name on his office door and his pay grade should be that of the Director. Dexter oversees the day-to-day operations and makes sure personnel are content with their roles and responsibilities, and is on top of every communication effort from press releases to social media blasts. The actual director spends most of his days on the golf course or trying to put a spin on whatever asinine thing the attorney general has publicly said that week.

Dexter joined the Department of Justice after spending most of his post-grad career in the communications and marketing departments of a handful of Fortune 500 companies based in New York City. His ability to hobnob with the likes of Wall Street and manipulate public perception over billion-dollar transactions had kept him bouncing from one profitable company to the next and made him a sure fit for handling politicians in DC.

Dexter had been a standout track star at Syracuse University, competing in the 110-meter hurdles and 4 x 100 relay team for the Orange men. It had been sixteen years since he had suited up for the Orange, but Dexter still keeps his body in runner's condition. During his college days, he and his good friend, Coleman, were a duo to behold. Dexter's smooth mahogany skin seemed to pour right over his sinewy muscles. His smile was disarming, the type that makes an already attractive man irresistible.

When Dexter lived in NYC, they were still a dynamic duo, but their jobs kept them busy and afforded far less time for womanizing. Dexter's move to DC had lessened communication, but social media and Coleman's annoying but hilarious texts still popped up on Dexter's phone almost daily.

Coleman, however, has recently gone radio silent. It's been six days since his last message, causing Dexter to first send texts joking about Coleman being on the run, to eventually calling him last night. Dexter's cell phone rings and the ID notes that it is a New York City call, but he almost ignores it. Something, intuition maybe, leads him to reconsider.

"This is Dexter," he answers, putting the phone up to his ear and spinning in his chair to face his computer screen again.

"Dexter," the voice responds.

"Coleman?" As soon as he recognizes his voice, he is in the mood for a little light-hearted ribbing. "Been a few days. What's up with the new number? You get black-out drunk on a beach in Tijuana and lose your phone or maybe a hooker lifted it off you in some massage parlor?"

"Dexter," Coleman repeats. The curtness of his response and the gravity of his tone do not go unnoticed. Dexter sits up straight in his desk chair. "This is my boss's cell phone."

"Man, what's going on?"

"I need your help, and under no circumstances can you contact the FBI."

The hazard lights flash on Lydia's Lexus, and Alex presses down harder on the gas pedal. Crimson stains her hands, the bottom of her shirt, and her jeans.

Almost twenty minutes before, Oliver's head had been lying in her lap, his skin white as printer paper as the wound on his head oozed with the dark, warm liquid; his eyes shut, his breathing shallow, his pulse fading.

Alex's cries echoed in the parking garage. Lydia stared back at Alex, her mouth agape in shock and awe, watching as Alex frantically tried to bring her back to the present. Lydia's eyes had traveled around the parking garage in a stupor: her father slumped motionless between two cement pillars, her husband's body contorted and bleeding in Alex's arms.

The sounds of a car speeding away and out of the building were as faint as a whisper. Alex screamed Lydia's name repeatedly, and she latched onto reality with a slow shake of her head. She rose to her feet, crying out as she tried to use her right arm to help her to stand. Lydia's arm dangled limply at her side as she hobbled to her car. With another shrill cry of agony, Lydia opened the door and grabbed her cell phone. She slumped onto the seat and dialed for help. Over the sounds of her own sobs, Alex heard Lydia plead with the operator to send ambulances.

"They pinpointed the location, Alex. They are on the way!" Lydia's shout was broken but the message received as Alex gave an appreciative nod.

Lydia made a second call. "Delta-9-6-3-0-Alpha," she said, her voice sounding hoarse and weaker. "One person with gunshot wounds and Senator Michaels was struck by a vehicle."

Lydia collapsed in the car seat.

"Lydia?" Alex called out to her again, but soon realized Lydia's injuries had taken their toll. Alex slammed her eyes shut; she had never felt more alone as she did then in the eerie silence with three motionless people around her. "I'm so sorry! Oliver, I love you!" Alex wailed.

As black vehicles swirled up to the fourth level of the parking garage, Alex faintly heard the wail of sirens growing as they neared.

Alex was reaching into her pocket for her phone to call 911 again when the Secret Service arrived. She had turned her phone off before her flight to DC, leaving it off out of concern that whoever had harmed Coleman would likely have the capabilities to triangulate her location also.

Oliver's limp body was placed onto a stretcher, his body strapped down, and his neck braced as paramedics immediately began working on his head wound.

They told Alex they detected a weak pulse on Jamison, and he was placed on a stretcher and loaded into a second ambulance.

A member of the Secret Service lifted Lydia's frail frame out of the car and loaded her carefully into the back of an SUV to take her to the hospital.

Alex hopped into Lydia's car. Specks of blood dotted the driver's seat. She followed the two ambulances, flanked by black cars and SUVs as tires whirled towards Walter Reed Medical Center.

She didn't bother to park, pulling the Lexus up to the emergency room entrance where Jamison was taken to a trauma room, and Lydia is carried by a Secret Service member to a triage. Alex jogs alongside Oliver's stretcher as one of the EMT's continues to squeeze the oxygen pump mask over Oliver's nose and mouth, forcing air into his lungs.

A set of double doors open automatically as a team of doctors and nurses surround the stretcher, guiding it into an operating room. Alex tries to follow and squeeze between the doors as they begin to shut, but a nurse stops her.

"Oliver!" Alex shouts as the nurse puts gentle hands on her shoulders and guides the tearful woman away.

The doors shut with a thud.

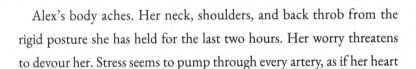

Alex's body aches. Her neck, shoulders, and back throb from the rigid posture she has held for the last two hours. Her worry threatens to devour her. Stress seems to pump through every artery, as if her heart were nothing more than a generator of anxiety.

There is still no word on Oliver's condition. Even if there is a reasonable update, the doctors will not provide it to her. Alex is not family or listed as next of kin. After pleading with an RN at the nurses' station for the fifth time that night, Alex finally begins to accept that she will not be provided with any details about Oliver's injuries. As the agitated nurse demonstratively stated yet again that Alex was not related to Oliver, a sobering and hurtful thought hit Alex: *I am not his family, I am not his anything*.

Lydia remained in treatment. They at least shared that much with Alex.

Secret Service had questioned Alex, and she provided the few details she could. A black SUV had come barreling through the parking garage;

no, she couldn't recall a license plate number; no, she could not provide information on why they were meeting in the garage; no, she was not sure if Senator Michaels was the target.

She had finally gone to the bathroom to rinse the blood from her hands. As she scrubs her palms and under her nails, the cold, soapy water swirls with the red of Oliver's blood as it disappears down the drain. She had involved Oliver in this situation, and now she has his blood on her hands.

After rinsing the last traces of red away, she dampens a paper towel and presses the coolness to her face, taking what felt like the first breath in hours.

She sits in the waiting room with Secret Service outside the door. Several suited men linger near the waiting area, monitoring the halls to the ER, and standing outside each of the medical center's entrances and exits.

Alex realizes that she has not checked in with anyone at the paper since she left NYC the night before. She has to call Pat.

She observes the closed door to the waiting room, with the back of a Secret Service agent visible out of the window. Her phone comes to life, glowing in her hand as she scrolls to her contacts and selects Pat's number. As she is about press CALL, her phone begins to chime with several missed texts and voicemails from the twelve hours she has gone without her phone turned on.

She ignores them all and listens as the phone rings. Where does she start? How does she tell him? Her racing thoughts are interrupted when the deep voice of her mentor, boss, and friend answers.

"Alex! Thank God!" He exhales sharply. "I've been trying to call and text you! I was scared to death that someone had gotten to you!"

"I ..." Alex begins. She opens her mouth, stammering as she tries to will herself to recount the horror of the last few hours. She rubs at her forehead. She fears speaking the words will make this ordeal real. She looks down at the blood-soaked jeans she is wearing. This is worse than a nightmare.

"Alex? Are you all right?"

"No." She crumbles. Tears spill down her cheeks as she suddenly gasps for breath, sobs violently seizing her body.

The Secret Service agent outside the door clearly hears her agony and opens the door. Alex puts her hand up, shaking her head for him to stay out. He retreats from the room, shutting the door.

"Alex, talk to me. What's going on?" Pat urges. His voice is fatherly, concerned, and calm as if to ease her grief.

"My contact ... here in DC ... the one helping me with the story," Alex blubbers between gasps. She squeezes her eyes shut as tears roll over her cheeks. She puts a hand to her lips, smelling the clinical scent of the surgical soap she scrubbed Oliver's blood away with. She steels her nerves and takes a deep breath.

"My DC contact is Senator Oliver Michaels," Alex explains.

"Michaels?"

"Yes. A little while ago, he and I were meeting with a source for this story, and someone ran us down." Alex twists and pulls at one of her coils.

"Dear, God. Are you okay?" The question comes again.

"I'm fine. But ... Oliver ... the vehicle struck him. He's been in surgery for a couple of hours. I have no idea what's going to happen to him. It's really bad, Pat."

"Alex, where are you?"

"Walter Reed. Secret Service is here. Oliver's wife called them but there's something else," Alex cautions. "Our source was with us, the vehicle stopped, and someone fired shots at him. He's in surgery. I don't know if he's going to make it either."

"I'm glad you are all right." Pat's voice is full of remorse. "I'm sorry about Senator Michaels. He's an old college friend, right?"

Alex pauses: a friend. Such a simple term to describe the complex emotions and feelings she has held for years for this man.

"Yes. How is Coleman? Any update on him? Pat, we've got to make sure he's—"

"You can ask him yourself." There is a rustling as the phone is passed, and when Alex hears Coleman's voice she begins to weep again, this time releasing the fear she held for him.

"Alex."

"Coleman," she bellows. "I have been so worried. I couldn't take it if something happened to you too!"

"Me too? What else has happened?"

Chapter 23

A nurse walks Alex through the pristine halls of Walter Reed to a private room at the end of the hall. A Secret Service agent is stationed outside the door and tips his head to her and the nurse before stepping out of the way.

The same nurse took pity on the distraught Alex and offered her a pair of scrubs to change into and out of the bloody clothes she was wearing. Alex gladly accepted them and changed into the pale blue shirt and pants. Alex's clothes had been bagged and would be kept as evidence in the case. No one knew if it would be a murder or an attempted murder case yet.

"She's groggy but awake," the nurse explains. The change of scrubs was as much for Alex's sake as it had been for Lydia's. She was emotionally battered enough; she did not need to see the blood-soaked reminder of the day's events on Alex's body.

"Thank you." Alex nods as the nurse gives her a sympathetic smile and turns and heads back up the hall. Alex steps quietly into the room, shutting the door with a soft click.

A dim fluorescent light is on just above the hospital bed where Lydia lies. The green vinyl sitting chairs, the geometric patterns of the green and blue curtains around the window, and the sanitary fragrance of Lysol reminds Alex of just how much she hates hospitals. Everything is so clinical, too schematic to reflect life and beauty, a constant reminder of sickness and death in her eyes.

She apprehensively approaches the bed. Lydia's blonde hair fans out around her head on the pillow. She is sitting almost upright in the bed. From underneath the hospital gown she is wearing, Alex can see the large bandage over her collarbone and shoulder. An oxygen tube curves over her ears and slopes across her cheeks and underneath her nose, and an IV bag hangs on a hook beside the bed, the tube running down to her thin wrist. Lydia had always sported a golden tan in college. She had looked pale when Alex saw her at Oliver's apartment last night, but now her skin is a shade lighter than snow.

At the swooshing of Alex's clothes, Lydia opens her eyelids, barely turning her head to look at Alex.

"How are you feeling?"

"I'm so drugged up I can barely feel," Lydia answers groggily. "Broken collarbone and dislocated shoulder. They put pins in the bones to fix them. They told me Oliver and Daddy were both still in surgery. They won't tell me anything else right now." Her words are slow and seem to fall out of her mouth rather than be spoken. Her voice is scratchy and her eyes are narrow slits as she fights off drugged sleep.

A heavy silence falls in the room as both women consider who they may lose this night.

"Lydia, I'm sorry," Alex offers respectfully. "For everything, for all of this, and for Oliver." Wild regret forces Alex's shoulders down.

Lydia lifts the hand of her unbandaged arm, waving it dismissively.

"Not now," she says, and Alex simply nods.

The room is silent again.

"You know Oliver had an opportunity to take Secret Service protection full time and he said no." Lydia huffs and shakes her head a little. "Said he wasn't a big deal and wanted to save taxpayer dollars. Some other congressmen tried to tell him that he could be a target with his popularity, but Oliver wouldn't listen. He said he wanted to remain accessible to the people."

"That sounds like a very Oliver thing to say and do."

The two women exchange a knowing glance before Lydia snorts.

After a few silent moments, Lydia raises her hand and points to the small cabinet beside the bed.

"Open that drawer," she instructs.

Alex peers back at her curiously before stepping forward and sliding the drawer open. Inside is a Zip-Lock bag with several items sealed in. There are car keys, a wallet, a folded-up boarding pass, and what appears to be a flash drive. There are splotches of a dried, red substance on a few of the items.

"Nurse brought those in. They are some personal items that were on Daddy. My father is not someone who carries around any type of technology other than a cell phone. I'm venturing to guess he wanted to keep the information he had safe and with him at all times. I can't be sure, but what you need is probably on that drive. It sounds so simple and archaic, but that's Daddy. Take it. Take it before the CIA or FBI come after it."

Alex's eyes flash with surprise.

"Take it, take his wallet, too. There may be stuff in there that can help."

"Lydia, this is your dad's stuff, are you sure you—"

"The people he had worked with obviously tried to have him killed today. They shot *him*. They weren't there for you or Oliver, but my father. They had to have been keeping tabs on where he was going and who he was talking to. They can't get away with this. Even if he ... just take it, okay?"

Alex reaches into the drawer and opens the bag. She slips the flash drive into the pocket of the scrubs and slides the wallet into the other.

She puts a gentle hand on top of Lydia's. "Thank you."

Lydia didn't stay lucid for long as the painkillers she was given post-surgery delivered her to a deep sleep once again. Alex was grateful Lydia was able to find a peaceful respite from all of this, even if medically induced. Lydia wasn't awake like Alex to be terrified each time a door opened that it was a doctor bearing bad news. She wasn't so filled with stress that she didn't know how to sit still or had paced a ravine into the floor. That all fell on Alex.

She sits on a sofa in the waiting room still guarded by Secret Service, her knee bouncing.

She hears voices in the hall and suddenly the door to the waiting area swings open.

A man and a woman enter the room. The silver-haired man's face is vacant of expression. The woman's face is plain, no makeup, her brown hair greasy and flat. The pant suit she wears is as no nonsense as her facial expression.

Alex's eyes go slightly wide as they enter the room. There is no polite greeting, only stoic faces as she peers up at the two looming over her.

"Alex?" the woman asks in a slightly hoarse voice that might indicate she is a smoker.

"Yes?"

The woman reaches into her pocket and pulls out a leather fold, opening it to show her badge. "Agent Karla Patterson, Federal Bureau of Investigations. We need to speak with you about the nature of the story you have been working on."

"FBI?" Alex's eyes narrow. She searches for Agent Patterson to make sure the Secret Service agent is still visible at the door. She can see the back of his head through the window.

"FBI and DCPD are on this case. Agents and officers are over at the parking garage right now gathering evidence," the man says flatly. "Agent Bowen," he introduces himself. "We've got some additional questions for you regarding the nature of this story that you've been working on. Our New York contacts relayed they had been working with you on locating another reporter at *The Times*. What is your connection to Jamison Ainsworth?"

Alex looks back and forth between them.

"Did Ainsworth say or give you any information in support of your story?" Patterson asks.

"I am not at liberty to discuss my sources."

"Ma'am, a US senator may die because of this," Bowen spits out, agitated. "At this point, you are interfering with a federal investigation and—"

A commotion echoes from out in the hall and raised voices spill into the waiting room. The four people in the waiting room turn as the door opens and a well-dressed gentleman walks in with two other men and a woman.

"Thanks fellas, but this is no longer an FBI investigation. Department of Justice will handle interviewing the lady," the tailored suit says.

Patterson and Bowen look at each other, stunned. "You're public affairs, you have no right to take over anything," Patterson begins bitterly.

"This order from the Attorney General says I do," he responds, holding up a piece of paper. Bowens and Patterson exchange another concerned glance before silently stepping to the side.

The man folds the paper up and tucks it into the inner pocket of his suit jacket. "Alex?"

He gives her a comforting smile.

"Dexter Adkins, Department of Justice. Our mutual friend Coleman asked that I come see you."

CHAPTER 24

Kentucky Senator Travis Chickman kisses Charlotte goodnight, then flips off the light switch and closes the door to her room.

He takes a deep breath as he inspects the hall leading towards the primary bedroom where Lena is already in bed reading, the same thing she has done every night at bedtime in their twenty-six-year marriage.

He has had trouble sleeping for the last six months—so many sleepless nights, or nights spent tossing and turning. Even making love to Lena, once a sure-fire elixir to help send him to dreamland, has not helped in recent weeks.

He softly pads down the stairs of their townhome, his memory foam slippers making little noise on the hardwood steps as he eases towards his office.

There should be an update by now.

He peeks up at the stairs before closing the door to the office and locking it behind him. He heads to the safe hidden by a faux wood panel in the wall. He lifts the panel and turns the knob on the safe, spinning it with the combination.

Reaching inside, he retrieves the cell phone he stores there. He waits a few impatient seconds as it powers on, and then selects one of only four numbers he has in the phone.

"Yes?" the reply comes hoarsely.

"Ainsworth is no longer a threat?" Chickman asks, scratching at his eyebrow.

"Negative. He is in the hospital, in intensive care."

"What?" Chickman interrupts. His own outburst rattles him, and he inhales slowly to calm himself. "How is that possible?"

"There were others there. We attempted to neutralize him, and it appeared we were successful, but we have no confirmation."

"Then you make sure this is taken care of! Get over there and finish the job!" Chickman growls into the phone. His mouth suddenly foams with thick saliva. He feels dehydrated, like a junkyard dog on a chain leash.

"Negative," is the short reply he receives.

"What the fuck do you mean—"

"Too much heat on this. Senator Michaels was injured in the attempt."

Chickman freezes, the blood running cold from his head to his toes. "Michaels?"

"Word will soon be public. There are those who already believe this was an assassination attempt on a US senator. We can't be connected to this. You are on your own now, Congressman."

A beep ends the call.

Chickman holds the dead phone to his ear, blinking slowly, no longer seeing the objects in his office. *No. No, this can't be, and it cannot end this way.*

He dials Rupert Ingelman's number. An automated greeting tells him to leave a voicemail. He curses that coward Ingelman who has been flakey since he and Eisenhower leaned on him. He must reach Eisenhower. The phone rings several times before he hears the same automated message. He doesn't bother to record a response.

He paces to the other side of his office before spinning wildly and launching the cell phone against the wall. It shatters on impact. He walks with his hands on top of his head, groaning and wincing as his fate becomes evident.

He has to get out of here. But where will he go? How would he leave the country? What resources does he have? Can he still access the crypto accounts? He has means to take care of them. Or he did.

When Chickman logs into the account on his laptop the balance is $0 USD. Has Ainsworth taken the cash and moved it? How could he get money for his wife and daughter's care without raising suspicion?

As he thinks of his family, he fears the disgrace he has caused them. He can already see the headlines, the breaking news tickers, the top trends on social media all being his name. The women in his life he has given his last name to don't deserve this.

"Travis?"

A soft knock breaks his racing thoughts. The doorknob turns only slightly before the visitor seems to realize it's locked.

"Travis? Are you all right?" Lena calls from the other side. "I heard a noise."

He walks to the door and puts his hand against the wood, closing his eyes as they water. "Yes, Lena. Everything is alright. Go back to bed, sweetheart."

While they do not know where the leak came from, Alex's only surprise is that it took this long for it to happen. Six and a half hours after she cradled the love of her life's body in her arms, word that Senator Michaels of Maine was struck by a vehicle has made national news. The twenty-four-hour news stations did cut-ins and the bottom of television screens across the country flashed with breaking news: *US Senator Oliver Michaels Critically Injured, Possible Attack.*

Workers at the office buildings and warehouses near the parking garage had seen the buzz of activity as FBI and DCPD vehicles blocked off the area and began marking signs of evidence. A few pictures from social media and shaky vertical cell phone videos outside the crime scene were all the media had to use in the first hour that the news broke.

Alex briefly watched the footage in the waiting room before turning off the television. She wanted no more reminders.

Dexter is on the phone out in the hall, already rallying his team to respond with statements from the Department of Justice on the investigation and the compliance of the FBI in this process.

The hour grows late, and Alex is more tired than she has ever been in her life. She is weary. She has prayed and begged God, pleading for Oliver to be okay.

She wraps her arms around herself as she tucks her feet under her legs on the sofa and tries to rest her head on a pillow. Each time she tries to close her eyes, she relives the horror of watching Oliver's body lift unnaturally into the air and crumple when it strikes the ground.

She tries to think of something happier, like the last kiss they shared, but all she can feel is hopelessness. She may never feel the warmth of his lips on hers again.

The waiting room door opens, and Alex sits up. The Secret Service agent holds it wide as a nurse pushes Lydia into the room, sitting in a wheelchair.

"Lydia!" Alex raises up on the hospital sofa. "You should be resting!"

She dismisses her statement. "They took me to see Oliver." Her eyes water.

Alex feels faint. "Lydia. No. Is he?" She can't let her mind think it nor allow her mouth to form the words to speak it.

"He's unconscious," Lydia relays, "but alive."

The gasp that escapes Alex's lips is like the release of a steam kettle. All the anxiety, all the worry, all her fears escape with the rush of air that leaves her body. She covers her face and tilts her head back. "Thank you, God!"

"He's not out of the woods though," Lydia halts the rejoicing. "He suffered a brain hemorrhage and contusion. They were able to stop the bleeding, but we won't know what type of damage it may have left Oliver with. His right leg was broken in three places, and he also had a break in his pelvic bone and femur. They put him in a medical coma to allow the swelling on his brain to go down. It could be several days before we know if he's really going to make it, Alex."

Lydia's eyes water again, and she purses her lips, fighting off another wave of tears. Alex takes in Lydia's words, wondering if the Oliver they both know will return to them.

"Your father?" Alex asks softly.

"In the ICU. One of the bullets pierced his sternum and bone pieces punctured his lung. He's on a breathing machine. It was incredible luck that a bullet didn't hit him in the heart but still, it doesn't look good."

"I'm so sorry, Lydia. I truly am," Alex repeats, crossing her arms over her stomach.

"Alex, I've said it before, I don't like you. We both know why. But I appreciate you being here and being concerned." Lydia toys with her fingernail. "They have contacted his mom and brother and sister. They are all trying to make arrangements to get here."

Alex stares down at the top of her shoes.

Lydia huffs and seems annoyed by her own emotions. "You don't owe me a thing. But please Alex, I'm begging you: bury the sons of bitches who did this to them," she spits.

When Alex lifts her eyes to Lydia's face, it is stern and twisted with vengeance.

"I will," Alex says with conviction. "You can bet I will."

"You can go see him now."

"They told me earlier I couldn't go back."

"I told them to let you. I told them you were, after all, his family." Lydia licks her lips and turns her head as she closes her eyes.

Alex rises to her feet. "Thank you."

She opens the door to the waiting room and eyeballs the Secret Service agent. He motions to her before he turns and heads towards Oliver's room. She surveys the end of the hall and sees Dexter leaning against a wall on the phone.

With each step she takes, her emotions grapple within her. Alex wants to see Oliver, to touch him, to hold him, to kiss his face. What will she find when she enters his room? She tries to take deep breaths, finding it difficult to inhale and exhale for longer than two seconds, as she moves behind the agent towards a door guarded by two other agents.

The agent in front of her steps aside, motioning his hand towards the door. Alex grips the handle, and there's trepidation in her movements as she enters.

A monitor beside his bed displays a neon green line that ticks up and down in a slow rhythm. The heart rate monitor is tracking his pulse. She is not sure why she focuses on the screen first but slowly her eyes shift to the man in the bed. Oliver's head is bandaged, a brace around his neck, an oxygen mask strapped over his nose and mouth, and a black contraption with pins and bolts hovers like a half halo over his hips, another over his leg.

Her lip trembles at the sight. She softly lets out a cry, tears filling her eyes as she moves towards his bed without feeling the steps she takes.

She puts her hand on top of Oliver's, finding it cooler to the touch than normal.

"Oliver." She squeezes his fingers before lifting her hand and caressing his cheek with the back of her fingers. "Sweetheart, I want to believe that you can hear me. That you know I'm here. I'll always be here, Oliver, right here at your side for the rest of ..." She is sobered by time. Their future seemed so promising. Now it may be reduced to days. The rest of their lives may not be as long as she hoped.

"I love you. I have loved you every day of my life since our first day together at UConn. No matter what, I'm going to do whatever I can to take care of you and make sure you are okay."

She leans forward, her face inches from his. His eyelashes rest on the top of pale cheeks and tears from her eyes land against his skin, above the oxygen mask strap. "I'm so sorry I got you into this mess. This is my fault.

All of it. I should have just stayed away, but I couldn't. I couldn't because I love you, and I needed you. Maybe I wanted an excuse for you to help me so that we could be together, I don't know, but Oliver, I need you. I need you to come back to me" Tears cascade unceasingly from her eyes as she rubs his arm. There are scrapes along his skin there, rough under her fingertips.

"I can't lose you now that we finally planned to be together. That's not fair to us. It's just not fair," she cries openly. She lays her head against his chest as she bends over the bed.

"Please Oliver, please. Don't leave me, too."

The nurses had to pull her away. They entered Oliver's room to tell her he needed to rest and no more visitors. When Alex arrives back in the waiting room, she feels no more relieved than she did when she first arrived at the hospital.

Dexter opens the door for her and ushers her inside. A young woman sits in a chair with a cup of coffee in her hand. Alex's steps slow as she eyes her.

"We contacted Oliver's assistant. Needed to interview her about anyone who may have had a vendetta against Oliver," Dexter says.

"Yvette Graham," the young woman says, standing up and extending her hand to Alex. "I wish we were meeting under better circumstances. How is he?"

Alex shakes her hand. "They put him under. He's got some pretty critical injuries."

"Yvette has backed up what Coleman told me about the story," Dexter says, looking at Alex. "If we can connect the dots, then it will go to the Attorney General, who will issue a warrant and records from Chickman, Eisenhower, and Ingelman will be seized. Next step will be their arrests. Colbert and Vitale as well. I'll be back, need to make some more calls." Dexter leaves the room.

"Can I get you a coffee or something?" Yvette offers.

"No but thank you." Alex sinks back down into a chair.

"When I got the call from the DOJ, it was like having a heart attack," Yvette says. "I couldn't believe that someone would hurt Oliver. He's so caring and selfless, and now this."

"It's because of me." Alex sighs.

Yvette wrinkles her nose. "Don't think that." Long, quiet reflection follows. "I have a spare key to his apartment. He gave it to me not long after he confided in me that he and Lydia had split. I go by and take care of Montana when he's stuck in session or has to go out of town. When they say I can go, I'm gonna go get Montana and take him to my place or wherever they take me. Dexter said it might not be safe for me at my apartment either." Yvette sighs.

"It's good he has you. Oliver must really trust you to confide in you. He doesn't do that so easily with people."

"Oliver is more like a big brother to me than a boss. When I tell people I work for Senator Michaels, they get all gooey-eyed like he's some movie star, but he's just Oliver. He's kind of a dork really." Yvette chuckles.

Alex joins in. "He is that." Their laughter soothes her.

"You know, he's been really down until you came to him about the story. He was so depressed; it was like watching a zombie go off to the Capitol every day. When you came around, it lit a fire in him. He was motivated again; he wanted to work and help people and he dove into this. Don't blame yourself, Alex. Oliver wanted to be a part of this. He chose to. That's the Senator Michaels I know. The one fighting injustice. It just happened to be that he was fighting it with you and that made him happy again."

Alex smiles. "Thank you for that."

An abrupt knock rattles the door.

Alex peers through the window of the door. Before the knob begins to turn, she jumps to her feet.

"Coleman!" She pushes the door open and Alex squeals with joy. "Pat!"

She rushes to Coleman and throws her arms around him.

"Hey, hey. Careful now, I'm walking wounded." His single arm lifts around her like a warm blanket on a cold, fretful night. His warmth envelopes her in peace and comfort. She pulls back and examines the bandage on his head and the cast on his arm.

"Are you okay?" she asks with concern, still holding him. "Jesus, what are you wearing?"

"I'm a little woozy here and there but better. The Armani suit is at the cleaners. Pat stopped and bought me these killer duds in Illinois."

"You look like a million bucks to me right now." Alex lays her head against his chest and squeezes him again, this time carefully.

After some time, she pulls away and practically collapses around her boss, hugging him too.

"I'm glad you are okay, kiddo. Both of you. Something just didn't feel right," Pat says as he pulls back to hold her at arm's length. He looks directly into her eyes. "I had to make sure you were safe."

"How did you get here?" Alex asks.

"Friends in high places," Dexter says, entering the room.

"After I called Dexter, he arranged for a charter to meet Pat and me in Ohio, after we drove from Chicago. Flew us to DC and they drove us from the airport here," Coleman explains.

"Thank you, Dexter," Alex says. "I can't say thank you enough. You have actually saved our lives."

"Just add it to the other lists of reasons Coleman owes me." Dexter grins. "We are working on getting warrants to search Chickman, Eisenhower, and Ingelman's homes and offices. The Attorney General is up and awake and briefed on the situation. I have pulled a few people from the FBI that I trust to help and recommended them to the director to assemble a team of investigators."

"Dexter, I have one more favor to ask of you," Coleman says. "I know I can't repay you but if you could do me this solid, I'd be grateful."

Dexter nods emphatically. "What's up?"

"There's a family in Marktown, the Fischers. I can give you the address. Can you send someone to look after them? To watch their house? I interviewed the mother. Whoever took my recorder, notes, and camera knows about them too. They have a little girl, man. There's a doctor, too. Dr. Calvin Peterson. He stuck his neck out there and was willing to talk to me. If you could make sure they have some kind of protection, I'd be grateful."

"Consider it done."

"Thank you, Dex." Coleman says.

"Anything I can get you guys while you wait? Food, drinks?"

"How about a laptop?" Alex asks.

Coleman frowns slightly at his colleague. She reaches into her pocket and holds the blood-spattered flash drive up to his face.

CHAPTER 25

The motorcade stopped outside of the Army Navy Club on Eye Street. Alex and Coleman huddle in the back seat of a black SUV as they roll through the dark streets of DC. They say little, saving their conversation for when they are inside the walls of *The Times* Washington Bureau. Alex holds Coleman's hand as he rests his head against the seat back and closes his eyes. It would be hours before a chance to rest would present itself again.

Pat sits on a row in front of them. He phoned Ezrah, JB, and the rest of the team with the investigative research unit. It was all hands on deck in both the NYC and Washington offices.

Dexter had arranged for a DOJ escort for Alex, Coleman, and Pat. After two attacks on Coleman and the attempts on Jamison and Oliver's lives, no one affiliated with the story was being left unguarded. An escort went with Yvette to Oliver's apartment. A DC police officer was assigned to keep watch outside of her apartment building once they determined she could return.

The motorcade stops at the side entrance of the bureau and the trio file inside.

Alex crouches over the laptop. She has not slept but doesn't care. Two empty coffee cups litter the conference table where she and Coleman are working. She doesn't need food or rest—she needs to write.

Pat is seated across the table from her and scrolling through his phone.

Coleman ends a call and gingerly takes a seat beside her, resting the arm in the sling on the table. "Chickman and Eisenhower's communications directors both called back. Neither had a comment other than to say they will cooperate with the DOJ investigation should it get to that point. They are in panic mode, I can tell."

"EPA? Takestrom?"

The information Colbert had promised Alex is as likely to arrive as the *Titanic* was to its destination. She skimmed her emails and searched for his assistant's name, finding no new messages.

"No response. Put in that we tried to reach them. They are going to take a while to get their ducks in a row."

"I'm adding in the following, 'We reached out to the communications offices of both Senators Chickman and Eisenhower and were told they had no comment but would cooperate with any requests from the Department of Justice. Representatives for the EPA and Takestrom Chemicals could not be reached.'"

"Perfect," Coleman replies. He leans back on the sofa and groans slightly, pulling at the bandage on his head. "Part one of a multi-story effort."

He had accessed the audio files from his interview with Dr. Peterson and the Fischers and the pictures he had snapped early in his trip to Marktown from the cloud. A backup to the backups.

The Times piece details Takestrom's alleged disregard for proper disposal of toxic chemicals and pollutants and how the EPA blatantly overlooked it and federal contract protocol, all so Chickman, Eisenhower, and Ingelman could pad their pockets.

Pat put his phone down with a thud that draws Alex's attention away from her computer screen.

"I hope I didn't do more harm than good by taking you out of the hospital before you were ready," Pat addresses Coleman.

"If I'd stayed there, I could be dead now." Coleman scratches at the stubble on his jawline with his unbound hand. "I don't think there is a best practice established for that type of situation."

"Yeah," Pat begins, "but if your injuries worsen—"

"Then please be gentle in my obituary for *The Times*." Coleman shrugs. "I want front page coverage, too. None of that bottom corner, last page BS."

Alex's shoulders hunch towards her ears and she gives a weary sigh.

Coleman reaches his hand out and places it on her shoulder. "I'm sorry, I don't mean to be insensitive to--"

"It's fine." She waves him off and he retracts his hand. Alex rereads her last sentence back to herself under her breath.

"I need some air," Pat announces. He was close to chewing a wad of gum the size of a baseball.

Coleman and Alex both know what 'air' meant: a cigarette. He paces outside the bureau, taking a puff with the DOJ looking on as he makes calls back to the web and legal department of *The Times*. It's just before dawn. A story is about to break, and everyone needs to be ready. Attorneys need to review Coleman and Alex's piece before it is published online. It's already too late to meet the day's print deadline.

Alex continues to type. "How are you feeling?"

"My head still hurts like a son of a bitch. I don't care though. Nurses gave me some children's acetaminophen earlier. Crazy how loopy this stuff makes you. It's helping some. You know, I can't believe Ainsworth had all this," he says of the financial files open on the laptop. "What idiots these guys are."

"I think Jamison took a few liberties in keeping up with electronic records, especially once he had issues with them."

"Is he going to make it?"

"Doesn't look like it."

"And Michaels?" Coleman asks cautiously.

"We can't be sure," Alex answers in a hush. She stops typing and sits back. She was keeping herself busy and worry for Oliver at bay. She was keeping her promise to Lydia. At the mention of Oliver's name, she is sick with anxiety again. "I'm glad you are safe," Alex remarks sincerely.

"Oh, that makes two of us. When I was at the hospital, someone paid me a visit and it wasn't to deliver flowers and balloons."

Alex whips her head around to look at him.

"Someone tried to hurt you again?" she half shouts.

He puts his hands up to calm her. "Yes. I didn't mention it earlier because I knew you were already dealing with a lot. I didn't want to add that to the load."

"Coleman!" Alex shrieks.

"It's going to be okay. They are looking for him. I told the investigators and they said they were going to pull surveillance footage from the hospital entrance and try to ID the guy. If I had to guess, one of Vitale's guys."

"I almost got you killed and may have gotten Oliver murdered." Alex covers her face in her hands. "I didn't tell you, but while you were in the hospital, I got a couple of death threats. I never stopped to think about the endgame of all this."

Coleman reaches out and pulls her hands from her face, holding them with his unbound hand.

"We both knew it was risky when we got involved. You are very convincing, Alex, but you didn't force the hands of two grown men to help you with this. Pat isn't here only because he's our boss. This matters. I can't speak for Oliver, but I was glad you asked for my help and that I've been able to work with you like this."

Alex turns and faces him, seeing sincerity in his eyes. The dip in his tone lets her know this is more than a conversation between co-workers. Alex slowly let's go of his hands, pulling hers free.

Coleman bites his lip as he thinks, and she watches his teeth pull at the flesh.

"You love him?" he asks of Oliver. He tugs at his ear lobe as he drops his gaze down at his thighs.

Alex looks towards eyes that won't meet hers. "I do. Coleman I'm sor—"

He gives a miniscule head shake, grimacing. "There's no need to apologize."

"He was planning to divorce Lydia so we could finally be together," Alex confesses. "Before all this with Oliver, before I knew there was a chance, Coleman I ..." she trails off again.

"Almost, huh?" he says, giving her a small smile. His dimples lift in his cheeks as he does.

"I'm sorry."

Coleman stares at her and reaches over and pats her knee. "Let's get back to work. We've got a story to publish."

The nurse wheels Lydia through the maze of corridors at Walter Reed. He shuttles her past serene murals of Midwest corn fields at sunset. Other generic, scenic oil paintings hang every five feet over the beige walls of the hospital. The flooring changes from buffed linoleum that mirrored the circle lights embedded in the ceiling overhead, to wood laminate under the hospital's most recent remodeling. The corridor has the pristine smell of antibacterial washes and sterilizers.

He pushes Lydia past a nurse's station framed by two tranquility water fountains, a meager sensory attempt to help visitors and patients feel less ensnared by the sterility of their surroundings. Lydia glances at a round brown clock suspended to the wall over the station. The hour of the day was not a burden she had troubled herself with until now. It was just after 9 p.m. The lone nurse seated behind the desk does not look up as she scrunches her nose to read a line more closely on her computer screen.

The nurse's pants make a swooshing sound with each step he takes and periodically a squeak issues from his sneakers catching on the hard floor. He pushes her chair through the ICU to her father's bedside and places a compassionate hand on her shoulder. His warm palm squeezes, and she turns her head to look up at him before a searing heat causes her to wince. The broken collar bone reminded her it was still there despite the heavy medications she was on. Her forearm and elbow were cradled in a sling, pulling against the opposite side of her neck. The nurse had helped her pull her blonde hair up into a ponytail before escorting her through the hospital to stop the constant tug and sting on her scalp each time a few strands of her hair got caught in the sling. Tiny red speckles of blood had dried in her limp hair like fire embers slowly drying, hardening, and darkening.

"May I have a few moments alone with him before you get the doctors?" She clears the gruffness from her voice from the heavy, drug-induced sleeping and hours alone in quiet.

"Of course." He gives her an empathetic glance before he zips the curtain hooks and pulls the cotton barrier into place behind him. As she studies her father's ashen face under the eerie glow of a single fluorescent light over his bed, she follows the plastic tubes extending from his mouth like industrial tentacles. The front of his gown is open to reveal thick bandages and gauze. The door to the room clicks shut behind her.

She reaches for her father's hand. She doesn't know if it was the frigid hospital air or the thread of space between his life and the grave, but his hand feels like she is holding a scoop of ice cream—cold and without grip.

"Daddy," Lydia whispers. She half expects to feel him squeeze her hand back, but it remains unmoving.

His unresponsiveness opens a door, a gateway to darkness once bolted, that Lydia had been trying to force shut. As her shoulders began to jostle with her sobs, the pain in her chest radiates in all directions through her biceps and up her neck. A hot burn that reminds her she is still very much alive.

She feels so utterly alone. Through the bad times with Oliver, she had been her daddy's girl. Lydia and her mother had never been close, not even during her cancer battle when Lydia had been dutiful as the eldest child in seeing to her care. When her parents divorced, she had sided with Jamison. She wanted to live with him, but her mother had filed for spousal support and Jamison said it was best if Lydia remained with her mother so that he could provide for her and her sister, Emily.'

Rather than turn her head, she shifts her gaze around the curtained enclosure, looking at the monitors next to Jamison. His pulse registers so slowly she knows he's almost gone.

She's losing her father. She may lose Oliver. She had almost lost her life. In that moment, Lydia weeps. She wishes it had been her.

There is no one there to hug her, no one to make her feel safe. The simple touch of the nurse had been her only comfort in the last few hours. Soon she will return to her own hospital bed and the black sleep of pain pills will take her.

Now, however, it's almost time to say goodbye. She feels paralyzed by the thought of choosing life or death for her father. Somehow, she knows no matter what she chooses she will carry the burden of the decision for the rest of her earthly days.

The thumping of hard soles on hard floors grows from a tap to a hard thwack close to the door before the handle jostles and men speaking in low voices interrupts a daughter's grief. Lydia wipes at her eyes before the curtain is pulled back.

Two doctors in white coats move towards Jamison's bed. She had spoken with one earlier.

"Lydia." Dr. Felix takes a deep breath, tilts his head, and forces a smile with the corners of his eyes at her. His skin is dark brown and there is a hint of an accent, possibly Dominican. "How are you feeling?"

"I'm in some pain but it's manageable," Lydia's voice is hoarse from the sobs she suppresses.

"If you need any additional pain medication or a change to the dosages, please let us know and we will get with your attending doctor. No need for you to suffer unnecessarily."

Suffer. She glances at her father then back at Dr. Felix. Watching your father get shot, your husband's mangled body run over by a three-ton vehicle, that is suffering. What did he know?

"This is Dr. Bonner, he's a neurologist on staff here," Dr. Felix introduces. "As I explained earlier in your room, he did a full diagnostic check of your father's neurological system."

Lydia blinks slowly. They made him sound like a computer.

The man, almost a half a foot shorter than Dr. Felix with brown hair and small eyes, magnified behind a pair of black-rimmed glasses, lifts a hand in greeting.

"Dr. Bonner has an update on your father's status," Dr. Felix explains.

Lydia waits. "Well?" she snaps.

"We ran all the required tests earlier and along with Dr. Felix's observations from surgery, I can say with certainty, that your father is permanently unconscious," Dr. Bonner says pedantically. There is no softness to his delivery, no cushion to pad the words; he is merely relaying facts.

Lydia's focus skips from the doctors to her father's face, barely visible behind the tubes. The rise and fall of his chest are only because of the ventilator pumping air into his lungs, keeping the blood pumping and the pulse faint.

"So, he's brain dead?" Lydia questions, needing the answer not for confirmation but to ease the mental war she is under with her morals and her love for her father.

"I'm afraid so ma'am," Dr. Bonner replies.

Dr. Felix steps forward as if moving closer might help her navigate her emotions. "Lydia, I know this is a lot to process right now. But you are listed as your father's primary emergency contact. As his daughter ..." Dr. Felix pauses when he sees Lydia's lip begin to tremble. "This doesn't have to be a decision you make right away."

"Yes, but the longer it's prolonged, the longer the impact on his body and your well-being, to be quite frank," Bonner adds.

"I understand," Lydia says solemnly. She doesn't need to call anyone to consult with them about the decision. There are no relatives to anger, no parents to mourn the loss of their son, or a sibling to grieve the loss of their brother. Emily had stopped speaking to her father when he filed for divorce from their mother. His ex-wife would not shed one tear in bereavement.

The burden of this decision is Lydia's and Lydia's alone.

"There's no need to drag this out. I know Daddy wouldn't want to suffer." She flicks a glance at Dr. Felix when she uses the word.

"We will have the nurse prepare the documents, get your signature. Then we will start the process," Felix says.

"How long ... does it usually take for someone ... to pass on? When they turn the machines off?"

"It varies," Dr. Bonner explains. "Some patients, it's only a few minutes. For some it can be a few hours, some several days. With your father's injuries and the lack of brain function, I wouldn't believe it would be a lengthy amount of time. His organs aren't getting the signals they need to function. He won't feel anything."

Lydia carefully nods. "I'll sign," she agrees.

"We're very sorry for your loss, Mrs. Michaels." Dr. Felix gives her a sympathetic stare. Lydia does not respond.

The two doctors pull the curtain behind them and exit the room.

Lydia holds her father's spiritless hand. With a heavy sigh, she glances down at her lap before lifting her head and flashing her famous smile.

"Daddy." Lydia clutches his thick fingers and knuckles with her frail slender hand. "We haven't always had the best relationship. I was so angry when you left Mama and me and Emily. I just wanted us to be a family. But you were always my hero. No matter what, you were my hero growing up. You still are." She pauses. "How could you do this though, Daddy? How could you do this to Oliver? To me? You fooled us all ..." Lydia's words draw out like the bridge of a song. There is a crescendo and then a beat, the symphony of emotions swelling.

"I know you made some mistakes, you made some bad choices, but that doesn't mean I don't love you because of it. Despite everything that's happened, I love you ... and I forgive you."

A tear plops onto her lap, a small circle that grows as the sadness seeps into the fabric. Soon, that single circle is joined by dozens more around it.

"It's time to say goodbye now. We will be together someday again."

Her face is wet with tears she doesn't wipe away. There was a time when Lydia would have eagerly reached for the painkillers to numb herself to the emotions swallowing her up whole. The alternative would have been something bottled and heavy. Neither of those appeals to her now. She doesn't check out; she forces herself to remain present.

She lifts his large knuckles to her lips and places a kiss on his hand. It has been just a few hours since she saw her father's body rocked violently by the bullets that penetrated his flesh so easily but left lethal damage. There is far too much trauma to his lungs for any hope of recovery. She can't prolong his life. She knows it is not what he would want. It is the hardest decision Jamison Ainsworth's daughter has ever had to make.

———————— •◦»— «◦• ————————

Travis Chickman couldn't handle the lines of questions from his wife. The phone in his home office had been ringing all night. The calls to the main house line had started. His communication director was beside herself. First, the Department of Justice wanted information from her, then *The New York Times* came calling. She was frantic and despite her pleas to her employer to understand what was going on, he would only offer little solace with a calm, "Everything will be okay."

He hugged Charlotte tight before she and Lena headed out the door for school. Lena told him they would talk more when she got back. There was no kiss goodbye, no I love you. Only a leer from a woman mindful of her husband's mood swings in all their years of marriage.

The phone rings in his office down the hall. He ignores it.

He heads out to the garage. The space next to his Audi where Lena parks is vacant. He knows it will take her at least an hour and a half to get Charlotte to school in DC morning traffic and return home. It's enough time.

He looks at the closed garage door before swiping the keys off the rack next to the back door and climbs into the Audi. He turns it on, rolling down both car windows.

He leans his head back against the seat and closes his eyes as he breathes deep ... and waits.

———————— •◦»— «◦• ————————

The special report from *The New York Times* reporters Alex Broussard and Coleman Chester was posted online at 10:48 p.m. eastern time. The headline: *EPA Head, Two US Senators Implicated in Kickback Scheme.*

The lawyers had approved it. Ezrah and the research department had received the uploads from Jamison's records that Alex provided. Copies of the first photos that had arrived with the anonymous mailing to her desk, and snippets of the travel and phone logs were embedded in various portions of the story. Extracts and clips were included in the online edition and would be available in a revised print edition on stands that afternoon.

The overnight headline had already made it onto the morning broadcasts for the *BBC* and *Sky News*. As the sun rose across North America, conversations at coffee shops, barber shops, salons, and around office water coolers across the nation were all about the report. Social media was spinning conspiracy theories.

The Times was getting calls to request Alex and Coleman for television interviews. The media relations department had taken a growing list of requests but could only respond that neither reporter would be available for at least three more day.

Jessie slips on his coveralls and is lacing up his work boots from his seat on the sofa as he watches a network morning show.

"Son of a bitch!" he exclaims.

"Jessie Fischer!" Aubrey struts from the kitchen where she is making oatmeal for Felicity before her morning nebulizer treatment. "You watch your mouth," she scolds through gritted teeth and tosses her head in

Felicity's direction. The toddler was having a conversation with Mr. Alligator, her diapered bottom and sock-wrapped feet planted on the floor near the television.

"Look!" Jessie jabs a finger in the air in the direction of the television, not caring about Aubrey's correction.

A breaking news banner is across the screen and still images of Takestrom Chemicals and the photos published of Marktown by the *Times* are full on the screen, one high-definition image after the other.

"Shit," Aubrey breaths out.

In the middle of the night, a knock had come at the door of their mobile home. Jessie looked out to see an East Chicago PD vehicle parked in his yard and he feared the worst.

Aubrey crept up behind him, sliding on her bathrobe and clutching his bicep as they looked at the officer at the door.

"Mr. and Mrs. Fischer?"

"Yes, officer?" Jessie replied defensively. Aubrey looked up the hall to make sure the banging on the door had not woken Felicity.

"We've been asked by the Department of Justice to keep watch over your property," the young officer explained. A holster was strapped around his waist and his shoulders, and he was armed with two pistols and a taser.

"Department of Justice?" Aubrey questioned and looked up at Jessie who was equally perplexed.

"Yes, ma'am. I'm Officer Ramirez. I'll be here until the next officer arrives in about eight hours. I don't have much detail, ma'am, other than we are to make sure there are no trespassers and keep an eye out for suspicious activity."

"Are we under surveillance?" Jessie questioned.

"No, sir. We're here to look after your family."

"What's this regarding?" Aubrey demanded.

"Ma'am. I'm just here doing what was asked of us," Officer Ramirez responded and shook his head.

Aubrey and Jessie had not slept that much, wondering why the cops were at their place. The neighbors up the highway were sure to be talking when the sun rose. Unable to rest, they whispered together, wondering if this had anything to do with that Chester fellow that had come by. They kept their voices low to not disturb their baby girl who could hear just about everything through the thin walls.

Now, they have their answer.

In Fort Wayne, Bonnie saw the news first. She returned from her weekday five a.m. jog through the streets of Cherry Hill and came back to her townhome to whip up a fresh smoothie. She tuned into Good Morning Indiana and stood with her sneakers rooted to the floor as the details of *The Time's* story were mapped out.

"We have crews headed to Marktown now for local reaction," the anchor announces.

Bonnie sprints to the kitchen and grabs her phone.

"Some people sleep, Bonnie." Grayson sounds very much like he was laying on his back and had been in a deep sleep.

"Turn on your TV!" Bonnie screeches.

"Wha—"

"Turn on your TV!"

"All right, all right!"

Bonnie makes out every grunt and groan he makes as he lifts himself out of the bed and shuffles across the floor.

"What channel?" he asks.

"Any channel."

Bonnie's tone wakes Grayson up like an energy drink. He flips to the cable news network he loves. Bonnie puts him on speaker and clicks an icon on her phone.

"Son of a bitch ..." Grayson breathes as he sees the story. "Coleman. Is this the—"

"Yes."

"Is it on—"

"Sending you the link now."

Grayson's phone chimes.

"I'll see you at the office in thirty minutes." He speaks alertly, no longer encumbered by the grogginess of waking. "We've got clients to call."

───────── •◦› — ‹◦• ─────────

Alex checks her phone, following what seems like cinematic updates to her and Coleman's story with every hour that passes: Senator Michaels, struck by a car and battling for his life the previous afternoon, may have been hit because his father-in-law had been involved in a corrupt cover-up. She reads coverage from multiple outlets before she feels like she is suffocating.

Pat enters the conference room with word that Senator Travis Chickman had been found dead in his home.

"A friend in DC tipped me off first. No confirmation on the circumstances surrounding his death. Wife found him. Friend only said foul play isn't suspected. They don't think it's whoever went after Jamison."

"Oh ..." Alex tugged at her earlobe.

"You okay, Ace?" Pat checked.

"Yeah ... just ... lots of lives lost with this story."

"You didn't create this situation, Alex. You exposed it for the crime that it is. You are not responsible for any body count." Pat offered for comfort.

But Alex felt differently.

The attorney general, reacting to the public outcry and the mounting evidence provided by the team Dexter had assembled, issued a warrant for the seizure of documents from Martin Eisenhower's home and offices. Eisenhower released a statement expressing his plan to resign as the senator from South Carolina effective immediately.

Rupert Ingelman had been brought in for questioning and the shame of his actions rippled through the EPA. An arrest of both he and Eisenhower was likely in the next few days.

Lonnie Colbert, head of Takestrom Chemicals, and Peter Vitale, don of the Insigne crime clan, were nowhere to be found on US soil.

It was just Part One of the story. Alex and Coleman had barely reviewed the last copy changes from the editors before they were making calls on Part Two. Coleman had phoned Grayson to follow up and the attorney had agreed to a few statements about the litigation. Thanks to interviews and statements from Aubrey Fischer, they had enough material to put together a follow-up piece that showed the scope of Vitale's misdeeds reaching into the judiciary branch, as well as near Marktown and Judge Skinner.

Aubrey and little Felicity humanized the story. It made the medical plight and environmental fallout from the rich and greedy more relatable and real to the general public.

Thanks to the link JB had found between Judge Skinner and Vitale's kids, calls were being made to the Lake County and Indiana state government offices.

"This is Alex Broussard with *The New York Times*," Alex identifies herself as she speaks to a stammering receptionist. "I'm trying to reach Judge Caroline Skinner or a representative of her office."

"Uh, yes, ma'am. Could you hold?" the girlish voice quavers.

"Sure can." Alex leans back in her seat and taps her pen against her notepad.

She ends up being on hold for a good chunk of the morning. She sits in the bureau's conference room staring up at the TV screen as she flips from one news channel to the next, listening to some orchestral melody on the hold meant to calm, but after thirty minutes of waiting and with her lack of sleep, it put Alex near rage. The young voice comes back to the line and tells her nervously that someone will get back to her soon and asks for a call back number.

"We have a deadline of tonight by 5 p.m. Eastern," Alex warns. "We will move forward with the story with or without comment from your offices."

"Yes, ma'am," the girl responds.

At 2:30 p.m., Lake County Commissioner Carson Gailus returns Alex's call. She can tell from the way each word leaves his mouth with preciseness and frequent pauses that he is being coached.

"Will there be a formal investigation into Judge Skinner's connection to Takestrom and her past involvement in hearing cases against the company?" Alex asks as diplomatically as possible. "Or, what about her alleged affiliation with a known criminal organization?"

"Mrs. Broussard," Commissioner Gailus begins.

"Miss," Alex corrects.

"Ms. Broussard," he relaunches what Alex assumes is a prepared statement. "We, of course, take these allegations, very, very seriously." Pause. "While we want to make sure all our county officials represent us in a manner of dignity and honor, at this time, these are just allegations as you said. There has been no formal complaint brought against Judge Skinner."

"Yes, about that ..." Alex draws a square on her notepad. "I've got a call into the governor's office about his appointment of Judge Skinner. I'm sure not long after our conversation, there will be an inquiry. As the leader of Lake County, is there any statement you'd like to give other than" Alex pauses as if reading but she recants the prepared bull from memory "you're 'taking these allegations very, very seriously?'"

Alex can hear the muffled sound of flesh covering the phone and assumes Gailus is consulting his team before she receives a reply.

"We would like to have time to formally respond more properly. Is there an email we could send a statement to after we consult with our legal counsel further?" Gailus stammers.

"Yes." Alex provides the e-mail address. "Would it be possible to speak with Judge Skinner now?" she asks wryly.

"We are acting on behalf of communications for Judge Skinner's office, but we will have a reply to you before your deadline. I assure you," Gailus says.

"Thank you. I'll be looking for it." She taps *end* on her phone. No new voicemails, no new emails since she began to reach out earlier.

———— •◊• — •◊• ————

The Times puts Pat up in a DC hotel. The same is offered to Alex and Coleman, who refused. They both wanted to return to Walter Reed.

Alex turns her attention back to the TV in the waiting room again. Every network has broken into programming to bring updates to the story. She feels a small pang of regret each time Chickman's photo is on the screen. She certainly never intended for anyone to lose their life over the story.

Coleman is given a bed in a vacant room to rest, the doctors checking his injury had determined that he still needed care and was showing symptoms from his concussion. Alex kisses his cheek gently as he fades into sleep, and she tiptoes out of the room.

She will not leave Walter Reed. She will not leave Oliver.

———— •◊• — •◊• ————

Grayson transforms the office suite into a war room. He and Bonnie reach out to seven clients, the very first being Aubrey Fischer.

"Yes sir, I'm looking at it right now," she says into the phone. "They sent a police officer over," Aubrey tells Grayson. "Keeping guard out front. They've been changing shifts every few hours, but they've got someone looking after us."

"Coleman," Grayson says.

Grayson and Bonnie drive from Fort Wayne to Marktown that afternoon. Grayson sits on the floor, cross-legged, and holds Mr. Alligator in front of his face as he speaks in a high-pitched voice that makes Felicity giggle. Bonnie takes notes, helping Aubrey gather medical bills and make a checklist of everything they would need from her.

"You were with us before, you stayed in touch, and you weren't in it for the dime," Aubrey tells Grayson while sitting in the living room later that evening as he and Jessie sat side by side on the sofa with beers in hand. Bonnie is in the rocker working through her notes, Felicity tucked into bed for the night. "We're sticking with you. This time we're gon' win." Aubrey nods at him.

"Damn right we are," Grayson says with conviction. "I should have fought harder for you Aubrey. For you, for Felicity, for Jessie, for the whole town."

Aubrey balls her hand into a fist and puts it against her hip, shifting her weight from one foot to the other.

"You been watching the same news as I have?" Her brow ticks upward. "Because from what I'm seeing, we didn't stand a snowball's chance in hell with that judge and them senators. The cards were stacked against us. Always is for folks like us," Aubrey scolds. "You stop being so hard on yourself."

"I could have done more. I could have stopped this from getting worse a long time ago." Grayson runs a hand over his face.

"One thing I've come to learn, Grayson," Aubrey levels a look at him that reminds him of his mother, full of truth and wisdom well beyond her years, "is that people with power will do anything to stay in power. They don't care how, just as long as they keep it."

"Grayson, about the fees," Jessie begins.

"Ah!" Grayson shakes his head and cuts him off. "Same deal as before. Not a cent goes to Bonnie and me unless we win you a settlement."

"Yes sir, it's just, how long do you think this is going to drag on?" Jessie asks.

"Hard to say," Bonnie chimes in, "with the news and the whole world watching, maybe sooner than later, but it could take up to ten years."

"If Takestrom files for bankruptcy, it could take longer. I'm sure those cowards are going to do everything they can to avoid shelling out even a dollar. They have no leadership and no operations as of yesterday afternoon, thanks, for once, to the feds."

"I really thought that after we couldn't get the case to jury the first time, Takestrom was going to outlive all of us. We'd be in the city cemetery, and they'd keep plucking along." Jessie scratches at the back of his neck.

"Never would have thought that day a reporter came knocking that it was going to change everything. You know, I almost didn't open the door? Wasn't going to let him in. But something in my gut said, 'Aubrey, this is it.'"

"Coleman's still fighting for this town. Still fighting for you all. Still reporting and updating even the smallest details. He's a good guy," Grayson adds.

"Easy on the eyes, too. Prettiest man I think I've ever seen." Aubrey nods at Bonnie who only tucks her lips and fights back a smile.

"Hey!" Jessie protests.

"Second prettiest." Aubrey rolls her eyes and rests her hands on his shoulders, causing both of them to laugh. Then the hacking cough hit, then the wheezing. Grayson gets up from the sofa and offers his spot to Aubrey, helping her to sit down as she coughs into her hands.

"I'm sorry, y'all." Her words are broken by the raucous coughing in her lungs that causes her shoulders to hunch and her belly to crunch in on itself.

Grayson kneels in front of her as the shaking and wheezing subside. He takes both her hands in his. "You just hold on. We're going to make sure no one else has to feel the way you do. That no more children have to go through what Felicity goes through every day."

Aubrey glittering eyes meet Grayson's stare. "I feel something I ain't felt in seven years: hope."

PART VII

THE HEADLINES

PART VII

CHAPTER 26

The lack of sleep and the dissipation of her adrenaline is starting to take its toll. Alex could use a hot shower and a bed. She's been in the same pair of scrubs for two days. She clicks the remote, turning off the TV, and considers lounging on the waiting room sofa.

She is surprised when Lydia walks into the room unassisted. Lydia's countenance bears no hint of emotion. Her shoulder is still bandaged and her arm in a sling now across her body.

"I wanted to come and say thank you." Lydia says. "Thank you for exposing this and thank you for writing it so that it seemed like my father tried to do good in the end. He would have wanted to be remembered for something positive."

"You're welcome, but that doesn't really feel like the right thing to say now honestly, Lydia. How are you holding up?"

"I talked to him before they turned the machine off," Lydia says distantly. "I'm at peace with it, as much as I can be."

"Losing a father, it's hard. Sometimes it's like losing our first hero." For the first time in the years since they met at UConn, Alex and Lydia's eyes meet in an appreciated gaze of shared experience.

"Nurses say Oliver's vitals are stronger. They did a scan and the swelling on his brain is down. They have stopped giving him the medicine to keep him under," Lydia explains.

Alex feels hope for the first time in days.

"Why don't you go see him? I can wait till later. I kind of want a minute to myself really."

"Oh, absolutely, of course." Alex hops up. She hurries towards the door as she leaves Lydia to privacy. Before she exits the room, she peeks over her shoulder. Lydia eases down onto a chair, her face in her hand.

Secret Service is still present but not in the numbers they were on the first two nights. She knows the way easily now and walks to Oliver's room in the ICU. She opens the door, finding him in the same position he had been in the last time she visited. Part of her hoped he would be sitting upright and greeting her with the smile she loved. She slides a chair up to the bed and sits down, taking his hand in hers.

"Hey you." She swears for a fleeting second, she can feel him squeeze her hand. "So, here's the thing, there's a new musical opening on Broadway in a few weeks. I really want to go and you're the only one I want to take me. So, you've got to wake up. Okay, Michaels? The clock is ticking, and I need you with me." She studies his blank features.

"Got an update for you. We finished the first two stories. They're published and the world knows the truth now. I couldn't have done it without you. You were the key to helping us. I wish I could hear your voice again, that's all."

She closes her eyes and drops her head. She lifts Oliver's hand to her cheek, nuzzling her face against it.

Alex flinches. She believes she dreamed it, but it happens again. His index finger graces her cheek on his own. She lifts her head hopefully and lifts her gaze.

Long lashes veil narrowly opened green eyes, the word from his mouth muffled under the oxygen mask. It is gruff and coarse with sleep and ailment, but it is the most beautiful sound she has ever heard.

"Alex."

CHAPTER 27

In a conference room of the New York Times Building, before every cable and national broadcast network camera, before reporters from all the largest papers, Alex Broussard thanks "the People's Champion." It is a title that stuck.

"Senator Michaels is not able to be here today." Alex reviews her pointform notes as she stands poised at the podium, cameras and audio recordings rolling. "He's not able to be here because his commitment to democracy, to the American citizens who for too long have felt unseen and unheard by Washington DC politicians, almost cost him his life." Alex lifts her head and looks directly into the feed camera in front of her. "Without the assistance of Senator Michael's office, we would never have found the connection between Takestrom Chemicals, Senators Eisenhower and Chickman, and EPA head Ingelman. Without Senator Michael's help, the citizens of Marktown would remain another point on the map, where hard-working people are not given a fighting chance in this country to access a basic human need: survival."

Alex held the index cards in her hands and then put them down, going off script for a moment. "I've known Oliver since college. This is just who he is," Alex says.

———————— •❦ — ❦• ————————

Lydia watches the press conference from her mother's living room in California. In the last two weeks, she'd faded quietly away from the DC political scene and returned home where she scattered her father's ashes in the Pacific Ocean.

She found a listing in the local paper's classified section for AA meetings in the basement of one of the town's historic churches.

Lydia was determined to make things right. Not for Jamison, not for Alex, not for Oliver. But for her.

———————— •❦ — ❦• ————————

Six weeks later, Coleman is back at Walter Reed surrounded by a chorus of clanking metal, grinding gears, grunts, and laughter. He stands beside one of a dozen bench presses in the rehabilitation center.

Oliver's face flushes pink then maroon, his brown hair wet and sticking to his sweat-slicked forehead and the scar near his hairline. He grits his teeth and his lips stretch back towards his ears as he growls.

"It's all you, OM. Punch it! Two more reps," a dark-haired man in tan and green pixelated camouflage encourages. He leans over the bar and Oliver, his arms and hands outstretched and ready to spot the senator as he lifts the weight. At the start of the physical therapy session, he'd introduced himself to Coleman as Lieutenant Alfonso Duran of Maine.

Oliver's biceps tighten and his T-shirt gathers sweat around the neck as he lifts and lowers the bar, repeats, and with a groan and Alfonso's help, drops the bar back down onto the bench with a bang.

"Ayuh! That's how you do it. Show them you still got the muscle, Senator!" Alfonso extends his hand and Oliver grips it as he sits up in a huff on the incline bench, his chest and shoulders heaving. Oliver wipes the back of his hand on his forehead and rests his hands on his knees.

"Thanks, Lieutenant," Oliver pants.

"Is it safe to say this is a huge change to your lifestyle?" Coleman holds out the voice recorder a foot away from Oliver's face.

"For sure." Oliver licks his lips and reaches for a water bottle. He takes a swig and a long gulp. "I've played football since I was in the fifth grade and trained for NFL seasons. I'm used to being in the gym or going to therapy to bounce back from an injury. This isn't like recovering from a torn ACL. I could never imagine that one day I would be conditioning my arms to be able to hold my toothbrush steady or comb my hair."

"Not accustomed to this kind of struggle?"

"Yes and no. Not being able to be as active as I'd like, it's a struggle. I grew up with a single mom and low income. That's a different kind of struggle. Had the turf knocked out of my cleats by the New Orleans Saints defense. Struggle is hard to define and measure. All of it is different for each of us as people. I feel my struggles are nothing compared to some of the men and women here. They put their lives on the line and lost limbs."

Coleman's head swivels to the half dozen veterans working on physical therapy to walk in prosthetics or exercising in wheelchairs.

Oliver stands with Alfonso's help. His gait is uneven, his right leg stiff and pulled along by the left as he crosses the black rubber mat to a medicine ball. It's stamped with "14 lbs."

"Some, like Alex, would say you put your life on the line?" Coleman draws close with the recorder held out but stands off to the side to give Oliver and Alfonso room to work.

"I don't look at it as being the same." Oliver rests with his hands on his hips, tilting his head back in preparation.

"Why not?"

"Because it was a split-second decision to protect people I care about. I didn't enter military service like the men and women in this room." Oliver motions around him.

Alfonso hands Oliver the medicine ball. He lifts it over his head and slams it down to the floor with enough force to launch it back up towards his hands. He does this over and over.

Today is the first day of Coleman following Oliver for a series he is putting together on Oliver's journey back from the attack. Coleman will document Oliver's recovery as he works with the best neuropsychologists and physical therapists at Walter Reed to rebuild strength from his head injury, broken pelvic bone and leg.

"You usually use a walker? But not at the moment?"

"Short distances I'm okay with for now. When I move back and forth from my room to here, longer distances, I still need it." Oliver points to the silver contraption with tennis balls on the legs stationed in the corner of the room. Seated beside the walker is Montana. The dog's ears prick upwards and his tail begins to whack the floor when Oliver motions in his direction.

"I had Montana registered as an emotional support animal." Oliver smiles for the first time that afternoon and puts the medicine ball down. "My assistant Yvette has been keeping him while I'm still in the hospital, but on rehab days she brings him over for a visit along with any documents or paperwork I might need to read. He's allowed to be here."

"Who gets more attention, you or Montana?" Coleman chuckles.

"With good reason, Montana. No contest." Oliver pats his thigh and Montana hops up and trots to his owner for petting.

"How many surgeries did you have in all?" Coleman asks.

"When I was brought in, it was something like three or four? Two more since then and more are likely." Oliver bends forward as he scratches behind Montana's ears. He balls his hand into a fist and presses it against his chest clearing his throat. Oliver grimaces before breathlessly motioning for Montana to sit.

"How's he doing?" Coleman questions Lieutenant Duran.

"Two weeks after the accident, I was helping him to get out of bed. We worked on mobility and flexibility after the surgeries, strength and hand grips while Senator Michaels was still confined to his bed and healing. Then, it was helping him to get into a chair. Now, he's standing here tossing this medicine ball. This is one tough man right here. That's why I asked to be assigned to him." Duran lifts his chin.

"You requested to work with him?"

"Yes, sir. When I heard he would be doing his rehabilitation here, I asked that I be on the list of Senator Michael's therapists. We Mainers stick together. Need a break, OM?"

"Yeah ... need ... a minute," Oliver replies.

Coleman pulls his pen and small notepad from the back pocket of his jeans and scribbles down a note. "How long of a road does he still have ahead of him?"

"Depends on any additional procedures he may have," Duran explains. "Our goal with any patient is to have them as functional as possible before they go home."

When the hullabaloo over the EPA and congressional scandal started to fade from daily talk shows with the waning attention of the instant gratification public, Coleman reached out to Oliver wanting to put together stories on his return to health and politics. Oliver had one condition: The stories should be about more than his recovery, spotlighting the work of healthcare professionals and the plight of injured veterans.

Coleman's attention returns to Oliver when he sits back down on the incline bench. "You could have gone home to do your rehabilitation in Maine, why have you chosen to stay in DC?"

"Sometimes out of tragedy comes ... opportunity." Oliver exhales deeply and his breathlessness seems to subside. "Being here is a chance to spotlight something much bigger than me. I want to thank the incredible staff of surgeons, nurses, therapists and mental health specialists here at Walter Reed who have been working with me since that day. They are bringing me back. Also, it's a chance to spotlight the conditions for those who are not dignitaries or members of congress."

"Meaning?"

"I'm training beside veterans who are triathletes now and competing in adaptive sports. They are real warriors. In talking to them, it's opened my eyes to the plight of veterans. I will get a pension from the NFL and can afford healthcare. As a congressman, I receive services immediately at this facility. Sadly, most veterans don't have access to such prompt responses or what we call Ward 72."

"Ward 72?"

"It's quarters here, high security and reserved for so-called VIPs. Lawmakers can check in here and have a private bath in a suite. In my eyes, that same luxury should be afforded to those who have served our nation on the frontlines. You're right, I could be rehabbing in a different part of the medical center or even back home. The real VIPs are the men and women in this room who have a title in front of their name because they signed up to protect our nation and fight in our wars. Not me because I wear a suit and sit at a desk most of the day."

Coleman balances the notepad against his thigh as he scribbles down a few more notes. He lifts his gaze to Oliver, seeing his chest rise and fall steadily now before Coleman continues his interview. "What do you remember about the attack?"

"You know, it's foggy at best. It's like a moment in time that is missing from my memory but the reality of it has been with me every single day afterwards."

"Earlier, you said your plan of care includes working with a neuropsychologist and occupational therapists?"

"Yeah. Today, so far, I've felt okay. Sometimes there's a pause when I'm trying to think. Like the thoughts and the next words won't link up. Doc says it may be like that for a bit."

"Do you see that impacting your job?"

"No. That's another reason why I wanted to stay in DC. I intend to be back on the senate floor as soon as I can, with the walker if needed. Yvette is leading the office. The documents she brings or the updates she provides keep me abreast of committee happenings. I will be voting by proxy this week on some items with the Agriculture, Nutrition and Forestry Committee."

Coleman scratches at his arm. "You know, you could take time off from your job. No one is banging at the door demanding you go back. I think the American people and the folks back in Maine will be pretty understanding of what you've been through and that you need time."

"That sounds like a comment and not a question." Oliver grins.

"You're not in danger of being removed from office. You've been incapacitated after trying to expose corruption. You don't think you should take a break from politics for a while?"

"I need to get back to the Senate floor." Oliver lifts his hand to stop Coleman as he opens his mouth to interrupt. "There's still work to be done. It's my duty. The folks here have reminded me that duty is everything and there are many ways to serve."

Coleman's questioning halts when a shout rings out near the sliding glass doors of the rehabilitation center. "Senator! You want to toss the ball around today?"

"With my best receiver? You know it." Oliver laughs, barely looking over his shoulder before he rises to his feet. He winces but limps towards a bald man standing on two prosthetic legs.

"Coleman, this is Army Master Sergeant Delroy Hardt. Sergeant, this is Coleman Chester with *The New York Times*."

"Nice to meet you," Coleman extends his hand, and the two men shake. "I'm writing about Senator Michaels and his comeback. Do you mind if I get a few words from you?" Coleman holds up the audio recorder.

"Not at all." Sergeant Hardt grins.

"We'll get things set up." Lieutenant Duran claps the sergeant on the back as he and Oliver grab two very large bolster-like pieces of equipment and pull them across the floor. Montana follows at Oliver's heels, inspecting their work.

"You seem to have befriended Oliver?" Coleman asks the sergeant.

"He's a good dude. You know, I think when we first found out he was coming in, we thought he'd be a diva. You know, former pro baller, congress and all that. He's as down to earth as they come." Sergeant Hardt grabs a clean towel. "We've been talking with him about the care available to us. He's really been listening, really wants to do something about it."

"How long were you in?"

"I did two tours in Iraq." Sergeant Hardt drapes the towel over his shoulder. "I was a division one athlete in college and went into the military afterwards. Our convoy was hit by an IED. Lost both legs below the knees. Trying some new prosthetics out, more functional. So, I'm back here working to get conditioned."

Oliver takes a seat on the end of one of the uneven bolsters, straddling it. Sergeant Hardt moves into position on the second bolster about fifty yards away.

"These are intentionally off balance when you sit on them," Lieutenant Duran tells Coleman. "It forces the patient to stabilize their core to be able to sit without falling over and to be able to throw."

Duran hands Oliver a neon green Nerf football. Oliver rears his hand back by his ear and it spirals over to the sergeant.

"Not what I had in mind when I hoped to catch passes from an NFL quarterback, but this is still fun," Hardt says.

Coleman continues to mill around, jotting down notes and talking with Sergeant Hardt as he works with Lieutenant Duran and Oliver.

Once they finish the game of catch, Oliver sits in a cushioned chair in the middle of the room. Montana rests his head on his owner's shoes and falls asleep.

Coleman takes a seat across from Oliver. "Thank you for doing this."

"I appreciate your coverage. If it can bring awareness to the issues veterans face, that's what's important. Maybe it'll encourage others to keep up the fight during their recovery as well. Maybe I can help people be less afraid about healing after an accident or violence."

"What have you learned through all of this experience?"

"That I need to run faster?" Oliver gives a sly grin. Coleman is hesitant to laugh but seeing Oliver's expression he quakes with humor. "Truthfully, I've learned the old saying isn't true. What doesn't kill you can make you stronger. I'm quite frankly happy to be alive. Did I ask for this to happen to me? No. Am I facing it and dealing with it? Yes. Doesn't mean I don't feel down about it or wish I was back at one hundred percent. That may never be the case for me physically. I have a second chance at life, and I want to spend it helping others."

Coleman turns off the recorder, the red light switching off, and he puts it away in his pocket. They sit and watch Duran leading Hardt as he walks over foam pads of differing heights.

After several minutes pass, Coleman speaks, "My colleague has been spending all of her weekends here."

"Yes, she has. I'm worried she is going to wear herself thin by traveling back and forth between here and New York so much, but she insists."

"You mean Alex is being stubborn? Nah ..." Coleman blinks, feigning ignorance.

Oliver lets out a boisterous laugh. "You already know."

"She is something."

Oliver's laughter dissipates. "Yes. Yes, she is."

They both observe the other therapy sessions in progress before Oliver eases his feet from under Montana's head to stretch his aching legs. "When Alex visits, we try not to talk shop too much. We both need a break from it sometimes. It's been hard on her, too. How are things coming along with the case?"

"Judge Skinner resigned and was charged with perverting the course of justice. Indiana Governor, Mathers, appointed her replacement last week."

"The family with the little girl? They were your contacts, right?"

"Yes, the Fischer's. I am pretty fond of that family. A philanthropist started a GoFundMe to help with their medical bills. People have been pouring in support for the mom, Aubrey, and the little girl, Felicity. Grayson and Bonnie—the attorney and his paralegal—have the original seven cases, including the Fischer's, plus two hundred and twenty-eight former and current employees of Takestrom and local citizens who had evidence of health issues."

Oliver whistles. "The power of the press."

"I want the case to move forward quickly but you know how these things go. Could be ten years before it goes to trial, but Grayson assured him that McAllen Industries will face the people they've poisoned for decades."

"Coleman, that's outstanding. Do you see what you and Alex did? You've changed that community forever." Oliver's eyebrows flash up and hold.

"There's a lot of people in Marktown that want to see Takestrom have their comeuppance," Coleman retorts. "Sadly, there's a Marktown in every state."

"You sound like Alex. Plagued by the will to turn over every stone and make everything right."

"That's pretty rich coming from you. You two were made for each other."

Oliver does not reply.

Coleman clears his throat. "You know what? I wanted to do these stories. I'm not here because Alex asked me to be or anything like that. It was my idea. I knew she couldn't because, well it would be a conflict of interest with you two—"

"Yes." Oliver rubs at the back of his neck.

"For the story, I had no idea you were Alex's DC source until you were in the hospital. That's how closely she protected your involvement. When everything first happened, the hit and run and the shooting, I trusted you and supported you because Alex trusts you and supports you. But now I see, you are a lot more than talk."

Oliver's eyes gleam, before his lips curl into a tiny smile.

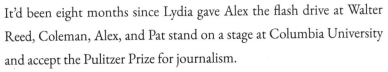

It'd been eight months since Lydia gave Alex the flash drive at Walter Reed, Coleman, Alex, and Pat stand on a stage at Columbia University and accept the Pulitzer Prize for journalism.

"It is with a mixture of emotions that we accept this award," Alex says to the crowd. "As journalists, we are elated to have our work recognized with this prestigious award. But also, as journalists, we do not show up to the office each day, we do not sit down for interviews, with the goal of winning awards. It is our duty, our responsibility, to the integrity of our field that we share stories like that of the people of Marktown, Indiana.

"There is a reason that freedom of the press is explicitly named in the US Constitution," Alex continues. The stage spotlight is so bright, the hundreds of faces in the auditorium are silhouettes, outlines of human forms, faceless to Alex. "It is because this country was established with the belief that if democratic governments were to succeed, a checks and balance system needed to be in place. It should not be commonplace for corruption to take precedence over decency, empathy, and humanity. Our elected officials work on behalf of the will of the American people. When they do not, it is our duty as journalists to tell the story. To dig beyond press releases and prepared statements and ask the questions that get the answers we as citizens have a right to know. Pat, Coleman, and I want to thank the tech team at *The Times* for their tireless efforts and review of documents to help us expose the truth. We also want to dedicate this award to the people of Marktown, Indiana. We want to dedicate it to factory workers and industrial communities. For too long, corporate progress has come at the cost of your health and safety. We will continue to tell your stories, we will continue to ask the tough questions of our elected officials, and we will continue to shine a light on injustice. Thank you."

Alex turns to take a spot on the stage beside Coleman and Pat, but not before her boss wraps his arms around her in a celebratory hug.

"Congratulations, Ace," he says in her ear as the audience rises to their feet and applauds.

CHAPTER 28

He finally finds the right door.

Rounding corners and turning down one wrong hall to the next, Oliver Michaels was lost in his own home. He was struggling to remember the way. His memory is often fuddled, but he has challenged himself over the last seven years with Brain Gym exercises to keep the cloudiness at bay.

He stood in a dimly lit hall for two solid minutes as he tried to recall the tour his chief of staff had given him. He had been distracted as Yvette spoke, thinking more about an upcoming address than focusing on her directions. He curses under his breath, irritated with himself for not paying closer attention.

He would be too embarrassed to admit it to anyone other than his wife that he had gotten lost. She would surely get a good chuckle from his harrowing ordeal in this residential maze. But he could always handle looking like a fool in front of her; it was his team and the public he feared making an ass out of himself in front of.

His wife can't fault him. It is their third day in their new residence. It will take them some time to get acclimated and for the structure to feel less like an institution and more like home. While they will enjoy lunch in one part of the building, hundreds of visitors and travelers from other nations will tour the main halls and front rooms.

He crosses the living space and raps softly on the door.

"Come in."

He smiles at the sound of her voice. It is angelic, tiny, and filled with pureness. Any time she speaks, it is like the flapping of butterfly wings: beautiful, light, and airy.

He opens the door, stepping inside and gives his daughter a smile. Montana doesn't bother to lift his head from his position curled up beside her legs at the foot of the bed.

"Hey Beetle Bug," Oliver greets. He loosens the tie around his neck, walking towards the bed. The sleeves on his collared shirt are rolled up to his elbows, his pressed slacks slightly wrinkled after a day of work. The polish on his black dress shoes is somewhat scuffed and not as vibrant and reflective as when he first started his day in them.

"Hi, Daddy." She beams. She recently lost her first tooth and when she flashes her bright and disarming smile, he grins at the sight of the gaping hole in the bottom row of her teeth.

Oliver pets Montana's head and rubs his gray snout before he sits on the edge of Hartley's bed as she sits up. He assesses the room and the incredibly swift and accurate job the staff did in prepping her new bedroom. Oliver was adamant that it replicated her room at their townhome. He wanted the transition for her to be as smooth as possible and making sure she was comfortable was paramount. He wanted Hartley to have as normal of an existence as a five-year-old could in her situation.

The pink and white décor of her princess room was recreated down to the thread count. The crowned bed canopy with its sheer pink and white curtains parts in the middle, just where she rests her head each night.

"Did you have a good day?" Oliver asks her.

She nods her head emphatically. "Mama took me to the kitchen and guess what?" She beams, bouncing slightly. Her long-sleeved *Frozen* pajamas are a wardrobe staple, and it would be odd if she weren't wearing them. Oliver delights in her elation.

"What?" He tilts his head quizzically and smirks.

"We can order whatever we want, whenever we want! They will make it!" she says in a rush of words almost too fast for him to understand.

Oliver's head tosses back slightly as he laughs. "What did you order?"

"Peanut butter and jelly sandwich with Cheetos!" she reports seriously. Her eyes widen and she makes a show of holding her hands out. "It was so good."

Oliver bites into his lip as he tries to keep from laughing. "Whatever you wanted, and you ordered a PB and J?"

"Mmhm. They asked what I want for breakfast, and I said chocolate ice cream, but Mama said no. She told them oatmeal with fruit and stuff." She scrunches her face as if she has smelled something horrible and then sticks her tongue out.

Oliver chuckles again. "Well, a healthy breakfast is a good way to start the day." He raises his eyebrows for emphasis. "Mama and I just want you to be healthy and happy and the best you can be."

"I know." She shrugs, uninterested.

Oliver stares at her, not realizing he is smiling. She has his eyes and long lashes, but the rest of her features are drawn from her mother. Including her can't lose attitude. He leans forward and kisses her forehead and reaches out a hand, smoothing her hair. "Time for sleep now," he says. If he is in town and at home, even before their move, she will not turn out her light until her father comes to tuck her in.

She fluffs her pillow and turns onto her side as Oliver stands and lifts her bed sheet and comforter. She snuggles her cheek into the downy pillow before Oliver lays the warming blankets across her body.

"Do you like your room?" Oliver leans over the bed.

"It's just like my other one!" She grins, and he focuses on the gap in her teeth again. It feels like just yesterday he was holding her as a tiny newborn in his arms. Time has flown by way too fast. He appreciates these moments with her.

"We wanted it that way, Mama and me."

"How long are we going to be here?" Hartley asks, looking up at him expectantly.

"At least four years, but hopefully if I do my job right, eight."

"How old will I be then?"

"Thirteen," Oliver explains.

Hartley blinks as she thinks, trying to imagine herself at age thirteen. Oliver's heart beats faster: *thirteen*, a teenager. He wants to slow the clock down.

"I think I like it here," Hartley muses.

"Good." Oliver smooths her hair again before giving her cheek a kiss. "Sweet dreams, baby girl."

He reaches over and turns out the lamp and the night light plugged in beside the bed glows as darkness falls over the room.

"Goodnight Daddy," her tiny voice says as he turns and walks away. When he nears the door, she stops him. "Daddy?"

"Yes?"

"Do we live in a castle?"

"Well, something similar to a castle."

"A big white castle and Mama is queen, and you are king, and I'm the princess!" she exclaims in a tumble of words again.

Oliver laughs. "No, sweetheart. Mama and I aren't a king and queen, but you are our princess, okay?"

"Okay," she says and yawns.

"Goodnight," Oliver repeats and opens the door. He waves with his fingers at her as he closes the door behind him.

He sighs and rolls his neck and shoulders as he crosses the living space with a slight limp and heads to the other side of the room. The lag in his leg movement is discernible but not prominent. He is able to fake a confident stride when in front of the cameras, but the drag in his gait is a symbol of recovery and hope for so many.

He opens the door and steps into the bedroom, finding the bathroom door open and a light on. He shuts and locks their door.

"Is she asleep?" his wife asks from inside the bathroom.

"Awake but tucked in." Oliver sighs. He unfastens his tie and pulls it from around his neck, tossing it over a wingback chair in the corner.

He unbuttons and untucks his shirt, tossing it next to the tie. He sits on the edge of the bed and unlaces his shoes. His neck feels stiff, and his hip aches. The pain in his joints is a familiar aftereffect from years before.

He takes off his shoes and pulls his socks off, stuffing them inside. He flexes and balls his toes against the fibers of the area rug, feeling the relief of freeing them from confining shoes. He would take a good pair of Nike's over Brooks Brothers' any day. Stripped down to just his white tank and slacks, he feels free from the shackles of his business clothes.

Oliver looks over at the dresser in his new bedroom and finds it lined with framed pictures. Alex has done everything she can to help make the transition to life here in the White House feel like any other move.

Oliver stands, unbuckling his belt and whipping it off his pants, laying it in the seat of the chair. He focuses on a few of the pictures: Him smiling and holding Hartley for the first time; an old picture of him and Alex with their old college suitemates at UConn; and a few posed pictures from Christmas and holidays of him and Alex with Hartley. Their daughter transforms from a baby to the kindergartner she is now in the series of photos. One photo is of Oliver on the day of his release from Walter Reed with Alex at his side.

Alex was with him throughout his recovery process. When it was publicly confirmed that Oliver and Lydia Michaels were divorcing, most did not fault him. Lydia's father had taken advantage of Oliver's position to align himself with some money hungry, greedy politicians. Oliver had almost died because of Jamison. To those looking from the outside in, it was easy to understand how that could impact a marriage. Lydia contacted her attorney and signed the papers the day after Oliver was released from the rehabilitation center.

The first pictures of Oliver and Alex as a couple did not appear until seven months after she accepted the Pulitzer. It had been two full years since his divorce from Lydia, and though he and Alex were together long before the public was aware of it, they had been discreet in their romance, partly out of respect for Lydia and also for the sake of public perception.

A year after their honeymoon, Alex and Oliver learned they were going to welcome a baby. Hartley Angelica Michaels was born to Oliver and Alex on a warm morning in June.

The public push for Oliver to run for president had elevated from a whisper to a shout. Polls showed Michaels was who the people wanted. Alex was a woman of the people as well. They were the power couple the country needed.

After Hartley's third birthday, Oliver Michaels declared his run for US presidency. Alex resigned from her position at *The Times* to help her husband campaign and to raise their child. It was her choice, not one Oliver pressured her into. Alex sometimes brought Hartley along on the campaign bus. Americans fell in love with the images of the tiny little girl holding her father's world-weary face between her hands and smiling at him adoringly as he campaigned across the country.

He glances into the mirror above the dresser and sees Alex's reflection from the bathroom. She is brushing her teeth, leaning over the sink as her arm moves the brush vigorously. She rises onto her toes, a habit she is oblivious to. Oliver visually trails her long, toned, brown legs stretching out from under the satin slip she is wearing. He admires his wife's beauty, silently drinking in every detail of her, though he has her features memorized.

Two days ago, he, Alex, and Hartley stood before the nation as he was sworn into office. Andrea Michaels, his mother, and his siblings, Leah and Andrew, were on hand to watch son and brother make history.

The temperature was hovering at freezing as Hartley was bundled up in a hooded, wool peacoat of blue, custom-made for her. Alex cradled her against her hip as Oliver placed his hand on a book of law and took the oath of office for the highest elected position in the land. Aubrey, Jessie, and now ten-year-old Felicity Fischer stood with the other dignitaries as Oliver was sworn into office.

"I have been given the nickname 'The People's Champion,'" Oliver said during his inaugural speech. A crowd of 1.4 million gathered on The Mall, stretching back for miles beyond the spot where Oliver spoke. Speakers posted throughout the area broadcast his message of hope as supporters waved little American flags in the air. "I want to say, the American people need no champion. There are heroes in communities across this great nation. They don't have a podium or a stage. They have their hands, their voices, and their convictions. My job as president is to ensure that the voices of those working to provide resources and support to their communities are heard and they have the support they need. My job as president is to make sure that those whose voices have been silenced, that the marginalized, the stigmatized, and the ostracized citizens of this great country have their rights secured because that, that is what makes America great."

Oliver holds the picture in his hands, staring at Alex's confident smile. Her strength, bravado, intelligence, and ambition are the sexiest things Oliver has ever known and he thanks God every day she is his now.

"What are you looking at?" She flips the light switch off in the bathroom, closing the door.

"Just reminiscing."

She approaches and takes the framed photo from his hands.

She smiles when she realizes what he has been staring at. "This was a good day."

"Every day with you is a good day," he says. He steps up behind her and slides his hands over her hips, moving the satin fabric she is wearing as his arms wrap around her waist and he pulls her back against him. She puts the photo down on the dresser.

He places a soft kiss against her shoulder, bringing a devilish smile to her lips. He continues his course, brushing gentle kisses one right after the other from her shoulder up her neck, before pressing his lips against her ear. Alex moans at the feel of his warm, smooth lips delightfully tickling her skin.

"Mr. President, what would the people say if they saw you like this?" she moans.

"I'd hope they would be happy the First Lady is being well tended to," Oliver says softly before nipping at her neck.

"Oliver," she groans again.

"Ah, ah," he pretends to chide. "That's Mr. President," he says in a low, husky voice.

"My commander-in-chief," she says with a light chuckle.

"Are we going to do this thing now where we make presidential puns all through sex?" Oliver's humored eyes inspect her face.

"I mean, how could we not?" Alex laughs. Oliver gives a soft laugh before spinning her around and kissing her lips.

"How much sex do you think has been had in the White House?" he asks.

"You mean between the president and the actual first lady or just the president and some broad?" Alex cocks a brow.

A throaty laugh escapes him. "President and first lady."

"I would think with the blue hairs and old stuffy guys that have been through here, not much. Even if there is some sexual record, we will beat it and then some." She winks.

Oliver smiles and becomes reflective.

"Did you really think we would make it here someday?" His face is still bright with enjoyment.

"I did." She nods. She reaches up and takes his face in her hands. "I did because I believed in you, and I always knew you could do this. Me and Hartley have your back always, don't ever forget that. We are Team Michaels through and through."

Oliver's smile is broad and wide. "Thank you, Alex. With you, I feel like I can do anything." He leans in and gives her a slow, sweet kiss. "Now, what's say we test out this whole twenty-four-hour kitchen thing and get a big plate of french fries?"

She giggles. "You really are the love of my life."

EPILOGUE

The blisters on his hands tore open and bled. The rusty hacksaw's teeth had been ground down as smooth as the edge of a fingernail file as it penetrated the thick rolled steel. As the raw flesh of his palm met the flakes of rust and dried toilet water that concealed the tool in its tank, Peter was certain he would catch tetanus.

So be it. Once he was free, he could have access to any medical care he needed.

He rests the hacksaw on the base of the reinforced concrete window seal. Gritting his teeth like a rabid dog, his forearms and biceps burn as he pulls at the steel. The bars crack open one by one. It's an opening narrow enough for his body to squeeze through. On the diet of prison food, he'd shed twenty pounds since his imprisonment in Pagliarelli.

He pulls the pillow from his cot and folds it over his elbow. He tucks his lips hard as he drives the makeshift pad into the glass. It doesn't make a crack.

Peter stands solidly, driving his elbow over and over against the glass. The skin on his joint bursts open, the bone of his elbow tearing through the flesh until at last there is a fracture in glass.

Tightening his core, he slams his elbow and the pillow into the glass once more before it shatters. Glancing back at his cell door, he waits before carefully pulling the jagged shards away. He lays them flat on the floor, one piece at a time.

The echo of footsteps amplifies from a light tap to a stomp drawing closer up the hall.

"*Tu, inutile maiale!*" *You useless pig*, a shout rings out. It starts with a duo of voices then spreads to an entire choir. Inmates begin to beat on cell doors and shout profanities. It is as they'd discussed.

Peter sits down on the musty, flattened mattress of the cot in his cell. He watches as guards in red striped pants run up the hallway, batons in hand yelling back at the prisoners.

"*Stai zitto! Abbassa i toni!*" *Shut up! Quiet down!*

Peter reaches between the cot and the wall and begins to uncoil a chain of white sheets. The Romanians in the cell beside him had helped in gathering the soiled linens and passing them to him before heading towards dinner a week before.

After last night's cell inspections before bedtime, Peter had tied and knotted the sheets. The piss-stained bedding would be his liberation.

During his last face-to-face visit, Roberto told Peter the other clans were seeing the Insigne as weak and vulnerable. They were circling, necks craning and wings beating like buzzards, waiting for the death of the newest family in the ranks. The families might bring the Insigne extinction. Roberto is the muscle but he doesn't have the intelligence of his older brother. The operation was taking on water without Peter at the helm.

He'd been on the run for six years, hunted by Interpol. He'd found refuge in Colombia, Brazil, and then Sicily before his arrest last year. Someone had snitched.

The Insigne weren't disbanded, only reorganizing until Peter's return. In his cell, he thought every night about how he would make it back to his family. Laura had threatened divorce. He wouldn't allow it. His children would not grow up without a father the way he had.

Takestrom was supposed to make operations legit. Roberto and Colbert had made things messy. When *The New York Times* story broke, Colbert fled to Amsterdam, then the Bahamas.

Roberto delivered the updates to Peter. A Southern District of Indiana court charged Colbert with conspiracy, securities fraud, and money laundering. The EPA's Criminal Enforcement offices had been able to add charges against MacAllen Industries and Colbert for violations of the *Clean Water Act*, the *Clean Air Act* and the *Resource Conservation and Recovery Act*.

Bahamian authorities caught up with him at the airport, bringing him in for questioning before a flight to Venezuela. He'd also been charged with evading arrest and seven counts of fraud and conspiracy. After extradition, Colbert was set to face trial for the illegal activities that contaminated the air, land and water and threatened people's health.

Then, he cut a deal. In exchange for a lesser sentence, Colbert told the authorities all he knew: Vitale had dispatched the thug to Coleman's bedside and Vitale had kept tabs on Jamison Ainsworth and ordered the hit on him.

From a hideout in a Brazilian Favela, Vitale learned of Colbert's betrayal. He also learned the gravity of the crimes he was being charged with. President Michaels was collateral damage, but costly collateral. In addition to the same crimes Colbert was charged with, Vitale's global network of trafficking and drugs, now had the additional and most heinous count of attempted assassination of a US senator.

Vitale had been watching the news in prison, following Oliver Michaels' ascension to "leader of the free world" while he himself was in shackles. The Insigne clan was not one of Peter's wounded racehorses waiting to be put down. Peter was at the starting gate, ready to victoriously gallop across the globe.

As the ruckus in the hall escalates, Peter binds the sheets to one of the unsawed bars, wrapping and yanking on it tightly for leverage. He tugs and pushes his foot into the wall to test the chain of sheet's ability to hold weight.

Peter lifts bloody hands up onto the sill and tosses the sheets out the window. He peers down from the fourth story window.

Angling, he squeezes through the bars. The jagged edge of glass slices along his rib cage and then hip bone as he wiggles through. His hands tighten around the sheets, the flesh searing, flecks of blood being absorbed by the cotton.

Peter regards the fifty-foot drop. He suppresses a shriek of pain from the cuts in his hands and the flesh of his torso. He slides down three stories, but his hands can't maintain the hold on the sheets as blood slickens them. When he reaches the final story, he drops to the earth.

The sensation of a hundred push pins driving into his ankle forces him to clutch his leg. It's a possible sprain. He can't let it slow him. He falls on his butt and rolls onto his side.

His heart is pounding. He digs his fingers into the grass, soil caking under his nails and over his wounded hands, as he pushes himself to standing. He scans the facade of the building and scrambles into a clumsy run, a limp slowing him as his ankle cannot bear the full weight of his body. He hobbles towards the chain fence.

It is broad daylight. The flush of adrenaline accelerates the function of his lungs and heart. The stale air, cleaning disinfectants, mildew, and body odor of the prison are replaced by the salty air blowing in from the Tyrrhenian Sea.

He finds the cut at the bottom of the fence, enough space for him to push through and belly crawl under the metal. His fate is liberation. He wills it to be. He would die before he was sent back to prison. He'd been a lab rat, prodded and questioned, targeted for connections and knowledge.

He did not feel pain. He was prey running for his survival with tunnel vision for only life outside of a cage.

The front of his jumpsuit is caked with dust, grass stains, and soil as he staggers on one strong leg. The Madonie mountain range fills his view up ahead. Pagliarrelli Prison was situated behind the ancient rock, a spattering of trees and wildflowers around it. Peter exhales but there is no relief. He must make it to the other side of those mountains and down to the Palermo coast where Roberto has arranged for a tourist boat, clean clothes, and altered ID cards to give him passage.

They replay the footage. The clip is no longer than sixteen seconds but it's enough time for the gravity of its depiction to leech onto their consciousness. The new director of the Department of Justice, Dexter Adkins, stands beside Jeff Grimes, Deputy Director of the US National Central Bureau—Interpol Washington—incredulously watching the security camera footage sent by the Sicilians.

Peter Vitale drops down the side of the maximum-security prison with the sun shining and not one guard in the vicinity. Palermo and Europol authorities were investigating, Dexter was told.

Vitale was one of the ten most wanted men in Interpol's crime list until his capture a year prior. Like a dandelion seedling on a breeze, he vanishes from sight.

Dexter's hands rest on his hips. "Notify the CIA. Put surveillance on the Vitale family. Notify the Secret Service, too."

Dexter looks up at the round, brown clock on the wall at the bureau office. It's just after midnight. Grimes picks up the office phone. Dexter steps out into the hallway.

He knows this call will not be a disruption. Usually at this hour, his friend is looking over the agenda for the correspondent's press briefing for the next day.

"Yeah?"

"Coleman."

"That's who you dialed."

"Got some news. It could be cause for concern."

"What's up?" says the White House press secretary, his voice sounding fully alert.

"Peter Vitale escaped from prison. We don't know where he is."

Coleman speaks in a quiet voice. "I don't think we tell the president. Not yet. But keep me updated."

END

Acknowledgments

Writing *The Senator* has been an unusual journey. From my first attempts at writing this story in 2018 while sitting in my SUV during afternoon carpool, to my first beta read with my friend Erin Irvin, I maneuvered through parenthood and a major detour of writing my first memoir. I was grateful to get back to fiction.

To my husband, "Buster," my constant best friend, my sometimes therapist, and my forever partner, for helping me to believe I could do this and for giving me the time and space to do so. To my son, for showing me wisdom and joy even in the chaos.

To my Mom, Dad, "D," Joe and Gloria: Thank you for your love, endless support, and understanding.

My Ainty, for being by far the biggest cheerleader of my work.

Thank you to the team at Rising Action Publishing Collective for their brazen support of this novel and women in publishing. Tina Beier and Alexandria Brown, for encouraging a dream. Special thanks to the marketing teams at RAPC and Simon & Schuster.

Thanks to Marthese Fenech for your immense knowledge, friendship and expertise. You have made so many of us better at what we do because of the light within you.

Special thanks to *The Senator* beta readers Nicole Brown, Chris Panatier, and Read Cook for their invaluable feedback and guidance. Attorney Crystal Strickland, thank you for your help!

Appreciation and gratitude to authors KC Carmichael, Maria Alejandro Barrios, and Bianca Marais. To Fred Markham, Michelle Coburn,

Tracy Phelps, and Lauren Bean for being true allies in the evolution of my career.

The Dallas and East Texas writing communities for embracing me, including Aaron Glover at the Writer's Garrett, Alex Temblador, and Logen Cure.

Tumblr writers and fandoms for buoying me in my early tests of the fiction waters. The pipeline is real.

Lastly, I'd like to thank the city of New Orleans and the survivors of Hurricane Katrina. It was your tenacity, friendliness and resiliency in the weeks that I covered the aftermath of the storm that I wanted to honor in this book. You showed warmth and humor, and were welcoming even in the darkest of times.

ABOUT THE AUTHOR

Maya Golden Bethany is an Associated Press winning and Emmy nominated multimedia journalist. Her debut memoir, *The Return Trip*, released in 2023. Maya is the winner of the Excellence in My Market Award (EMMA) from the National Academy of Television Arts and Sciences. She is the founder of the 1 in 3 Foundation, a non-profit organization that provides recovery and counseling resources to survivors of sexual trauma with little to no income in East Texas. The Texas A&M alum's career includes experiences as a sports anchor/reporter and television production editor, newscast writer, field producer and print writer. Maya has been featured on Bally Sports, Fox Sports College, and ESPN 2 and 3. She has written for Newsweek, Salon, Insider and BlackGirlNerd s.com. Maya speaks as a survivor for organizations such as the Children's Advocacy Center, CASA (Court Appointed Special Advocates), and Kids Aspiring to Dream. Maya is a member of the Writer's League of Texas and a second-place winner of the Martha's Vineyard Institute of Creative Writing 2024 Parent-Writer Fellowship.

Looking for more thrillers? Check out Rising Action's other suspenseful reads on the next page!

And don't forget to follow us on our socials for cover reveals, giveaways, and announcements:

X: @RAPubCollective

Instagram: @risingactionpublishingco

TikTok: @risingactionpublishingco

Website: http://www.risingactionpublishingco.com

RISING ACTION

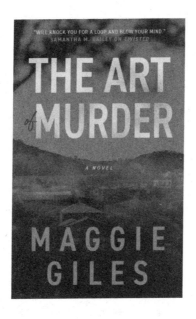

THE ART *of* MURDER

A NOVEL

MAGGIE GILES

In the tranquil town of Cedar Plains, where safety and community are sacred, Courtney Faith's ideal life is upended by a body found on a local farm, shattering her peaceful existence. Her friend, Alexa Huston, intimately familiar with chaos, gets entangled in an accidental murder that escalates her spiraling life into deeper darkness. Alexa wrestles with a disturbing question: Is murder justifiable if it targets the deserving?

As bodies accumulate, the local police scramble for answers. Torn between loyalty and justice, Courtney discovers evidence linking Alexa to the crimes. Their friendship frays as Courtney grapples with a dire choice: expose Alexa and risk her own darkest secret, or protect a friend and possibly destroy everything she cherishes.

In Cedar Plains, some truths are too perilous to unearth. Caught in a deadly dance of secrets and lies, Courtney must decide whether to confront the monster behind a familiar face or let their secrets stay hidden, buried within the town's heart. Their darkest deeds are cloaked in silence, and no one truly knows anything.

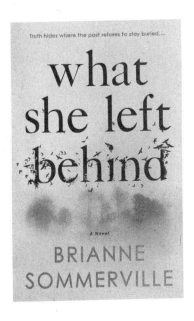

Truth hides where the past refuses to stay buried....

what she left behind

A Novel

BRIANNE SOMMERVILLE

Recently fired and adrift, Charlotte Boyd agrees to oversee renovations on her parents' small-town summer home that holds a tragic past. After discovering an enthralling diary hidden amidst junk the previous owners left behind, Charlotte connects with the author—a troubled teen named Lark Peters who died by suicide at the house sixteen years ago.

When an unsettling incident forces Charlotte to seek refuge at the local pub, regulars, including the police, warn her of Lark's older brother, Darryl, who has become a recluse since Lark's death, and may know more than he's letting on. But Charlotte sees a side of Darryl others don't, being an outsider herself.

In a search to uncover the truth, Charlotte must question those closest to Lark and reconcile her own past trauma. Because if Lark was actually murdered, then whoever is responsible might be lurking in Charlotte's own backyard.